Greyla

CW00548265

THE ENCIRC____

'Josephine Elder' was the pseudonym of Dr. Olive Potter. She was born in Croydon in 1895, educated at Croydon High School, where an inspirational Botany mistress helped her to win her scholarship to Girton. She completed her medical training at the London Hospital in Whitechapel, one of the first four women there. After a couple of years in hospital doctor posts, she set up as a G.P. in Surrey. Patients were slow to come to women doctors in the 1920s, so she turned to writing. Her first book, *Erica Wins Through* (1924) was followed by nine more school stories for girls, and six adult novels (two under the further pen-name 'Margaret Potter'), including *Lady of Letters* (1949) and *The Encircled Heart* (1951). She didn't retire until she was eighty-eight, and died five years later, in 1988.

The people in these pages
are just types – no more.

THE ENCIRLCED HEART

JOSEPHINE ELDER

Greyladies

Published by
Greyladies
an imprint of The Old Children's Bookshelf
175 Canongate, Edinburgh EH8 8BN

This edition is published by arrangement with
The Lutterworth Press
© Lutterworth Press 1951

This edition first published 2009
Reprinted 2012
Design and layout © Shirley Neilson 2009
Preface © Hilary Clare 2008
'A Woman Doctor's Training' © Olive Potter 1987

ISBN 978-0-9559413-4-4

Set in Sylfaen / Perpetua
Printed and bound by the MPG Books Group,
Bodmin and Kings Lynn.

CONTENTS

Preface

In *The Encircled Heart* 'Josephine Elder' – in real life Dr. Olive Potter – drew largely on her own professional experience to create the picture of a woman doctor in the days before the Second World War and the post-war creation of the National Health Service. Like Marion, the book's heroine, Dr. Potter was Cambridge and London trained, and became a general practitioner. Her practice was in Sutton, Surrey; Marion's is not specifically located but despite being described as 'eighty main-line miles from London' seems to be in the Home Counties and is not unnaturally similar to Dr. Potter's; there is in consequence no picture of health care – or the lack of it – in urban or industrial surroundings similar to that given in the contemporary novels of A.J.Cronin (e.g. *The Citadel,* 1937) or Francis Brett Young (e.g. *My Brother Jonathan,* 1931; *Dr. Bradley Remembers,* 1938). But where Cronin was certainly writing to expose the system 'Josephine Elder' was concerned not with a state of affairs which had been superceded but with the particular problems of being a woman doctor. The early part of *The Encircled Heart* clearly derives from her own experiences, though of course she must have changed details in the interests of professional confidence – a subject of which Marion is obliged to speak trenchantly to Paul early on in their marriage.

But though Marion is based on Olive she is not a self-portrait. To begin with, she must be a good ten years younger, since the story opens in the early 1930s when she is only in her mid-twenties. Olive Potter was born in 1895 and qualified in 1922; Marion could not have followed exactly in her footsteps since in the early 1920s the London Hospital medical school stopped taking women students (they interfered with the hospital's rugger prospects). Marion would have had to train at the Royal Free (women) or at University College London (the only co-educational London medical school of the period).

And Olive Potter did not marry. The plot of *The Encircled Heart* demands Marion's marriage to Paul and her attempts to juggle matrimony, motherhood and medicine, but although the details seem well-observed, Marion's emotional turmoil does not altogether carry conviction. The problems are certainly there, but her physical and mental attraction to Paul, and her commitment to her children, are stated rather than experienced. What rings very true is her social relationship as a university wife with the wives of her husband's colleagues, who are chiefly interested in bridge and servant problems; Marion's only hope of real friendship in these circles, like Olive Potter's, is to be treated as an honorary man.

An important part of *The Encircled Heart* is Marion's relationship with Philippa, the friend from student days with whom she shares a house and who, later on, presents her with an agonising ethical dilemma. The account Olive Potter gave to a W.I. of her own student days (see page xiii) gives us some clues as to whom Philippa was based on, for she describes her in almost exactly the same terms as she does her unnamed Cambridge friend, who also refused to dress discreetly – 'I'm a woman, and proud of it!'. This must have been Dorothy Gibson, Olive's contemporary at Cambridge (but Newnham, not Girton) and at the London Hospital. Like Olive herself she went into general practice, working in Bow in East London; born in 1896, she died unmarried in 1974. Philippa, however, like Olive Potter's slightly younger contemporary at Girton and the London, Dorothy Stuart Russell (see her entry in *The Oxford Dictionary of National* Biography) has chosen to become a pathologist. It is perhaps surprising that Olive did not include the experience of another fellow student at the London (who can be identified as Dr. Gladys M.Wauchope), who was one of the earliest diabetic patients in this country to be treated with insulin; she merely refers to the discovery in passing.

The Encircled Heart is set late enough for Olive Potter to incorporate some of the striking medical advances of her time – the discovery of insulin in the early 1920s and the treatment of pernicious anaemia a decade later, the development of antibiotics and of the sulphur drugs in the 1940s. The book opens with a childbirth which demonstrates up-to-date practice, but later in the book we are reminded of how far obstetrics have since moved on – nowadays Mrs. Tuson would almost certainly not have lost her longed-for baby but have had it safely delivered by Caesarian section. It is noticeable, incidentally, that contraception is viewed as entirely a male preserve: Marion attributes her own first pregnancy to a deliberate act on Paul's part, not to a failure of any device of her own; otherwise the subject is not dealt with.

The domestic details of Marion's practice are emphatically of their period and must seem extraordinary to the modern reader accustomed to large group practices and purpose-built health centres. Marion runs her practice from the house she shares with Philippa. She does have a consulting room, but the patients wait in the dining-room and are admitted by Ethel in her parlour-maid's cap and apron. There is no receptionist, no practice nurse, and, at the beginning, no regular cover for time off. Yet, within living memory, this is how it really was.

Like Marion, Olive Potter had set up on her own, and, when in her early days patients were slow to come, she took to writing school stories to pass the time and make ends meet – she was able to buy a car with the proceeds of her first book. Marion is soon successful and able to employ an assistant; Olive Potter ended by having three partners, all women. Unlike Marion she remained in general practice, finally retiring in 1983 at the age of 88 and dying in 1988 at the age of 93. Marion gives up when expecting her first child, and sells her practice to her assistant. This was normal in pre NHS days. (After 1948 those doctors who had bought their practices were compensated on retirement or death, though the amount allocated was not uncontroversial.)

Most of Marion's patients are fee-paying, and 'Josephine Elder' demonstrates both the advantages and drawbacks of the system. On the one hand there was continuity of care (for the fortunate rich); on the other was the imperious way some patients behaved, and the difficulty doctors often experienced in getting their bills paid (not a subject dwelt on in *The Encircled Heart).* Marion's 'panel' patients are the men covered by insurance for the bread-winner of the family, a system introduced by Lloyd George; their wives and children were not covered, though Marion seems to treat them for free. We do not hear of her having 'club' patients, where working-men's clubs made contracts with doctors to treat whole families for payment of a small sum; perhaps this was only common in industrial areas. *The Encircled Heart* does not deal either with the question of 'poaching', where unscrupulous doctors would try to get fee-paying patients from their neighbours; Olive Potter scorned the habit, and when during World War Two she looked after neighbouring practices was able to boast that she had handed them back without gaining a single patient from them.

The book ends too soon to cover the transition to the National Health Service in 1948. On her husband's return from the war Marion intends not to go back to general practice but to go into public health, where she can work regular hours and not be subject to calling-out. It was a decision many married women doctors made, understandably enough, though to the scorn of some of their male contemporaries. Some were able to work part-time in general practice. At least one of Olive Potter's student contemporaries continued to work as a G.P., despite husband and children, but she was married to another G.P. and certainly employed a nanny to look after her children, something Marion does not seem to contemplate. 'Josephine Elder' was to treat the problems of a woman doctor again in her next book, *Doctor's Children*

(1954). One aspect of having a doctor in the family is mentioned, a tendency for them to be treated with the samples given out by the 'reps' from pharmaceutical companies. Another is a certain lack of sympathy with minor ailments!

It is the slant on a woman in medicine which gives particular significance to *The Encircled Heart*. As a picture of a pre NHS G.P. in an 'ordinary' southern England setting it is a valuable testimony, and the more so for being by and about a woman. Marion's marriage takes her where 'Josephine Elder' had not been, perhaps to the book's detriment, but her experiences otherwise are unquestionably authentic and deserve recognition as a witness to the work of her and Olive Potter's generation.

Hilary Clare, 2008.

A Woman Doctor's Training

A talk given to the Women's Institute by Dr Olive Potter in 1987.

Madam President – Ladies –

I ask you to imagine – if you can – that you are looking at a young, eager woman, in her early twenties. She is thin. Her hair is strained back from her face and screwed into a tight bun at the back of her head. She is wearing a white shirt blouse with a high neck, tucked firmly into a long skirt, right down to her ankles and almost covering her sensible shoes.

That was me, a Medical Student, in 1917.

It was not easy for a woman at that time, to get as far as that.

It wasn't easy for her even to get an education anything like that of today. If she went to school at all, she went to one where she learned perhaps to read and write and know her tables, and to sing a little and sketch a little, and to have good manners, and to please her father and any eligible young men she might meet.

I was lucky. My Father had ideas in advance of his time. The Girls' Public Day School Trust schools had just been launched. He wanted his only daughter to go to one of them. He insisted on his own way, in spite of my mother's horrified protests. I went to the Croydon Girls' High School, and stayed there until I was eighteen.

I managed to win a Scholarship to Girton – and there, to my surprise, difficulties began again.

I had already made up my mind that I wanted to be a doctor. That meant I had to study Human Anatomy and Physiology at the labs in Cambridge. No woman had ever done this at Cambridge before, and my attendance at the labs was sternly refused. If a woman so much as put a foot there, it was said, the male students would go on strike.

However, Girton at that time was ruled by a very determined High Mistress. To her, any refusal to the rights of her students was a challenge. She had a quick temper – she had been known to hurl a heavy Greek Lexicon at anyone who disagreed with her. I don't think she went to that length with the Cambridge authorities, but she sarcastically brushed aside all their objections, and to the labs I went, three miles on a bicycle in and three miles out at the end of the day.

I remember the Dissecting Room very well. It was a big, high room with narrow windows and a floor of scrubbed wood. In it were rows of trestle tables. On each one of them lay a human body, thin and yellow. They were said to have been those of vagrants whom nobody claimed.

Students worked there in pairs, teasing out blood vessels, nerves and muscles to learn exactly where they were.

I had been paired with a man. I believe he was a Chinaman, but I never saw him. No woman should have been there, no man would work with one. So I climbed on my high stool and sat looking down at the arm I was going to dissect and reading my Grey's Anatomy.

I began to dissect. I'd been at it some time before I realised that there was a curly head – a female-looking head – bent over the opposite side of the table. Was it? Could it be – another woman? She looked up and smiled.

"Hullo, where have you come from? I thought I was the only one — "

"I thought I was," I told her. "I've come in from Girton."

"I'm a Newnhamite," she said, and then, "I'm jolly glad to see you."

I agreed. "Me too." We both went on with our dissecting.

After a while she looked up again. "I suppose," she said, "You couldn't find the ulnar nerve for me?"

I had just laid bare the white cord of that nerve. I told her so and leaned across towards her.

She giggled. "You can't reach! Aren't you little!"

I slipped off my stool. "I may have short arms, but I *can* walk!" I went round the body's head and showed her, and we both went back to our work.

Presently she looked up again. "Why don't we work together? It's easier with two, and if those blighters won't join us we'll get on without them."

So we did that. We exchanged names and bits of our history. We went on working together, and spent a contented three years finding out about the human body in that horrible smelly room. The only time I've ever smoked was there, it was the only thing that could get rid of the mingled smells of formalin and death.

Having been the first women to read Anatomy at Cambridge, we thought we would like to be among the first women Medical students at the London Hospital.

We were told to come for an interview.

We got off a bus at Whitechapel Station, and stood looking across the road at that great hospital, the oldest and the biggest of the London teaching hospitals, and, we were soon quite sure, the very best. We crossed the tram-lined road, dodged between stalls which sold jellied eels and a poisonous-looking drink and whelks and all sorts of things, and went up the steps, to be stopped by a porter in a tall hat with gold on it and a gold-striped uniform. "Not visiting hours now, ladies," he said.

We told him what we had come for and after a startled look of unbelief, he directed us along a passage and into a little waiting room, where we were presently joined by two more women. One was a tall Scot from St Andrews, the other a small dark Welsh girl.

We were interviewed by the Dean. I've forgotten his name, he was always known as Old Bill, a big square man sitting behind a desk. He looked us over before he spoke, almost angrily it seemed. He said "You – *ladies* – are here purely as an experiment. You must not expect any privileges due to your sex. You must make yourselves inconspicuous by dressing as far as possible like men."

That was a tall order in those days, with our long hair pinned up in buns and our long skirts. No-one seemed to have thought of short hair or of slacks.

He went on, "You've all been very highly recommended to us. So I suppose I shall have to accept you. You will present yourselves at the Medical School at nine a.m. on today week."

He waved a hand, and we filed out, perhaps rather

appalled by our reception.

We did our best about the dressing, with dark coats and skirts and white shirt blouses – the male students all wore suits then, though I'm sure they don't now. Or rather, three of us did our best. My Newnhamite friend said, "No-one's going to make me dress like a man. I'm a woman, and proud of it." She turned up in an emerald green dress, black silk stockings and high heels. The men students loved it.

Their treatment of us varied. Some ignored us, some made silly jokes, a few were pleasant and friendly.

We had a little common room of our own, out of bounds for them as theirs was for us. When we passed the glass doors of theirs, newspapers would drop, feet would come down from tables. They took a good look at us, and burst into conversation as we passed out of earshot.

At lectures, we sat together in a bunch – until one day when the lecturer, a surgeon renowned for his bad manners, passed us over when he asked questions round the class. After that, we split up, and answered his question, briskly and very often right, when he pointed at the young man next beyond us.

After a few weeks of lectures and demonstrations, we were allowed into the wards.

Here, each student had a patient allotted to his or her care. One examined them – at that time by feeling, looking, even smelling sometimes, there were very few tests or X-rays then – one asked them questions and made notes on their progress from day to day.

We had to read out these notes to our chief, a Consultant Physician or Surgeon, when he did his ward round once or twice a week. This was a nerve-racking experience, for he was followed by a retinue of House doctors, students, Sisters and nurses. Some chiefs were very critical, and could be sarcastic and scathing, especially if they didn't like women students.

The Sisters, very powerful ladies then as now, were mostly kind and helpful. One adopted the tactic of silence to show how much she disliked having us, and never told us how our patients had fared during the night. But on the whole those six months in the wards passed peacefully, and we came to know each other and the men with whom we worked, and to make friends. We got used to the operating theatre, and did none of the things we were expected to do, like fainting under the table at the sight of blood.

There was sadness rather than horror in the medical wards, so very many illnesses were impossible to treat effectively then. The example I remember most was of a little girl of ten, in heart failure due to rheumatic disease of the heart. She sat propped up in bed, her face white and swollen, her lips blue, her breathing laboured. One treatment for it – a bad treatment – was bleeding. This was done by applying leeches over the heart and letting them suck one's blood. They are like big slugs, black and shiny. The child had six of them, all at once, clapped on to her little flat chest. Her eyes opened wide – and her mouth, as though to scream, but no sound came. She fell back dead – of fright. I can still see what she looked like when I think of her, and I shed tears for a long time in bed that night.

There was hope too, in that ward.

One day the Scotswoman came to me when I was alone in the little Common Room. She was a steady reliable person, very reserved. She spoke right out of character. She said, "I must talk to someone. I've only got a few months to live, and I can't bear it." She was almost crying.

I wasn't over sympathetic. When you're learning about diseases, you tend to think you've got each one as it comes along. I just grunted.

She said, "It's true. It really is."

I grunted again, an "Oh yea" sort of grunt.

But she persisted. "You must believe me. I've got Diabetes."

I was silent then. We hadn't been learning about Diabetes.

She said, "I really have. Acute Diabetes in a young person. It's always fatal."

It was, at that time. She went on, "I've been getting tired. I've never been a person to get tired, I thought perhaps I'd been worrying about exams or something. I've lost weight, too, and I'm terribly thirsty. It was when I found myself taking bottles of Squash up to be with me that I realised it added up to a syndrome – the syndromes of Acute Diabetes. So I tested my urine – and it was full of sugar. So in a few months I'll be dead."

I didn't know what to say then. It was all too true. I ventured, "You'd better tell Dr. Ogilvie." He was our Consultant.

She said, "What's the good? He can't do anything. You know he can't."

"Well, tell him, all the same," I said. "He can give you a diet to stick to."

She did tell Dr. Ogilvie, and the next day she was warded, in our own Medical ward.

Dr. Ogilvie's ward round was two days later. He ambled round, then stopped at the foot of the Scots student's bed.

I whispered, "He can't be going to demonstrate on *her!* It's too cruel — "

But he was, and she didn't look as though she minded.

He said, "Here we have a very interesting case. An acute Diabetes in a young adult. Always leading to death in a few months. Agree?"

We all nodded, too shocked, it seemed, to speak.

Dr. Ogilvie nodded too. Then he smiled – how could he? He said, "That's what it *did* lead to. But not now — "

A sort of sigh went up from his whole retinue. We didn't believe him. But he went on speaking. "You all know that your pancreas makes an enzyme which digests sugar, and makes it usable by your muscles, an enzyme which is lacking in the Diabetic. I have to tell you that our researchers, and those of other hospitals, have isolated this enzyme in a form which can be injected. I am going to inject some into this young lady – Sister."

Sister came forward with a tray. Dr. Ogilvie took up a hypodermic syringe. The Scots girl, smiling now, bared one shoulder – and in the needle went.

"In a few weeks," he told us, "this lady will be up, putting on weight, living a normal life. She'll have to have injections, she'll have to limit her sugar intake. But she'll be alive and well. We call the enzyme Insulin. The first injection of Insulin to be given in this hospital."

We still didn't know whether to believe him. It seemed like a miracle. It *was* a miracle, at that time. A killer disease had been cured.

The Scots girl lived to be 75 and became a Consultant in Diabetes and allied diseases.

Another killer was Pernicious Anaemia, an anaemia which couldn't be helped by taking iron pills as other types could.

It was found that it could be made better by eating raw liver – quite a lot of it, every single day. Some people could not bring themselves to do this, it was so nasty. They faded away and died, as they always had. But those who persisted lived and were well.

The enzyme from the raw liver was soon isolated. We call it Vitamin B12. Another killer has been controlled.

In the Surgical wards, where we were posted next, the outlook was quite different. Patients there were either made better or sent home to die – there were no Geriatric wards or Hospices then.

One thing I never liked was the tonsillectomies. Up to a dozen young children were done one after another. The tonsils were removed with a sharp instrument known as a guillotine. It simply cut the tops off them, resulting in a very bloody operation. The children were then wrapped in red blankets, still anaesthetized, and laid on the theatre floor in rows, regaining consciousness or taken home, as likely as not, on a bus.

After the Wards we had to learn about Midwifery. For the first month we were taught in the Hospital, how to deliver babies and even how to bath them, under the supervision of the Chief Midwife, Sister Victor. She was a great person, very fat, very strict, and very kind. She taught us more about normal deliveries than all the Consultants put together.

Then we were sent out, in twos, to Maternity cases on 'The District' as it was called. Our District was the heart of London's East End. It was inhabited then by Jewish tailors, and Irish families who kept small shops. There were also tumbledown tenements, let out to labourers and street women, all very poor indeed.

The Jews and the Irish detested each other, and there were often fights between them. Even policemen and Nurses went about in twos, and carried whistles. The authorities were much concerned for our safety – Nurses wore uniform, male students were thought to be doctors, both were respected. But what about young women in mufti?

Some of the House Governors wanted to prevent our going on the District at all. We of course insisted that we would do the same as all Medical Students did, we couldn't get qualified without.

They temporised by providing us with the green cloaks and bonnets which the nurses wore.

The first couple from our group was the Scots girl and a tall young man called Donald Joy. They both put on the cloaks and caps, and came to show themselves, very solemnly, to the rest of us. They looked so funny that we shouted with laughter.

With equal solemnity they took off the nurses' clothes and dropped them on the floor before they sped off to the District. I don't know what happened to the cloaks and caps, they were never seen again. We never wore them and we were never attacked.

I still remember my first District case. The man who should have gone with me was ill, and the other two had been out earlier that night, so I had to go alone. That in itself was alarming, at three o'clock in the morning.

The patient's husband, who had come for me, was a taciturn man. He wheeled my bicycle with the Midder Bag on its carrier, and spoke no word until we arrived at the tenement where he lived. Then he said "Upstairs. Mind the 'oles."

The stairs were steep and narrow, and very dark. One tread was entirely missing. After a stumble, I climbed over it to the next.

I found myself in a gloomy little room, lit by four guttering candles. Nothing was in it but a crooked bed and two dilapidated chairs.

The girl on the bed was covered only by a thin, grubby blanket. She looked up at me through a tangle of hair, her eyes terrified.

In a minute she screamed, "It's coming again! 'Elp me doctor, 'elp me!"

The elderly Sary Gamp who was in charge of her grunted "Push, girl, push!"

I began to take off my hat, but the Sary Gamp stopped me. "You keep that on. You'll get things on yer 'ead. An' put yer coat on that chair, *under* the brown paper, or you'll get things on that too — "

I looked about for "things" that flew, but found none. What I did find was that the walls and ceiling were rippling with movement.

They were covered with bugs.

Still, the baby came out quickly and easily. The Sary Gamp and the young mother laughed when it began to cry.

When I came downstairs, the patient's husband was sitting in the kitchen, beside a table on which lay a large kitchen knife. He looked up and said,

"She all right?"

"She's fine," I said. "And you've got a little boy."

"But is *she* all right?"

"I told you. She's fine."

He fingered the knife. "This were for you, if she hadn't a bin," he said.

We stared at each other. Then his face was split by a great smile.

"An' we've got a boy? We've really got a boy?" And he was off up the stairs in a flash.

I went back to the hospital then, by myself this time, on my bicycle, well pleased with my first case – though I must say I didn't like those little narrow dark streets between the tall tenements.

When I got back to the hospital, I began to do what we had to do, clean out the Midder bag and make it ready for the next call. But Louie, the woman who looked after the Midder students, in the hostel where we lived, sailed down on me.

"You leave that a while," she said, "Look after yerself. What about yer hair?"

"What about it?" I said.

"You'll have things in it. You take it down and let me look."

She pulled out all my hairpins, poked about with a comb – and extracted a creature like a miniature brown crab.

"There. That come off your hat. Now strip & see if there are any more. No need to be shy, I've done it more times that you've got years, an' I know what a girl looks like — "

So I stripped, and she found four more bugs. She attacked me with a damp cake of soap – "The only way you can pick 'em up," she explained. "There, now you can dress."

I couldn't stop scratching all that night, I was sure I'd been bitten.

I did the required twenty cases on the District without mishap, though I did have to send once for the registrar for a baby which was upside down. He arrived in a horse-drawn cab, at the gallop, with the patient's husband running beside him. And that baby arrived safely too.

In the hilarity which always follows a successful confinement, I was given several presents – a large plaice or a bag of whelks from porters from the docks, an occasional bottle of cherry brandy, the usual gift of a Jew at the birth of his first son. Carrying those back without breakage in one's bicycle basket was quite a job, the plaice even worse than the cherry brandy.

After that, we had a month of Casualty. At the London, patients came in, at that time, when they wanted to. They were never sent in by their own doctors even if they had one. There again, we learned more from Casualty Sister than from anyone else. She seemed to know exactly what everyone had the matter and put them all in their proper places – infectious diseases in the isolation cubicles, broken bones in the splint room, very ill people on stretchers ready to come in.

Then it was all over. There were exams, then holidays, the coming back to get results. We had all four passed, the Scots girl with distinction. We were qualified doctors.

The experiment had evidently been a success, for by the time we were qualified the number of women students was about fifty. But as soon as the war was over no women were taken – because, they said, having them interfered with the Hospital Rugger.

I'm still glad I did it.

I've had a interesting life.

I did several House Jobs, in various different places – a whole year in Plymouth, for one. Then I decided to do General Practice. And there, to my surprise, there began to be difficulties again. The male doctors were not prepared to accept me.

But gradually patients began to come – all women except for one young man, who came because, he said, women were kinder than me. He stayed with me till he died, when he was 69, just before I retired.

After a very few years, I had three partners, all women, and the practice is still going strong, after 60 years. But that is another story.

Thank you very much for asking me to tell you about it.

BIBLIOGRAPHY

Girls' school stories
by 'Josephine Elder'
Erica Wins Through. Chambers, 1924
The Scholarship Girl. Chambers, 1925
The Scholarship Girl at Cambridge. Chambers, 1926
Thomasina Toddy. Chambers, 1927
Evelyn Finds Herself. OUP, 1929
Barbara at School. Blackie, 1930
The Redheads. OUP, 1931
Exile for Annis. Collins, 1938
Cherry Tree Perch. Collins, 1939
Strangers at the Farm School. Collins, 1940.

Adult novels
by 'Margaret Potter':
Sister Anne Resigns. Selwyn & Blount, 1931
The Mystery of the Purple Bentley. Selwyn & Blount, 1932

by 'Josephine Elder':
Lady of Letters. Lutterworth, 1949
The Encircled Heart. Lutterworth, 1951
Doctor's Children. Lutterworth, 1954.
Fantastic Honeymoon. Robert Hale, 1961

THE ENCIRCLED HEART

PART ONE
*
Marion

MARION BLAKE drove cautiously in the half-light of summer midnight, looking for a house. Much of the little terrace was already asleep, but some way ahead light shone from an open front door. She accelerated, and drew up in the bright beam, and a young man came out quickly. An older woman, stout and tousled, waited uncertainly in the doorway.

"I'm glad to see you, Doctor! You haven't been long."

She smiled at him as she turned off her headlights and reached for her bag. He snatched at the car door as though he could hardly wait for her to get out.

"You'll be even more glad when it's all over," she said, and he grunted assent, unable to assemble words, and stood back for her to pass in front of him into the house.

Upstairs, a door opened suddenly, and a nurse shut it behind her and came down. She pulled a mask from her face as she came, and left it dangling from one ear. Her face was drawn and anxious.

"Sorry to get you out, Doctor, but there's some obstruction. She's been in labour just over forty-eight hours now — " She waved the young man and the stout woman peremptorily away, and began to give details of the labour's progress.

Following her presently into the bedroom, Marion Blake encountered at once the questioning gaze of a pair of terrified grey-green eyes in a childish face. Then the face was withdrawn, to be buried in the pillow, a hand shot out, gripping the sheet, and the girl groaned, and moved jerkily about on the bed.

A pupil midwife, sitting beside her, remarked with an exasperated resignation, "She won't help herself a bit!"

The older nurse said, "It isn't generally won't, it's generally can't. That's what I'm worrying about. She oughtn't to be able to avoid helping herself, by this time!"

The girl's tensed body had gone limp, and she swept the damp hair back from her brow. Looking at Dr. Blake, she said tearfully, "I'm a coward. I know I'm a coward, but I can't do a thing more!"

Marion Blake turned away from her and called down the stairway to the girl's husband, and in a minute he came up, carrying the square case of her gas-and-air machine, and handed it through the door, and a spare cylinder of gas after it.

His wife watched her as she arranged it on a corner of the bed.

"It looks like a gramophone."

"You'll enjoy it just as much as if it were. See, now – as soon as you feel the very beginning of a pain, hold this thing on your face as tight as ever you can and take big breaths into it."

"I can feel it now – it's coming now. Oh, stop it, please stop it — " She stretched an eager hand.

"Other way up – that's right – clamp it on tight, if it leaks it doesn't do much good."

There was no sound in the room but the girl's deep breathing and the click-click of the machine. The nurses stood back watching.

Marion Blake said, "I'll examine her," and moved round the bed.

While she was washing her hands, the pain passed and the girl came, blinking, back to life.

"Was that better?" Dr. Blake asked her.

The girl smiled, the delighted smile of successful 'laughing gas'. "It was *lovely.*"

"Well, breathe it up again," she was told, "while I find out how you're getting on."

The examination over, the doctor stood drying her hands and thinking. The nurses, eyeing her silently, were, she was sure, hoping that she would send the girl to hospital, or at any rate put on forceps and pull the baby out quickly and bring their long vigil to an end.

She said, "I'll listen to its heart."

The older nurse told her, "It's all right, but it's getting rather slow, I thought."

Just to let me know she really thinks something ought to be done, Marion Blake thought amusedly. Aloud she said after a minute, "It's O.K. now, anyway. The head's low and in a good position; I don't see why she shouldn't push it out herself, with the gas to quiet her." Then, with a twinkle in her eye at the sudden wilting of the pupil midwife, who had been doing most of the watching, "We'll see how she gets on with half a dozen pains, and if we're not happy about her then, you can boil up the forceps."

To the girl, she said, "All right, now? You can do a bit more with the gas to help you? Push when I tell you?"

"I'm afraid to push," the girl said positively. "It hurts. It'll hurt when it comes out. It'll hurt *horribly!* This stuff

5

doesn't send you right off, does it? Can't you put me right off and get it out for me, Doctor? Please?" She began to move about again restlessly, and her lip trembled.

Marion Blake bent down to her. "Listen. It doesn't come out with a plop, you know, it slides out gently, and it's all covered with grease to make it come easily. Did you know that?"

The girl was listening intently and managed a smile. "No, I didn't know. It feels as though I'm going to split myself, every time."

"You won't, if you do as we tell you. And there's a button on this machine – here – that gives you much stronger gas if we press it – see? – and puts you right out for a few minutes if you need it."

The girl stared at her, appraising. "All right. I'll try. It's coming again — "

Before the sixth pain it was apparent that Dr. Blake's judgment was correct. The girl was taking the gas well, not fighting any more, responding to the directions: "Four big breaths – one – two – three – four. Now hold your breath and push – that's good – another – can you manage another?"

The pupil midwife said, "I can see the head."

The older nurse abandoned her attitude of disapproval and bustled about the room, straightening things up, getting hot water. The tense atmosphere relaxed. A daddy-long-legs wavered across the bed, and one of the nurses flapped at it. "Go away, you horrid thing!" The creature flew, immediately, straight up to the picture-rail and hung there. Marion Blake said absently, "He heard!" A ripple of amusement ran round.

The pupil midwife looked up and whispered, "May I deliver her, Doctor? She was my case — "

The older nurse put in, "Such a job, to get enough normal cases for the pupils!"

Dr. Blake nodded. "Yes. I'll just stay and keep an eye on the anaesthetic, now I'm here."

The senior nurse asked anxiously, "You do think I did right to send? She was getting so unmanageable!"

"I think you had to send. She would have tired herself out, as she was, and p'raps produced a dead baby after a very long time."

The nurse looked gratified. It would have hurt her pride, had anyone thought she had sent for medical aid unnecessarily, especially in front of a pupil. They settled down to wait a little longer.

Marion Blake looked around the room: an ordinary little jerry-built room, littered now with the paraphernalia of childbirth – enamel basins, piles of towels, tossed blankets, little clothes; its own small ornaments pushed aside.

On the wall opposite her hung a print of part of Leonardo da Vinci's Holy Family, the sweet-faced Virgin seated with the Baby on her knee, the little St. John running to her side. She spoke the thought which came into her head, "Queer to think of – that confinement. Just an ordinary labour, but a nice, normal, joyous one."

The older nurse spoke chirpily into the rather embarrassed silence. "Nice and normal – yes, that's how it would have been. No complications there – and no anesthetic either!"

Marion Blake looked tenderly at the serene Madonna. "No need for it, I expect. She was a healthy young country-woman . . . and there must have been a great sense of safety, of being looked after, in spite of the manger, and the inn being full up and all that. Not any fear." She glanced at the nurse's thin-lipped, efficient-looking face. "It's fear that's generally the cause of these troubles."

The nurse was not quite ready to give up her theory of mechanical obstruction. She said so. "And even now it's not getting on as fast as I would like."

The doctor, perfectly cheerful because she was quite sure of herself, said, "Fast enough. You'll see," and went round to the patient's head to make certain that she was not being disturbed by the murmured conversation. She was not. She was breathing deeply into her mask, alternately sleeping and drowsing as her grasp on it tightened and gave.

The nurse pursued her own line of thought. "Give me a nice normal labour with no interference. No anæsthetic to slow up the pains. That's what I like."

Dr. Blake said, "I'm never satisfied with my conduct of a labour if the mother says, a few days later, that she'll never have another baby."

The nurse, startled out of careful argument, cried out, "But they *all* say that!" And Dr. Blake, spreading out her hands comically, rejoined, "Exactly! They all do, or nearly all, in this too-civilized age, unless you help them. Five years ago, it would have been chloroform and forceps, or nothing and a stillbirth, for this girl. Now, it's this, and she'll deliver herself naturally, be perfectly fit to-morrow, and be willing to have another, without apprehension, in a

8

couple of years."

The nurse said, with a cackle, "They all do that, too! Have another! And in less than a couple of years, most of them!"

Dr. Blake grinned. "I said, without apprehension! And you must admit there are far too many only children."

The pupil midwife, intent on what was happening in front of her, murmured, "Look at that! It's really coming, in another pain or two! And I've been sitting over it since teatime listening to her groans! I wouldn't have believed there could be such a change!"

The doctor moved round beside her, watching her eager face and careful hands; gave her a hint or two, and went back to regulate the flow of gas to the patient and to speak to her when, in her drowsy, contented state, she would be likely to obey. "A little push – steady – now don't push any more, just breathe."

A few anxious minutes, with the three women working wordlessly as a team, and then a small tense body was kicking and beating its fists beside its quiet mother. It opened its mouth and let out a great yell, and everyone laughed. "Funny little thing!"

The pupil remarked, with great satisfaction, "Not even the tiniest split!" The doctor said, "Good work!"

The senior midwife took command again. "Eyes, Nurse! The eye-swabs are behind you."

After a while the young mother stirred. "Is it born? Is it all right?"

Marion Blake smiled down at her. "It's a boy. And it's quite perfect."

A beatific look came over the girl's face, smoothing out

9

the strain, turning her into a child again. She slept.

She woke presently. "What are you waiting for? Didn't you say it was born?"

The nurse told her, "The afterbirth. And we'd be just as glad if you'd please hurry it up."

Fear glinted again in the girl's eyes. "Do I have to have some more pain?"

The nurse became jocular, bustling. "Bless you, no! Just a little pressure, here, that's all."

The girl tensed up at once. "I can't, I can't! Oh, please don't touch me!" The nurse shrugged and stood aside.

Marion Blake strolled over to her. "I shall have," she said conversationally, "to tell you my story about the land-girl."

She looked up languidly. Anything, she seemed to say, to take my mind off all this horribleness – and the attention of the nurses off me! "What's that?"

"It's not a very proper story."

"Having babies," the girl said, "doesn't seem to me a very proper business."

"Well, I was attending a young woman who had been a land-girl, and like you, she was a long time producing her afterbirth. She grew very tired of waiting, and said crossly, 'I wish I was a cow!' I, of course, asked why, and she said, 'Well, I've helped a lot of cows to have calves, and when it's time for the afterbirth to come, the cow just says "Moo!" and it comes'. Of course the only reply to that was, 'Well, for heaven's sake say "Moo!" ' – and she did – and it came!"

The girl gave the ghost of a smile. "D'you want me to say 'Moo'?"

"You can if you like. But I can't tell that tale to everyone,

10

so I generally just ask them to say 'Oh dear!' "

Still smiling, the girl said cautiously, "Oh, dear!"

"Oh come! Say it as if you meant it!"

She laughed this time, and ejaculated "Oh, dear!" on the gust of it – and then, with real concern, "Oh, *dear*!" and the business was over.

Marion Blake said, "Nicely done," and went and scooped up the baby, and showed his mother his crumpled, blinking face. He turned his head to her, and opened his mouth, and got a hand out, all its fingers stretched, and she laid one of her own on it, and laughed delightedly at his immediate grip. She stroked his petal cheek, and murmured, "John!" in great content. The nurse looked disapproving. She did not like her mothers to see the babies until they had been bathed.

As Marion dumped him back in his cradle the girl asked, "Did I do it all right?"

"Very well indeed," Dr. Blake told her. "You were very co-operative."

The pupil midwife, inclined to be hilarious now, chirruped, "*Co-operative*! You should have seen her before you came, Doctor! And heard her! I should think she woke the whole road!"

The girl looked ashamed of herself. "I was terrified! But that thing" – she nodded at the discarded gas-and-air machine – "that's magic! And" – shyly – "you gave me such confidence."

Marion Blake cocked an eye at the nurses. "What did I tell you? Well, I'll leave you now. Good night, Mrs. Elroy. Good night, Nurse."

11

"Good night, Doctor, and thank you," they chorused, and the doctor shouldered her way out, machine and all, and down to the little living-room, where the young husband was picking his way, like a caged animal, among a crowd of relatives. They turned mute, startled faces to her.

She smiled at them. "It's a boy. A nice, vigorous baby."

"And she's – all right?" The husband was not interested in the baby, yet.

"She's fine. I left her talking and laughing with the nurses."

The young man made a dash for the stairs.

"Wait a bit! She'll welcome you much more when she's been tidied up."

He grinned, and came and took her bag from her. "We do thank you, Doctor! It all seemed too awful, till you came, with her screaming and crying, and nothing getting on at all."

Grandmother bustled in with the teapot, Grandfather bent over a bureau and came up with a bundle of postcards. "Got these all addressed. Just left spaces to write boy or girl and the date!" He beamed upon them.

Funny, Marion Blake thought, to think of all the repercussions: people waiting for news, cards, presents, a paragraph in the paper. New titles for everyone, Granny, Grampa, Mummy and Daddy. For me, just a job safely over, and home, thankfully, to bed.

She excused herself from staying for a cup of tea on the ground that it would keep her awake, and drove home in the mood of exaltation that a successful confinement always induced in her. She considered the drama of it, the gay projection of one's own courage to sustain the labouring woman, the thought for her, exclusively and all the time, the intuitive interpretation of her mood; nice judgment, gentle handling, the right words; all these contributed to success, and at the end of it there was such gratitude, such joy, as the fear of what might be, what might have been, sank away and was forgotten.

She might have added to the catalogue of what was required and given, an utter forgetfulness of self; but did not, because she thought seldom about her own reactions. She jogged joyously, sleepily home, humming a little tuneful song. She loved her maternity work. It might get you out at midnight and keep you up till dawn, spoil your pleasures and interfere with your plans, but you got a kick out of it which nothing else could give you.

She put the car away and let herself in quietly, but in spite of her care she heard the click of a switch as she went upstairs, and a voice asked softly from a lighted room, "Hullo, have you got your baby?"

Marion tiptoed across the passage. It was a pity Philippa was such a light sleeper – but lovely to come back to someone who was willing to talk at any hour of the night, and ridiculously nice of her to leave her door ajar. She went in and shut it carefully behind her.

Philippa, her hair netted and her face creamed, had obviously just awoken. A white bull-terrier opened pink eyes, smiled, showing all his teeth, and thumped his tail on the bed, where he lay curled. Marion rubbed his head, and he at once jumped down and lumbered away to his basket in the corner.

13

Philippa laughed. "Funny old thing, isn't he, how he won't settle down till we're both in?"

Marion said affectionately, "You're rather like that yourself too, aren't you?"

"Not really. I've been to sleep, and noises always wake me whatever they are. I shall be asleep again in two ticks. There's some cocoa in the Thermos in your room."

"You shouldn't have . . . I shall enjoy it though, bless you; I'm always empty after these performances."

Philippa grunted and arranged herself for sleep. The bull-terrier was snoring already. Marion kissed her friend perfunctorily and left them.

She drank her cocoa as she undressed, thinking contentedly that she did, really, have rather a good life; and was soon asleep herself.

2

She was thinking much the same the next morning as she sat finishing her breakfast, the window wide open to the garden sunshine lighting the golden-yellow Heal cups and platters and the flowers on the table; the bull-terrier squatting on a stool with his chin on the window-sill, a pleasant smell of coffee, toast and bacon in the air.

Philippa had gone to her job as pathologist to the local municipal hospital. She was a good person to live with, Philippa. The two had been students together, and had maintained a close though unemotional friendship along the years. Marion smiled as she remembered the wary passage of the small number of women students through the great teaching hospital full of ribald, racketty men. She herself had been brilliant at her work and much taken up with it, so that most of her colleagues, after the first impact with her good looks, her quiet voice, and unexpected, humorous remarks, often alarmingly to the point, had sheered off and left her alone. Philippa, less clever, though a good all-rounder, had mixed better, and was continually in verbal battle with someone or other, man or woman. Philippa had been remarkable, too, for her defiance of authority's timid request that women students should dress quietly and be as unobtrusive as possible. "Ashamed of us, are they?" she had snorted. "Well, I'm a woman, even if I do choose to qualify myself for the hardest-used profession in the world. So what about it?" And she had lipsticked, pinked her nails, worn colourful jumpers and dainty stockings and shoes and careful curls from her first appearance there – and still did. Marion did not think that, man, or woman, clothes mattered much as long as you were tidy – and indeed they did not to her, because she had such good material to work on – and she stuck to coats and skirts. She never wore mannish ties, though, and her stockings matched Philippa's in silken sheen. Curiously, Philippa smoked a great deal, and Marion not at all. A funny couple, people called them. However, they agreed on many things, disagreed without rancour, and each treasured her own integrity and would have died rather than tamper, however gently, with that of the other.

"Why the dickens should we want to be alike, even if we

do go around together?" they asked, when people remarked on their differences. "I can think of nothing duller!"

Each had lived at home during the student years, though they had often gone on holiday together. After they had done their quota of hospital posts, they had looked for some way of setting up a common household. They had found it when Philippa had been appointed as pathologist to this big hospital some eighty main-line miles from London. (Fantastic to think of dainty Philippa growing microbes from pus and urine and doing postmortems, but there it was; she liked the stark truth of it, she said.) They had bought a small, pleasant house with a legacy of Philippa's from an aunt and a loan from Marion's people, and Marion had put up a plate. A new estate, and the fact that there was no other woman doctor within miles, had done the rest. Now, after four years, she was established, and had as much work as she could comfortably do.

She went from the breakfast-table to her surgery, passing on her way Ethel, the elderly maid – also a legacy from Philippa's aunt – who looked efficiently after them. Ethel was a prim and starchy person who belonged to one of those small religious sects which suspect all pleasure and most beauty, but compensate by a rigid sense of personal duty. She was, however, incongruously devoted to Philippa, put up with Marion, and dealt tolerantly with insistent patients.

"I suppose, Miss," she had said grimly to Marion one day at the beginning of their association, "we must behave as though the patient is always right?"

Marion had acceded with a twinkle. "I'm afraid we must,

Ethel, if we're to build up a practice."

Ethel had nodded, with pursed lips, realizing fully how much of success in such an enterprise lies in the hands of those who answer doors and telephones. She had loyally carried out the policy, and the practice had grown.

To-day, Marion paused and asked if there was anything Ethel wanted in the town.

"If you could bring in a lettuce, please, Miss, then I shouldn't have to go running out. Those in the garden have shot up, in the dry weather, and they'll be bitter."

"I will. And have we got any nice biscuits for to-night?"

Ethel's chin went down into her collar. The one disadvantage of her was her dislike of visitors, perhaps because they made more washing-up for her knobbly old hands, perhaps for the gaiety they seemed to symbolize. "I don't know, Miss, I'm sure."

"I'll look in the tin, and bring some if we want them," Marion said, and with her smile extorted the grimace which passed for one on the maid's pinched countenance. A blessing, that sense of duty, Marion thought. One knew Ethel would love to poison the coffee or pour the soup down some pretty dress. But one knew, too, that she would in fact never do more than swish round, with a face like a turkey-cock's and an occasional snort.

In the surgery, she arranged her list for the day, then went out. Bill, the bull-terrier, was waiting smugly by the garage door, and jumped into the back seat of the car before she could get in herself. He loved the car and, the mildest of dogs, would show his great teeth, lay back his ears, and growl fiercely if anyone so much as looked at it while he

17

was there.

Marion went to see last night's baby, and found the mother sitting up, the dimples coming and going in her chubby pink cheeks, the baby stolidly asleep in his cradle beside her.

"Like him?"

"He's *lovely* ! At least, I think so. I can't – it's funny, you know, I can't believe I *made* a thing like that. He seems so separate, so complete."

Marion nodded. "I know. And yet, if he were hurt you'd feel as if someone were cutting an arm or a leg off you."

"I suppose I should — "

They chatted on, while Marion satisfied herself that all was well with them.

She blew in to exchange chaff with a schoolgirl recovering from an acute appendix in a nursing home, and into a house where three children whooped dismally at her one after another, gave Bill a run on a bit of waste ground, then went back for her consulting hour at home.

On the way in she pulled a face. She had seen through the waiting-room window the grim old figure of Mrs. Williams, who lived by herself down the road because no one would live with her, and came in once or twice a week to moan over some part of her healthy but ancient anatomy and go off, if she had a chance, with the newest papers from the table.

"It's my *spine*, Doctor! The pains run *up* it and *down* it." She illustrated the pain's passage with twittering fingers, and Marion settled herself to argue away all possible diseases of the spine which the old lady might have read up in her *Home Doctor*, before she sent her away with a prescription for liniment and a deal of healthful suggestion.

Then came Miss Ferrers, her head up, limping in, a rheumatoid arthritic who was still teaching history at the local High School; a plucky, smiling woman with a sharp tongue and lines of pain marked deeply on her face. Marion admired her. She really had something to grouse about, and she never groused, her friends said. She just kept herself busy or amused, to the extent of being a Girl Guide Commissioner out of school hours and always being ready to play a hand of bridge. Getting ready a gold injection for her, Marion pondered about rheumatoid arthritis. She had a theory that it was due, always, to loss of courage as much as to septic teeth or what-have-you of that kind as the consultants said, and here was this woman upsetting her ideas. Although, one could regain lost courage after the damage had been done and, if one did, one might over-compensate just like this.

"Just coming – there – worse to wait for than to have — "

Miss Ferrers agreed, with her radiant smile. "I still hate waiting for it, and I still sigh with relief when it's over. That's the last of this series, anyway."

"Yes. Let me see you from time to time – I'm sure to, you'll be in for something."

"Alas, yes. Though I enjoy coming, if it isn't for a prick!"

An ante-natal examination, full of encouragement and re-assurance for all its thoroughness, a couple of panel certificates, a septic finger that needed opening, and the hour was over.

Ethel brought in a cup of coffee and another visit for the

list, and Marion was away out of the house again.

She would go to Mrs. Bowen first, because she couldn't make up her mind what was the matter there. A healthy, hard-working woman in her late forties, with two sons and a daughter, suddenly smitten with blinding headaches, so bad that they sent her moaning to bed, made her vomit, seemed to deprive her of all sense. Cerebral hæmorrhage, meningitis, tumour of the brain, migraine – Dr. Blake had thought of them all, even carefully read them up in case she might have missed some fine pointer, and none of them fitted. Meanwhile she had the woman in bed for safety; the daughter, grumbling, away from work to look after her. But that couldn't go on for more than a few days. If ordinary observation could not lead to a diagnosis, Mrs. Bowen must go to hospital, and this Mrs. Bowen stoutly refused to consider.

She found the front door ajar, the daughter having gone shopping, Mrs. Bowen was sitting up in bed, looking much more sensible and with a purposeful light in her eyes.

Dr. Blake said to her, "You're better."

Mrs. Bowen nodded, then rushed into speech, brushing the doctor's comment aside.

"I must tell you, Doctor. It's no good you examining me and doin' me jerks and lookin' at me eyes and takin' me temperature. It's nothing physical that's wrong with me, nothing at all. It's me nerves, that's all, just me nerves."

She stopped, breathless with the effort of having made herself say what she wanted to say. Dr. Blake, watching her, wondering whether the outburst was truth or wishful thinking, put in mildly, "I wouldn't have said you were a

20

nervous subject. And you've not had headaches before, have you?"

"No, I haven't. And I wouldn't have called myself a nervous subject, either. Nor am I not, but we must all have our limits, mustn't we? And I've reached mine. I must tell you, Doctor. I've sent Florrie out on purpose. It's me husband — "

Dr. Blake sent her mind back to Mrs. Bowen's husband, a pleasant-spoken, quiet man, to the three upstanding children, the respectable, well-kept house, and wondered if the woman were going out of her mind. But that, like the other diagnoses, did not fit.

She listened, then, to an ordered account of the life of the wife of a gambler; a man in a good job who spent the whole of his spare time and most of his earnings betting; drinking rather more than was good for him, though not enough to make him really drunk; how he would make promises and break them; save to be married – it went back as far as that, though then she had not known of it – for the babies as they were coming, for holidays, spending the lot each time before it could be used, looking to her to scrimp and pay the bills; how several little legacies, or so he had called them, she thought now they must have been lucky bets, had been gambled away with no benefit to anyone; except one, a big one, with which she had managed to persuade him to buy the little house they lived in.

"And now," she wound up, her bright eyes and a spot of colour in each cheek making her look young and pretty again if you did not peer too closely, "two things have happened. He's raised a mortgage on the house, and he's

21

lost his job. That means he's lost his pension. So we've no house, no income, no future. And he's no wife, for I'm through with him. All these twenty-two years I've kept silent, kept us all respectable, saved and planned and economized, and no one's known a thing was wrong. Such a *nice* man, everyone calls him, and I've never said a thing against him, though I've thought the more. It's not just the money, it's the slipperiness of him, how you can't trust a word he says. And now he's not working, he's in and out of the house at all hours, and I just can't bear it. There's no need for me here any more, I don't do him any good, and the children are on their own feet. I'm going away. The headache" – she turned her bright gaze on the doctor – "the headache was because I couldn't bring myself to tell him. He *is* a nice man, in some ways, he isn't all bad, or I'd have left him long ago. Well, now I've told him, and the headache's gone, and this afternoon I'm getting up and going to my sister's, and he must manage as best he may."

Through the professional part of Dr. Blake's brain flitted the dictum of one of her old teachers. "The label 'neurotic headache' is the refuge of the clinically destitute." The human part of it understood the situation perfectly, and allowed herself to have been properly had. Awful, she thought, to be dependent upon such a reed, to be concerned with keeping the family end up and never know from day to day when its nominal prop would let it sprawling down. To suspect his every assurance, to answer with fear every unexpected knock on the door lest it might be a policeman after him for swindling or for debt. Better, far, to rely on one's own efforts alone, hard work and lonely though that might be.

Aloud, she said, "You wouldn't have the slightest difficulty, of course, in getting a good job as a housekeeper. I'd give you a marvellous testimonial, if that would help."

The woman glanced, in a queer, appraising way, round the room. She said, "Thank you, Doctor. I shall hold you to that. It was what I was hoping for."

"Are you sleeping?"

"I shall, now. I haven't been. I've got some of those tablets you gave me."

Dr. Blake rose, and gave her a direct, encouraging glance. She was a little surprised when the woman, after meeting it, quickly turned away. Tired, after that outburst, she supposed. She let herself out, glad to find that the daughter, Florrie, had not yet come in.

The next few visits were not of great interest, and her thoughts kept returning to Mrs. Bowen. The last one before lunch was to a favourite patient of hers, a woman in her seventies, the widow of a headmaster, a gracious, wise, and charming person, kept tied to her chair by a failing heart. Marion Blake sat down contentedly in her lovely little room in which every article had a beauty of its own and which was filled with an atmosphere so harmonious that she called it, privately, the ante-room to heaven. Mrs. Gordon had been a handsome, lively woman, and was so still, within the limits of her restriction. When Dr. Blake had asked the necessary questions – and given appropriate advice, she was moved suddenly to tell the old lady Mrs. Bowen's story. She disguised it sufficiently to appease medical ethics, knowing that happenings down the hill were unlikely to be known at the top of it.

"And now," she finished up, "the children are off her hands, and she feels she can put an end to this awful life of uncertainty, and leave him and get herself a job and be dependent on herself."

The old lady surveyed her with shrewd and kindly eyes.

"That would mean leaving her home?"

Marion Blake allowed, "Well, yes, it would."

"I've always thought," Mrs. Gordon said, "that a home's more important – far more important – to a woman than a husband. A widow who can keep her home can be a useful, even a moderately happy person. One who loses her home is hardly ever either. I've noticed it repeatedly."

She peered pleasantly at the young doctor. "If your friend could only get her husband to walk out, instead of going herself! Couldn't she manage that?"

Marion Blake said seriously, "I very much doubt it."

"Then" – the old lady hitched herself judicially up in her chair – "I should strongly advise her to hold her horses. She'll only be exchanging one form of insecurity for another. It's not easy to walk on two legs when you've been accustomed to four, even if two of the four are wobbly. And it's less than ever easy when you're walking on strange ground. And there's the legal aspect of it, too. If she leaves the man without a proper agreement, she can't claim any form of separation allowance."

"I don't think she'd mind that," Marion Blake said. "She'd be unlikely to get it regularly, anyway, from him. She wants to be free of all the doubt and worry and know just where she stands."

24

The old lady spread out her hands. "I know, I know. But I still think she's rash. It isn't any fun to depend on oneself, suddenly, in middle age, never having done it before. You tell her" – the old eyes twinkled – "to make his life such a burden by jumping on all his little lapses that he'll go off and leave her the house and the children. Then she can take in lodgers, be the boss of her own home, and tell herself it's good riddance of bad rubbish. It's not so very unnatural for a man to go roving. For a woman I think it's so very contrary to nature that it almost never leads to happiness."

Driving along the road again, Marion felt deflated. She knew a whole lot about medicine, but precious little about practical living and less about law. She comforted herself by the thought that Mrs. Gordon belonged to another generation, and had been happily married. How could she put herself in the shoes of a woman like Mrs. Bowen or of a sturdy spinster whose two legs were her sole support?

She was, however, so disturbed that she turned in to a side street, and so went down the hill and back to Mrs. Bowen's house. People attached an importance out of all proportion to any casual word which a doctor might utter. "The doctor said — " And she had certainly shown approval of the woman's drastic plan. She would try to get her to think things over for a bit longer . . .

But the door was shut and there was no reply. A neighbour stuck her head out of a window and said, "Mrs. Bowen went out half an hour ago, and Florrie ain't in yet – what she'll say I *don't* know!"

3

In the afternoon, Marion went to the hospital to give anæsthetics; not the big municipal hospital where Philippa worked, but a smaller, voluntary hospital, longer established, and run mainly by the local doctors, who gave their services there free. To be one of its staff was an honour, for new members were elected on their merits by those who already worked there, and Marion, when she first put up her plate, had no idea that she would be welcome. Indeed, she had wondered how the local doctors would receive her, a stranger, and the first woman in the district. They had been quite surprisingly friendly. She had taken great care not to "pinch their patients", refusing any who already had a doctor unless it was for some purely female complaint, when she would see them, and pack them off back to their own practitioner with a report. She had been ready, too, to stand by for a colleague who wanted to play golf or go to a theatre when, perhaps, he had a confinement due. They had responded by sinking both sex and professional jealousy and, when an extra anæsthetist had been wanted at their beloved hospital and she had applied, by electing her to the post. And here again she was not above being "dog's body", to be called upon for emergency anæsthetics at times like Christmas Day and Bank Holidays, when no one else wanted to go.

To-day was her regular weekly afternoon at the hospital. She swung in, giving good day to the porter, looked in at the children's ward, where a child from her practice was getting over a tonsillectomy, and chatted with the sister;

met in the corridor a cleaner who was on her panel and smiled at her, and the Radiologist, a keen young man, who hailed her about a fracture case she had sent in; and on into the theatre, to get herself washed and gowned and her machine ready before the surgeon arrived. Sister Theatre greeted her cheerfully, a young nurse tied the strings of her gown for her. It was fun, to be in touch still with hospital life, and to be *persona grata* for no particular reason except that you were keen on your job.

The surgeon was an elderly, serious man, a little slow but very sound. He plated, carefully, a broken bone which would not knit. He removed a breast for cancer; a brutal, bloody, mutilating operation, but at best a life-saver, at least a comfort-maker for months or years. He filleted a couple of hammer-toes. All three operations with Marion Blake seated at the head of the table, watching the patient's breathing and pulse and the anæsthetic machine, a life, for the time being, in her keeping. When he was not doing the ticklish bits, the surgeon talked, to Marion and to the house-surgeon who was assisting him – shop, and rather proper funny stories, mostly about fishing or golf.

When they had finished, they had tea in the little room beside the theatre – the chippy toast, apparently fried, which hospitals always have, and jam, and sponge-cakes, which were probably, in the hospital balance sheet, intended for patients. Sister poured out the tea, and the talk was not shop any more, but current events, the pictures, hospital gossip. The surgeon thanked them all politely, as he always did, for their help; bent towards Marion Blake and said, still as though surprised, "Those were excellent

27

anæsthetics you gave me, excellent!" Marion smiled to herself. She had done this job so very often, in her years as a resident, that she could not help but be good at it. But the old boy *was* an old boy, a funny, formal old stick-in-the-mud, and he found it difficult to believe, even now, that a woman could be competent at anything outside a house, though woe betide her, most likely, if she was not most excellently so in one.

When she arrived home, Ethel came out of the kitchen. She always did, in a welcoming sort of way, when either of them had been out for any length of time. Bill jumped off the chair where he had been watching the garden gate, and pushed his pink nose into her hand.

"There are two patients waiting, Miss, and a lady going to ring you up. Wouldn't give her name." This last with disapproval. Ethel disliked bad manners as much as Marion did. "Have you had your tea?"

Marion nodded. "Yes, thank you, Ethel. Is Doctor Spencer in yet?"

"Not yet, Miss. But she did say she wouldn't be late, as you've got visitors coming."

Marion said, "Oh, yes. I'd forgotten them. I'd better get on with the surgery patients, then p'raps we'll get supper at the proper time . . . There's that 'phone!"

A cracked old voice came over the wire . . . eighty-year-old Mrs. Ingram. "Is that you, Doctor dear? I've got the most terrible cough! I don't want to drag you out to-night, so I'm sending my niece round for a prescription. I'm just going to cough into the 'phone, so that you can tell what to give me — "

A throat-rending, ear-splitting sound, which sent Marion Blake back, chuckling, from the receiver, then the cracked old voice again, anxiously. "Was that all right? Shall I cough again?"

"No, thank you, no indeed! It was quite all right, very good! Now I know exactly what to give you, and you must go to bed and I'll come and see you in the morning!"

Surgery: a dozen people with various complaints, one of them a husband who sat uneasily among the women until Ethel, on a word from Marion, entered and intoned, "I have a message for you, Mr. Hobbs!" at which he jumped to his feet in mingled panic and relief. In the hall, Ethel stonily indicated a chair, and Marion bobbed out and motioned him into the consulting-room before his turn. "It was only," she smiled, "that you looked so very unhappy in there! What's the trouble?"

The trouble was a boil, soon dealt with, and he was packed off. "I don't know why I do that," Marion told herself. "Really, I think they're awful idiots to come to a woman, and yet I get sorry for them. Women doctors for women, and men for men . . . and yet each to his choice." She opened the waiting-room door. "Who is coming in next?"

The last patient said, "You'll be glad to see the end of us! You must get fed up with all our ailments."

"I don't, you know," Marion told her. "You're all different, and all interesting!" And thinking it over later, she said to herself, "That's strictly true. The more of them I have, the better I like it."

29

A quick change into a dress instead of a coat and skirt – purely a concession to her visitors, she did not bother about changing on ordinary days, there just wasn't time – dinner, and gossip about the day with Philippa, who as usual contrived to look immaculate and exotic both at once; and soon after, the guests began to arrive.

First, Miss Black, the science mistress at the High School, in her twenties and pretty, if a thought prim; then Dr. Webster, the Radiologist and his wife, a few years older – Mrs. Webster was an Old Girtonian and so was Miss Black; Miss Ferrers, who played a good game of bridge and quickly banished the hollow feeling of pity one felt at the first sight of her by her quick, friendly intelligence; then, in a hurry, as he always was, Dr. Furnivall, the young house-surgeon from the local hospital. There was talk, animated, well-informed, initiated by Philippa, ably supported by the Websters, provocatively prodded by Marion and Miss Ferrers from time to time, and watched by Miss Black and young Furnivall, who plunged in cautiously after a while and soon became able contributors.

Marion went to the kitchen for the coffee, because old Ethel had to be humoured. She was dispensing it for young Furnivall to hand round when the telephone rang.

"Don't go!" Dr. Webster advised.

"It'll ring and ring if I don't."

"I'll go, and say you're out."

But she excused herself, regretfully, for it was a pleasant party, hoping the call could be dealt with verbally.

"It's Mother," came a worried voice – voices so often sounded worried, on that 'phone. "She's slipped down, in her bedroom. We've got her up into a chair, but she simply won't get into bed. Says if she once gets in she'll never get out again."

Marion said tentatively, "Mrs. Plowman, is it?" They were always so sure, patients, that they would be recognized by voice alone, that each was the one and only person in whom the doctor was really, lastingly, interested. Mrs. Plowman was a frail old lady of eighty, and the worried voice her already elderly daughter.

"Yes. Yes. Will you come?"

"Can't you coax her? If she won't do it for you, I don't see why she should for me."

"Oh, Doctor! She'll do almost anything for you!"

"Or just lift her in? You and your husband between you? She's very light."

"She won't let us touch her!" very positively. "Not get near her, even!"

Marion sighed and abandoned her evening's relaxation. "Right. I'll come."

The party turned expectant faces to her, and she told them the story.

Miss Black snorted. "Naughty old dame! Old people are much worse than children, aren't they? – you can just punish a child!"

"Must you go, really?" Mrs. Webster asked. "Won't she give in if she's left alone for a bit?"

"She may be just naughty," Marion said. "Or she may have fractured her thigh."

31

Young Furnivall heaved himself out of his chair. "May I come? I'm going into general practice when I've finished this job."

"Why, yes," Marion told him. "If it is a fracture, I'll be glad of you."

And she was. For the little, bird-like, terrified old lady greeted them tearfully. "A dreadful thing has happened to me, my dear. I've lost the use of my leg!"

"Does it hurt?" Marion inquired, holding the clawed, clutching hand in her own. The old lady, well known to her as one of those Spartans who consider complaints about their health as a lapse of taste, nodded. "Terribly!"

Furnivall's eyes met Marion's, and he stepped forward, very young, very large, very gentle.

"Now you let me hold you up, Gran, while they get your dress off and your nightie on!"

The old lady looked startled. "I'd be ashamed!"

"I'll keep my eyes shut!" he assured her gravely, and they got on with it and had her undressed and lying on her bed before she quite realized what was happening, the four of them lifting her with little pain. But there was no doubt about it, the thigh was broken, high up, in the way old peoples' thighs do break. Marion set the son-in-law telephoning to the hospital while she gave a shot of morphia, and young Furnivall helped her to splint the leg to a broomstick. The old lady was sleepy and did not care what happened by the time they left her, and an hour had gone out of their evening.

Marion said, "Busman's holiday for you, I'm afraid. You did help."

The young man told her, "I enjoyed it. Spunky old girl, not naughty at all."

"I didn't think it would be just naughtiness, from her," Marion said, and he commented, "I like the way you can get to know your patients, as a G.P. There isn't time for it in hospital. *This* one wouldn't be just naughty – but *that* one might. Still, you'd have to go, I suppose, even to the one that might!"

She nodded. "Even a Jew may have organic disease!" – and they were home.

The party was playing bridge, and a discussion as to whether young Furnivall should take Mrs. Webster's place was broken up by a message from the hospital – an acute appendix was to be done at ten, and would he please come and assist?

"Why does one take up medicine?" they agreed, and he went off.

The Websters lingered behind when Miss Black and Miss Ferrers had gone.

Mrs. Webster said, "We're planning a river picnic on Wednesday. Some old friends of Jim's, staying with us for a few days. Would you both come? I know you're good at rivers."

Marion and Philippa looked at each other. They liked the Websters, and they loved the river. Philippa said doubtfully, "I'd adore it. What time of day?"

"Start about five and take supper."

"Could do, I think. Thank you very much. Marion?"

"It's my half-day, so there's no surgery. I'd be off the 'phone an awful long time, though."

Dr. Webster hustled her. "Someone'll stand by for you. Smart, or Dodds. You're always doing it for them."

Mrs. Webster said, "Mustn't make yourself a slave. People don't think any more of you."

"Patients do," she corrected absently. "It's a crime, from their point of view, to sleep or have a meal, much more to go out and enjoy yourself! But I'll let 'em rip this time."

"Good. We'll give you a ring about the exact time and place."

5

Standing at the boat-house waiting for their hosts, the two young women had an impression of golden buttercup fields, blue sky, sun and dancing water, of freedom, and above all, of leisure: the boatman's slow movements across his raft of punts, to hook one here and swing another there, the poise and plunge of paddle or pole, all bespoke it. Marion drew a long breath and voiced her thought to her friend.

Philippa grunted. "You'll have to get a partner. It's a silly way to live, tied and rushed as you are."

"I suppose I shall. I'd rather like to, if I could find the right one . . . Look, here they are, friends and all . . . Hullo, what a lovely day we've got!"

The Websters, another married couple, and two young men came down the path from the car-park. Marion thought pleasantly, "Four to a punt, just right," before she was introduced to them.

"Mr. and Mrs. Ford – they're staying at Appledurham and are over with us for the day. Paul Shepherd and John Prior – they, I'm sorry to say, are rivals, so we'd better put them in separate punts to avoid any dirty work."

The two men laughed, shook hands, and explained. "We're both up for the education job at the University – no, there's only one job – no, we didn't know each other before, but Dr. Webster knew us both. He's kindly putting us up for the two nights. We've been having interviews this afternoon."

First one would speak and then the other, so that it was difficult to distinguish which was which. Yet, watching them, it could be seen that they were very different. Shepherd was a tall, loose-limbed, fair man, diffident in manner yet with a mouth which could shut up tight, and blue eyes, like a sailor's, looking far away. Prior had a pugnacious look about him, he was shorter, sturdier, and his dark hair stood on end. Marion thought he would get the University job.

Philippa was asking, "When will you know?"

They told her, "In a few days. The Selection committee, who saw us to-day, recommends, and a Board confirms. There were two other chaps as well."

Mrs. Webster said briskly, "Now forget it and come into the punts — "

They split up, with some amiable argument, and Marion found herself with Dr. Webster, Mrs. Ford, and Paul Shepherd. Dr. Webster took the pole and propelled them, efficiently but without grace, upstream.

The river was at its loveliest. Clear water rippled and splashed round the punt's nose, willows dipped golden-green fronds to meet their spreading roots of ruby red. Bent reeds made queer geometrical patterns with their own reflections. And away and away the buttercup fields stretched to the oak-woods which bordered them from the cloudless summer sky. Marion lay in the punt and loved it all.

At the other end of the punt Mrs. Ford was inclined to bright comment, and Paul Shepherd squatted beside her, grunting politely when it seemed fit. Both confessed to complete ignorance of punting, and this seemed not to worry the young man at all.

"You'll have to learn, if you come to live here," Marion teased him.

He was imperturbable. "I don't think it's very likely that I shall come. All the others seem to have strings to pull, and I have none. Anyway, it doesn't look very difficult."

Dr. Webster, stung, because, being a dumpy man, he had learned to punt with some trouble, said so firmly, "You come along right now and have a lesson, young fellow," that Shepherd could hardly refuse. He came cautiously from his own end, bent double, evidently unused to craft that floated. Trying to avoid treading on Marion, he swayed, and she put up a hand to save him, and he caught it thankfully and gave her an angry little smile. She flumped across into the place he had left.

The two men looked funny, standing together on the platform. Shepherd, tall, well built, sunburnt, the very

36

picture of an athlete, handled the pole so gingerly that Dr. Webster, balanced with his feet apart and his sturdy person planted squarely, roared at him like a sergeant major. "Oi! – steady, for the love of Pete – don't drop it, man – hold it straight – in – close to the boat – *push* — " He seized it himself, an energetic dwarf doing the lazy giant's work for him.

Shepherd said, "I'll get the hang of it in a minute – you let me go on trying." He held on more firmly now, and pushed strongly on the river's shingly bed. The punt checked, shivered, and swung across stream, offering its side to the second one, which was in the care of Philippa.

A yell went up – "Where the dickens — !"

"Tired, old man? Going home?"

Philippa avoided them deftly, and someone gave them a shove in passing, and started them round in the right direction. Shepherd, who had shown neither alarm nor amusement, dropped his pole again for another push – and they dashed headlong for a bed of rushes and stuck fast, sending Dr. Webster staggering down over the cushions. Mrs. Ford was squeaking, Marion helpless with laughter. Dr. Webster, righting himself, said, "Come, come!" very severely, and handed Marion a paddle, and, after groping a little for a hold, she pushed them off.

"*Now* — " Dr. Webster, puffing, mounted the platform again and laid hands on the pole. "No, don't give up. Nobody really minds. Do it with me. You'll soon get the hang of it — "

Half a dozen joint strokes and they were on their way again, and the Radiologist stood back. Shepherd did better now, and they slid cautiously forward. He looked down at them, a funny sheepish smile crinkling his lips and eyelids, like a little boy asking for applause.

Marion, catching his eye, said, "That's all right – that's fine – oh, my golly!"

For like the little boy showing off, he had given a joyous prod – his pole had stuck fast, and he was gripping with his hands and his toes, and approaching the horizontal more nearly every instant, with his eyes popping out of his head.

Marion grabbed the paddle, still mercifully near her, and with one swift stroke in the right direction, relieved the tension. Shepherd, still in possession of the pole, sat down heavily on the platform. His face, which had taken on a horrid solemnity, broke into the little boy smile. He said jauntily, "That was a near thing – a very near thing!"

He appeared to think he had retrieved matters all by himself, and no one undeceived him. Dr. Webster said, through his laughter, "If you give a little twist as you hit the bottom, that won't happen. Like this – see?"

After that they pursued a course which was safe, though erratic in direction and rather slow, so that the other punt was far ahead of them. Presently Dr. Webster said, "That's not a bad effort. I think I'd better take over now, if you don't mind, because I don't think my wife knows exactly where to make for unless I'm there to tell her. Or will you, Dr. Blake?"

"I'd love to," Marion said, and came and took the pole from the rather breathless and very wet young man. "Have another shot later?"

"P'raps," he temporized, grinning, and arranged his wet

side to catch the sun.

"Not as easy as you thought?" Dr. Webster twitted him.

He grinned again. "I shan't find it difficult very long!"

They went on, perhaps less fast than when Dr. Webster had punted, for Marion had less force behind her thrusts than he had. On the other hand, their progress was beautifully smooth and straight, for she had learnt to punt at Cambridge and had never lost the feel of it. She enjoyed the prod, push and swing, the guggle of the water as the punt's nose veered in answer to her will, and did it gracefully by reason of her length of limb.

The other punt was dawdling for them, John Prior having taken over competently from Philippa. Marion easily caught him up, and they went on side by side, exchanging jerky, easy conversation. Prior was, it seemed, an easy, competent person. He and Philippa had already established the friendly relationship of people who can do things and go to places and talk about them without trying all the time to score.

They tied up and landed on mossy turf under some oak trees. The Websters produced a pleasant supper from two big picnic-baskets: grapefruit doled out from tins into little bowls, hard-boiled eggs and salad with a slab of cheese for those who liked it; ice-cream with real strawberries in it, carried in a comic arrangement of two pails, a little and a big, with a layer of ice and salt between them; and lemonade and beer.

The sun obligingly set for them in a fantasy of gold and orange, with a wonderful rosy afterglow on clouds which floated in duck-egg blue.

They lounged and talked, and smoked to keep away the midges. A lace-wing settled on Mrs. Ford's skirt, and she squeaked and flipped at it.

Marion said lazily, "They don't bite. They're lovely things, if you look at them." When Mrs. Ford still showed signs of murderous distaste, she enticed the creature to climb on her own finger and to fly away.

Paul Shepherd said politely, "So are snakes, if you look at them. I saw one, as we came ashore. A grass-snake. They don't bite, either."

Mrs. Ford said, "Horrid thing? Did you really, though? Mightn't it have been an adder?" They embarked on an argument as to how to tell the one from the other. Paul puffed pipe-smoke at another lace-wing which flew past him, and it hastily changed its course.

Another party floated downstream, with a gramophone in loud support of their own singing. A noisy boat-load of young men rowed past. A half-moon swung daintily behind the trees. A little mist began to rise from the river, and the women reached into the punts for woolly coats and packed the supper things into the baskets.

John Prior and Philippa, still talking, stepped into a punt together, and Dr. Webster, who had seemed inclined to manœuvre a general post, gave in to them and joined Paul Shepherd as before.

"Take us down?"

"In the dark? Not much!" Shepherd slipped quickly past him and joined Mrs. Ford at the other end, leaving him to mutter that it wasn't dark at all with the moon up, and that it was a pity to miss a chance of learning to do a new thing.

Paul sat grinning obstinately, and Marion, to end the dispute, took up the pole and pushed off.

She was not self-conscious; she was too well-used both to punting and to doing whatever she did more or less in the public eye. But she had a curious feeling that Paul Shepherd, watching every movement, was intent not so much on learning to manage a pole as to pick holes, somehow, in her own behaviour.

Well, that was disagreeable of him, spoilt boy as he thereby appeared to her. But it did not matter at all, for she would most likely never see him again. She smiled at him contentedly, her face white and mysterious in the moonlight, and he jumped, and smiled back, it seemed unwillingly, at her.

6

Ethel had gone to bed when they came home, but, with consideration for Marion's known whim, had left a note by the telephone saying that the practice had kept quite quiet except for one lady who had promised to ring again in the morning. Marion was glad. She hated that anyone who wanted her should find her unavailable, however much she had been enjoying herself, and as a result of this she seldom went out for pleasure. She had enjoyed herself, this evening, and so had Philippa.

"Made one feel young and studentish again, didn't it?" they agreed. "Nice people."

Philippa said, "We ought to get out more often. Away from work."

But Marion, stretching her long arms above her head, said, "I don't know about that. A social life's disturbing, somehow. It's easier to keep single-minded without distractions. I like my rut."

"Get awfully dull, if you don't come out of it sometimes," was Philippa's opinion.

The next day's routine work was broken by a major operation – not an emergency but a planned affair – on one of Marion's own patients; a woman in her forties with certain symptoms which, harmful in themselves, might be the signal of malignant as well as of benign disease. Marion gave the anæsthetic, and a woman surgeon in whom she had great trust operated and brought her own assistant. The business went well and smoothly, the trouble was entirely eradicated, and the patient was trundled back to her room and slid into bed in excellent condition. Marion and the surgeon took off their theatre gowns and tidied themselves and went down to talk to the patient's husband.

He was sitting alone in the nursing-home's little waiting-room. When he saw them coming, he sprang up, one tense hand on the table, his face creased with anxiety, all conventional politeness forgotten, just waiting for a verdict.

The surgeon, a woman of quick sensibility, said at once, "She stood it very well indeed. And there was no sign of anything malignant at all. Just a big mass of fibroids which needed to be removed."

The whitened knuckles relaxed and the circulation came back into them. The man's eyes met hers, travelled to

Marion's, and smiled. "And – she's all right?"

"She's fine."

"And – she'll be quite well now? And it won't come back?"

"It can't possibly come back. And she should be very well indeed."

He smiled really broadly then. "Thank God. And thank *you*, both of you. More than I can say . . . How soon can I see her?"

Handshakings, reassurances, and he went out into the fresh air. Coffee in the Matron's room, a little gossip, then work of a more ordinary kind.

Everything remained ordinary until the evening, when a call came for a visit to a woman who had been, a few times, to surgeries, but whom Marion did not know well.

"Come at once, Doctor, will you, please?"

Marion temporized. There had been a time when she would have gone tearing off, in the middle of a meal or of anything else. Then she had learnt that some natures will dramatize any small abnormality, and that "come at once" might mean often fright, and sometimes nothing more than a thwarted sense of importance.

"I think – I think — " This voice was frightened, certainly, but diffident rather than aggressive. "I think she's poisoned herself. I'm a neighbour. I hadn't seen her all day, and I just went in – she looks awful."

"Oh, I'll be there in ten minutes. Don't give her anything at all, and warm her up with a hot-water bottle."

She really did hurry this time, pausing only to add a little to her equipment. She found the usual scene, as it might

43

have been set out in the Sunday papers – bottle which might have contained tablets, note stating, "I can bear it no longer" – and most noticeable, to her, the blue-grey face of the woman who lay, fully dressed, on the dishevelled bed. At first sight she appeared to be unconscious, but when Marion touched her the eyes flickered open. She stared in a drunken sort of way, and the face, which had been devoid of all expression, twitched into evident terror.

Afraid I'm going to bring her back? Marion wondered. Or that she's in Hades? She would have to be brought back. She was not so far gone that it was impossible. She closed her eyes again and became far away, impenetrable.

The neighbour, hovering at Marion's elbow, murmured, "She's a lonely person. I've never seen anyone else come to the house, never. She'll be better off dead, perhaps."

Marion said, "I shall want two good-sized bowls and some warm water." The neighbour, startled, seemed about to make some protest, but thought better of it and went downstairs. Marion gave an injection and put a finger on the pulse. It was feeble and irregular. The woman began to snore softly. There was no time to lose.

With some disapproving help from the neighbour, she went through the horrid business of using the stomach-tube. The woman offered no resistance, but at one time they thought she had escaped them. Then the stimulant injection began to work, and her condition improved. The pulse grew stronger, and a little colour came into her lips.

The house was well furnished and had a comfortable look about it. Hating the necessity, though recognizing it, Marion poked about in the drawers of a writing-desk, and presently found a letter from someone of the woman's own name, living at Harrow. She set the neighbour, still a little sulky that she had been done out of the greatest sensation of her life, to look through the telephone book to see if they could get in touch with him. After a while he was found, and Marion, using all her tact in the approach to him, ascertained that he was the woman's brother. There was silence for a while when she had told him the story, then he said, "She's always been a queer girl. I've heard nothing of her for twenty years, I should think." He agreed with Marion's intuition that she would hate a hospital ward, was sure she could afford two nurses and gave authority to get them, and promised to come over himself the next day.

"He sounded nice," Marion said to the neighbour. "I shouldn't think she need have been so lonely."

The neighbour shrugged. "She used to have a friend living with her. She went away – that'll be five years or so ago. This one's grown more and more eccentric and solitary ever since."

Marion said, "There are more people like that than you would imagine. We see them when they're ill, sometimes, even though no one else does. People with some kink, who are afraid of everyone. She's luckier than some, if she's got money and relatives."

The neighbour said grudgingly, "P'raps it's as well you didn't let her die. P'raps she'll have a better time, after this."

Marion said, cocking an eye at her, "Can't just let people die, you know, even if they think they want to. Unless they're obviously going to very soon, of an inoperable cancer or something and it would be cruel to pull them back and force them to go through it all again — "

She moved across the room, and sat watching her patient as she stirred, muttered, and at last focused her gaze on Marion, still with that expression of dreadful fear. Marion bent close to her, and the queer, slurred whisper took shape.

"Get – me – back. Please, get – me – back." A long pause, while the eyes drooped shut. Then they shot open again and she said, "I'm – frightened. I don't know where – I shall go. Definitely going – somewhere. Realize – that, now."

A flash of possible meaning, a back-look at the woman as she had seen her in the surgery, and Marion plunged. "You're going to get better. You're not going anywhere."

The, woman stared for many minutes. Then she said. "I'm not – going to die?"

Marion said, "No. We've given you something to make you well, and we're going to look after you here."

Her face suddenly smoothed out, her eyes closed, and she slept. Marion felt her pulse again. "She'll do now, I think. Is it too much to ask you to stay till the nurse comes?"

The neighbour said, "I'll be glad to." Marion left her bustling around, trying to recapture some of the thrill of assisting at a suicide by aiding the dramatic recovery.

It was late when Marion got home, and as she stood looking down at Philippa in her chair she was seized with an intense weariness.

Philippa, sensing it, glanced up. "Tired? No supper?"

"No. I forgot about it, really. Ethel hasn't gone to bed yet. She's bringing me some soup or something. Yes, I am tired, for once – something goes out of one, to a case like that — "

She told Philippa about the day. "It's a queer life one lives," she finished slowly, "isn't it? A life of entirely vicarious emotions. Other people's joys and sorrows and fights – the joy of a baby born – the happiness of that man this morning when he knew his wife hadn't got cancer – his worry about her until he did know – the terror of the woman just now, when she realized that even death wouldn't put an end to her, would only shoot her into another strange place – one lives them all, in a way, one has to. And yet, they're not one's own. One has no emotions of one's own."

Ethel came in with hot soup and some fruit, and Philippa silently arranged them so that Marion could get them without moving.

She said presently, "Quite seriously, I do wish you'd write to the Dean at the Free about someone to help you."

7

One day in September Marion Blake, coming in at tea-time, was met gloomily by Ethel with the news, "There's a visitor to see you, Doctor."

The new assistant, Doctor Eileen Roffey, had been found, and had cut her professional teeth on a missed fracture, the obstinate diagnosis of the rare and serious when the

47

common and curable stared in the eye; had learnt to disarm, with a ready smile, the disconcerting greeting, "Are *you* the doctor?" in a tone which might as well have meant, "Are you the doormat?" and was settling in. She was housed in rooms a short way away, for the greater privacy of both her principal and herself, and Marion certainly found her a great help. It was a comfort to be able to go out in the knowledge that her patients would be looked after in her own way even without her, and that there was little danger of losing them to a rival. She was beginning to go out more, but as yet had not made a habit of inviting many visitors, so she could not think who this one could be.

In her curiosity, she swung into the sitting-room without doing more than snatch off her hat and shake her hair. A long figure rose from an arm-chair as she did so, and she recognized, with surprise, Paul Shepherd.

She said, "Good gracious!" and then, "How nice to see you! Does this mean you got the University job?"

He nodded. "Yes. I didn't expect to."

Marion said frankly, "I didn't, either, somehow. The other man – John Prior – seemed so much more sure of himself."

Their eyes met, amused. "It doesn't follow, does it?"

He said, "I think perhaps it's being so big. I so often feel like apologizing for the room I take up — "

"And a little man has to strut and put on airs to make himself felt – yes. Sit down, anyway, you don't look so big then. Where are you living?"

He told her, and added, "Yes, I'm very comfortable. I'm going to like it, I think . . . I came to ask if it's too late in the season to ask you to come on the river."

Marion flashed, "In a pleasure steamer?" and the little-boy grin crinkled his pleasant features.

He said, "Not unless you'd feel safer that way. I've learnt to punt. Thought I'd better, when I knew I'd got the job . . . there were still quite a few punts about when I came over the bridge."

Marion said, "Yes, we're still snatching afternoons in one when we get a chance. Not quite as late in the day as we did that other time. It's been a lovely hot summer, hasn't it? – good for the river."

"Then you'll come?"

"Why yes, of course!"

They settled a time, and fell into talk about the University. Marion knew but little of it, for it was on the other side of the town. She still hoped that she might one day be M.O. to the women students, but did not know quite how to go about becoming it. She wondered if Paul Shepherd, rightly used, might prove a stepping-stone. With this in mind, she insisted on his staying to tea, and told him to look on the house as a second home and drop in when he pleased. He was easier to talk to this time; one of those people, she thought, who was better by himself than in a crowd.

This impression was borne out by the punting expedition, which was entirely successful. Except for a certain intentness of expression as he punted, one might have thought he had been used to it all his life. He had never lived near a river, he told her, and had not been in any sort of a small craft before the original picnic.

Marion said, "You're a quick learner!"

A little-boy look of pleasure flitted across his face. He said, "You must have thought I was an awful fool!"

"I didn't at all!" she protested. "One can't know how to do everything! As a matter of fact, I thought you were rather bored with the whole thing, and very disapproving of me in particular."

He flushed, the uncomfortable beetroot of the fair skin, but laughed. "I'm not a great talker, except along my own lines," he said. "And as for disapproving of you — " He drew a breath and looked away. Then, "I did think you were a bit precious about the lace-wing. Most annoying insects they are, I think."

She caught him up. "Annoying, maybe, but not worthy of death. I hate killing things, anyway. Curing, not killing, is my business. And – bodies are such wonderful things – insects' bodies just as much so as humans' and animals'?"

He blinked at her. "Frightfully difficult to be logical about that. Vegetarians? Mice? Mosquitoes?"

She said solemnly, "I know, I know! And liver extract and cod liver oil. I have got a patient who goes to the length of refusing to take those, although she'll eat eggs on the ground that 'the poor thing's never known what it means to be alive'. I'm not as logical as that; I'm not a vegetarian even. I just don't like killing things. And it *was* harmless, and it *was* beautiful."

He drew at his pipe. "Sentimental?" he suggested.

"Not in the least," she snapped.

"Merely that women don't have to be logical?"

"Neither more nor less than men . . . I don't agree that

you're not much of a talker!"

He said affably, "I can talk if I want to . . . my people have got a farm in Sussex, and I was wondering what they'd say to your views on vermin."

"They wouldn't *be* vermin if they kept in their right places," she argued. "If you wired your farm to keep out the rabbits and the rats and oiled your water to keep off the mosquitoes, there just wouldn't be any where you were and they wouldn't have to be killed."

"Something in that," he allowed. "Certainly, something in it." He went on, "I *was* trying to pick holes in you that evening. Because you'd caught me on the wrong foot about the punting. But I didn't think you'd notice it. I'm sorry."

She said briskly, "Nothing to be sorry about. I don't often get holes picked in me, I'm used to being an oracle. I expect that's why I noticed it, and I've no doubt it's good for me."

He looked embarrassed, and she began to talk about the river, and asked him what he had meant by his "own lines" a few conversations ago.

He said at once, "Education. And the theatre. I love acting, and my ambition is to write a good play." Led on by her interest, he talked of these things, and by the end of the afternoon she felt she knew a deal about him, and what she knew, she liked.

He accepted her casual invitation literally, and dropped in two or three times a week, sometimes for tea, sometimes in the evening. Marion took fright that he would soon be bored by what she called their hen-house, and if she knew he was coming she exerted herself to produce young Furnivall, the Websters, or some married couple from among her patients, for his entertainment. But the less formal the gathering, the more he seemed at ease, and the best evenings they had were when just she and Philippa, with perhaps young Furnivall and the new assistant, made up the whole party.

If neither Philippa nor Marion was in, he would drift into the kitchen and talk to Ethel, who had been one of a big family, mostly brothers, and was captivated by him. He was "Mr. Paul" to her before, though not long before, he became "Paul" to his real hostesses. If not precisely a hen-house with its inevitable peckings, squackettings, and dusty preoccupations, the household had been a little prim. With Paul Shepherd's adoption its atmosphere expanded and warmed. Instead of being overshadowed a little by the worries and sorrows of those who came and went, it acquired a light of its own which even the most doleful of its visitors could not fail to notice.

Old Ethel radiated it. Her facial grimace became a recognizable smile, more often on than off, and her tired old eyes held a kindly twinkle. Philippa wore a steadfast, guarded kind of happiness. And Marion seemed to spring from quiet competence to vivid life.

She sang or whistled on her way. She teased old Ethel into helpless laughter until she would flap feebly with her apron, as at insistent hens, to get her kitchen to herself. She tormented Bill until, ears back and eyes rolling, he ran madly round and round the garden in circles, then caught and hugged him while he washed her face ecstatically and collapsed in a panting heap. She so filled her patients with her own gaiety that they recovered twice as quickly as they should have done. The would-be suicide took hope for the future, made friends with her brother, and became a reasonable member of society. Patients recommended their relations to her, so that the practice flourished even more than before.

One day Paul told them that his parents were coming to stay near him for a week, and Marion divined that he was fishing for an invitation for them. She gave it at once, and asked him who should be invited too. "The Websters? Perhaps they know each other already?"

Paul looked down at her, and then, fleetingly, at Philippa. "They do," he acknowledged; and, after a pause, "Need there be anyone else? It's just – you – I'd so much like them to meet."

They came, and somehow they explained Paul exactly. His mother was a slender, charming woman with a quick, frank smile and a whimsical tongue. His father was as tall as Paul himself, and as gentle. They were quite evidently certain that Paul was a young king and were surprised and very much amused that they should have produced him. They had no other child. As for Paul, he also took his kingship for granted, and was surprised and very much amused that it should be so. There was no conceit in any one of them, it was just one of those things.

Another evening was given up to a dinner with the older Shepherds at their hotel, and this, too, was a great success. Marion never gave a thought to the practice all the evening. They all spoke each other's language, pounced on each other's points, and found more to talk about than would fit into the time.

That was always so, with Marion and Paul. She told herself that it was because they always had to break off in the middle of a conversation, for her to see a patient, or answer the 'phone, that she looked forward so eagerly, every time, to their next meeting.

She talked more than ever to Philippa, too, and "Paul says", "Paul likes", "Paul has done", this or that, slipped in unnoticed by her every few minutes.

Philippa was very gentle with her. It would have been brutal to have quelled this starry happiness, the more so because Marion seemed so unconscious of whence it came or whither it led. They had agreed long since that parting, for whatever cause, should not be allowed to jeopardize their friendship, and Philippa was content to stand by the agreement, if parting there should be.

One evening early in December, Marion caught sight of Paul's tall figure at the entrance to the hospital as she drove out after giving anæsthetics. She stopped, with a screech of brakes, and took him up.

"How did you happen to be here?" she asked him.

"Just – happened — "

"Nice," she said contentedly. "Now we can go on talking about that play. As usual, we had to leave off just when it was getting really interesting."

Instead, he said, "Have you got to go straight home?"

She considered. "Not really. I was going to do a visit on the way, but it can wait till to-morrow. Only one of my old chronics, she isn't particularly expecting me."

He said, "Let's go and look at the river. P'raps there'll be a moon."

54

She laughed at him. "Moon, at this time of the month! And you a countryman! The river will be as black as pitch, and it's going to rain!"

"Well, don't do your visit, and don't let's go in just yet."

"I'll leave the visit. But it would be much pleasanter in by the fire than driving around in the murky night!" she objected.

He said nothing to that, and she took him home. He helped her put the car away and locked up the garage for her, and went indoors behind her, all in silence and gloomily. She paused in the hall and turned to him. "You're very solemn. What's the matter with you?"

He stalked into the empty sitting-room, and drew a breath. "When does Philippa come in?"

Coaxing the fire into a blaze, Marion said, "Any time, now. Oh – no, to-night she's staying late for a staff meeting. About half-past seven, I expect. Why?" – turning up to him a vivid face flushed by the cold outside and the fire's sudden heat – "D'you want her?"

He became a little boy caught in a prank and almost, but not quite, sure that he would not be punished. He said, "No. That's just what I don't want. I want to talk to you."

"Well, you do that often enough," she said comfortably, and threw off her coat and subsided into a corner of the settee. "Sit you down, anyway. Cigarette?"

He shook his head, and remained standing, an elbow on the mantelpiece. "Term ends next week," he remarked into the fire. "They'll expect me to go home."

"Well!" Marion exploded. "Fancy saying it like that, when you've got those darling people to go home to! What's the

55

matter with home?"

"Nothing. Except that you're not there." He squinted down at her sideways. "It's leaving you that's the matter."

She had not thought of that. The weeks had slipped by so quickly, it had seemed as though they must go on in the same way for ever. Her habit had always been to live in the present, with little spontaneous thought of past or future. She said blankly, "You'll be coming back — " and glanced up at him.

The funny, shy, hungry look which met her made her heart quite suddenly miss a beat, then race. She was not used to her heart playing tricks, dismissed the phenomenon impatiently, and found she could say nothing, only wait in silence.

He said, "I wish you could come too. I know you can't, you're too busy. Unless perhaps, just for Christmas? But I should go – so much more happily – if you'd promise me first that you would marry me."

Marion found all at once that the happiness of the past few weeks had reached an undreamed-of yet quite inevitable peak. She put out a hand to him, wordlessly, and he took one stride and dropped beside her, and they stared at each other, lips trembling into smiles.

He turned her hand over and traced gentle patterns on its palm with one long finger. "You know," he said, "why I was really picking holes in you that very first day?"

She gave a small, uncertain laugh. "You said – because I could punt and you couldn't."

He shook his head. "It wasn't really that, at all. It was that I couldn't believe there could really be anyone so

56

completely perfect."

She flushed, and the smile she gave him was tremulous. She said presently, "Paul, I'm an awful ass, but I hadn't thought of this happening. I'd just – simply – been enjoying life most tremendously."

He insisted, pleading, "That's fine. It would last, you know. But, Marion, darling, will you – please?"

She thought confusedly that he had never called her "darling", or anything like it, before; that he had probably never asked for anything, humbly, like that, in his life, because everything he had wanted had tumbled unasked-for into his hands, and that even more than his sweetness and his good looks this humility became him; that Philippa must be thought of, and the practice; then, as her eyes came back to his, that neither of them mattered at all.

Her happiness bubbling over, she said, "I don't think we can help it, do you, Paul – dear Paul?"

"Help what? Oh Marion, do you mean you will? Oh – Marion!" He hugged her to him, kissed her, holding her carefully as though she were breakable and precious. She knew then that nothing mattered except herself and Paul, they two together.

After a time they sat back, beaming at each other, and talked. She gave him her thought that he had always had what he had wanted without asking for it, and he said, "It's true, I think I've been lucky. But – wouldn't you say it's true of you too?"

Surprised, she said, "Why, I believe it is. I've worked, of course. But so have you. I have had what I've wanted, by and large." And then, "What happens if we want different

57

things?"

"We shan't," he affirmed, and she believed him, and they found it all exquisitely funny and laughed again.

She said presently, "It's queer the way everything seems to have worked up to this. It was – or appeared to be – just chance that I came to this town. Philippa just happened to get the job at the County Hospital. And chance that you got your job, too – you didn't choose it for any special reason, did you? And chance that the Websters invited us both that evening – I so nearly didn't come – and that I was just busy enough to get an assistant, so that I had a bit of time to get to know you – I never had a minute, before."

He said, "The gods are on our side. Things that work out inevitably, like that, are always all right, now and forever. I don't believe it's chance at all. Do you?"

"I don't, really," she said, a little shamefacedly, for such a belief was surely one that a hard-boiled student of the sciences would prefer to keep to herself. It didn't seem quite in character for a Director of Education, either. She said so.

"One has these odd, deep convictions," he said. "I wouldn't be able to tell anyone but you."

When Philippa came in they had talked themselves out. But she sensed an unusual atmosphere, and turned a questioning look on them as she warmed her ankles.

Marion said, "We've suddenly fallen in love with each other, and Paul wants me to marry him."

Philippa grinned very broadly. "Not so suddenly. I've been watching it grow."

Marion was really startled. "Phil, you can't have. I didn't

know it myself until just now!"

Philippa said, "It's queer, that enchantment, isn't it? You're enmeshed in it – in the happiness of it. You never think to look out, and it doesn't occur to you that other people can look in. But they can."

She insisted on Paul staying to supper, and turned out a bottle of sherry to drink to their future, and brought old Ethel in to join in the toast.

Old Ethel looked from one to the other, and at Philippa. "Oh Miss – Oh, Mr. Paul – Oh, I do wish you every happiness!" and burst into tears and hid her crumpling face in her apron, and ran out, and had to be pursued and led in again to finish her drink.

Marion, having awoken to the possibility of other people's views about the matter, thought she saw Ethel's. From that she began to wonder about Philippa's. She looked suddenly so distracted that Paul caught her hand and asked, "Darling, what on earth's the matter?"

Marion had the same feeling which had invaded her once at the birth of a baby – of a central incident with unending repercussions. She began to say so, but found it too near the bone for explanation, and laughed and shook her head. "I realized – all at once – what a mass of things there'll be to think about. I've lived on the fringes of people's lives all this time – and now I'm suddenly right in the centre!"

Paul commented, "You are indeed. Right in the spotlight. But I'm there too."

8

When Paul had gone, Marion and Philippa talked far into the night.

Marion went straight to the point which old Ethel, unmeaning, had suggested to her. "Phil – I'm not butting in on a hope of yours?"

Philippa chuckled. "You are not. He's never even given me a look. I like him – you know that – but I'd want something more mature, myself. How old is he?"

Marion said, "Twenty-eight. Two years older than I am. I think it's living so much at home – and being an only – that makes him seem so very young. And his parents being so young, too. He can be quite authoritative about his own subject. The students don't seem to find him immature, from what I hear."

"I'm glad he's not younger than you are," Philippa said. "I'd wondered. I think Ethel's trouble was that she couldn't bear to be parted either from him or from me."

Marion considered that, and found it unanswerable. Parting was one of the horrid results of embarking on a new way of life. She said, "D'you mind, Phil? About the whole business?"

"Mind — ?" Philippa moved with a controlled unease, then laughed and spread out her hands. "Now what do you want me to say? If I say no, you'll be hurt. And if I say yes, you'll be sad because you'll think you're hurting me! Well, it stirs one up in an uncomfortable sort of way, of course. You've been under my skin for a good long time; but – and there are a whole lot of buts – although a spinster may make a very happy life for herself, there's no doubt a happy marriage is the best of all. And so, my dear, I can't grudge you it, can I?"

Marion said, "You're a nice bloke, Phil . . . " and they sat silent, each with her own preoccupation.

"I've been thinking about the future a bit, these last few weeks," Philippa went on presently. "I'd like to have a crack at a job in a London hospital. These provincial municipals are very limited. For one thing, you have to do as the Medical Super tells you, and if he's an old fossil like this one, that means you have to tread very softly indeed. And you're never in contact with really first-class brains, because they don't come to such places, and that means that if you're not careful your own standards go down and down from lack of criticism. Then I should get a flat in Town. We ought to be talking about you, not about me, but I thought you'd like to know."

Marion said, "Of course I like to know. Thank goodness we've never grown like some pairs of women living together, who can never do a thing without each other. We've always had our own separate interests, haven't we, as well as the lots we've had in common?"

Philippa, her eyes twinkling, said, "Of course we have. We're both far too self-willed not to."

Marion sat hugging her knees. "There are such millions of questions which arise – to work or not to work – I can't imagine life without the practice. I haven't an idea what Paul would like me to do."

Philippa looked as though she had intended to say one thing and then changed her mind and said another. "Lots of medical women do go on working when they're married."

"I don't know any who run a busy general practice" – Marion wrinkled her brow – "I know plenty who do clinics or part-time jobs – and consultants, who work by appointment." Then, definitely, "I shall keep it on if I possibly can. I should loathe to give it up, married or no."

PART TWO

*

Paul

1

THE months that followed seemed to Marion like a kaleidoscope before its shaken fragments have settled into a new pattern. The ordered routine which she had found the best way to regulate her busy days was always being broken into by the unheralded appearance of Paul outside a house or on a street-corner. Her professional reply to a 'phone call would be greeted by his unrespectful chuckle. It was fun, but unsettling. She wished she could have him only at times when she was free of the practice; and then, if she heard nothing of him for half a day, she felt a curious ache where her heart might be.

She was driving along one morning in a cheerful dream, her mind full of Paul, plans for the future, and only lastly, patients, when she heard a car's horn hooting – and hooting – and hooting. She turned, irritated, to see where the noise was coming from and whether it concerned her, and saw Eileen Roffey, her young assistant, getting out of her own car on the other side of the road. Marion pulled down her window and waited for the girl to come across.

"Something you wanted?"

The assistant blinked and smiled. "Weren't we – wasn't I going to help you with a minor op?"

Marion's mind came out of its dream with a click. "Good heavens yes! At half-past eleven – and now it's twelve and I'm going the wrong way!"

"I waited there for twenty minutes," the girl said. "And then – well, you never are late for things, so I was going see what had happened."

Marion said drily, "No. I never am late for things. It's a habit I detest, lateness. Can we do it now? Can you, I mean? I'm terribly sorry."

The girl's eyes danced. "Yes, I can do it now. I'll go and warn them."

Marion turned round, her lips pursed with annoyance at herself. She gathered, however, from the assistant's expression both then and later, that such lapses were expected of her at the present time; indeed that their absence would have caused surprise and disappointment. "You're sure to do things like that now! You're allowed to!" was the attitude. Her startled, if amused, response was, "I'm darned if I do!"

Yet when she arrived home, she found Ethel in the state of controlled fury which meant she had had to do battle with a patient. "Said you'd sent her in a bill, Doctor, which she'd already paid! I said such things didn't happen, not in this practice, and if she'd had a bill she must owe it to us. She was very testy about it. But" – triumphantly – "she couldn't produce no receipt!"

Marion said, "I'll look it up. Never mind, Ethel, she can't poison us!" And when she opened her ledger, the account had certainly been paid, and certainly sent in again, only a few days past. Forgetting appointments, sending in wrong accounts, just like any callow girl in love! It was not to be tolerated. She must pull up her socks.

It was Eileen Roffey who did the pulling up, she found in the next few weeks: reminding her of things, doing jobs for her, snatching her chestnuts back from burning. She gave way unwillingly, gratefully, to this good-humoured management of her too-crowded affairs.

Queerly, in this momentous interlude in her life, the incidents which stood out in her memory were connected with the practice rather than with her engagement. Perhaps this was because her work had been for so long the stable element in her life and seemed so still; that and old Ethel, who still stumped to the door and back again fifty times a day as though that were the most important thing in the world.

She came back from it one evening bubbling with wrath. "No respect for anyone, they haven't! Five of them, all together, filling up the waiting-room. So I said to them, do you *all* want to see the doctor – you and *all* the children – they was big enough, some of them, to have waited outside – and yes we do, she says, all of us – *we're the Royal Family!* And pushed past me, the whole lot of them! Patients! Impudent young arabs!"

There was the night when the fog was so thick that Marion had to leave her car by the roadside half-way to a confinement and walk the rest. The business over, she was walking back with her black bag when a shape loomed up beside her. "Now what," it demanded, "might you be doing with that bag, mum, at four o'clock in the morning?"

"Having a baby," Marion said at once. "I mean, helping someone else to!"

He looked very doubtful. "A nurse, are you?"

Marion grinned to herself, acknowledging that she must look like nothing on earth, buttoned up in an ancient Burberry, with an old hat crammed on her head and probably, by this time, pyjama trousers wandering down under her stockings. "No, a doctor," she told him.

Still he stood in front of her, his honest, pink young face wrinkled with anxiety. "Could you give me some evidence of that, Miss?"

"Oh, you want to look in the bag!" Marion said cheerfully. "I'm afraid you won't find the baby there, I've left that behind!" He snorted, but peered in as she opened the bag. Luckily the article which presented itself was a pair of obstetric forceps, which was evidently sufficiently surgical-looking to convince him that she was, at any rate, not a burglar.

He smiled self-consciously at her. "I'm sorry, Miss. Have to make sure, when we see people out with bags at night. We don't often see a doctor on foot these days." When she explained matters, he turned about and carried her bag for her all the way to the car, and told her about his wife's confinement a year ago.

There were such funny little bits of the practice that stayed in Marion's mind.

There was the nun who came one day with a pain, she said, in her heart. Marion was touched by the roughness of her underwear, the horrible heaviness of her habit.

She had indeed some cause for pain, an old rheumatic heart which was beginning to fail as a result of the rigorous life which she led.

"I didn't want to make a fuss," she said. "And yet, I just can't do some of the duties we're given – carrying all our water in pails up two flights of stairs, and kneeling for many hours, often in the night, and often in intense cold. One doesn't notice these things – if one's doing them for

God – but if this pain comes, one can't help noticing that."

Marion gave her directions about what she must and must not do, and she promised to obey them. "That's one thing we do learn, obedience," she said, smiling. "Not always easily, but we learn it. I shall have to tell the Reverend Mother, now, and put myself under the Convent doctor. I don't like him, he's one of those fat, coarse men who are always trying to be funny. But I don't think they'll let me go on coming to you."

She offered Marion a pound note. Marion, shaking her head, said, "I thought you people weren't allowed to have any money?"

The nun said, "My brother gave it to me. I did so want to see a woman doctor. He found out about you for me. It's so much easier to talk to a woman. You've been so kind — "

"You ought really to have a woman medical officer," Marion commented. The nun said, "I shall pray that we may," quite confidently, as though she were sure of the result.

When the money was refused, she tucked it away again, regretfully, and a few days later there came a little book about St. Theresa, and a note saying that she had been sent to bed, as Marion had advised, and that she would never have to work so hard again.

No, Marion could not give up practice, with its ardours and its interests – scientific, running like an accompaniment, mathematically exact, behind the human melody of sweet treble and ominous bass: the apparently miraculous recovery of a moribund diabetic when put on insulin, of a weary, breathless pernicious anæmia victim after a few injections of liver – both marked for early death but for modern science. She was still amazed when these wonders took place under her hand, the direct result of her thought and action. And, more profoundly, she would watch the relentless failure of a heart with coronary disease, rest it and medicine it how she might; and the despairing death of a body invaded by secondary cancer, perhaps long after the primary growth had been triumphantly removed. The surgeon might be and often was puffed up with conceit, he saved life dramatically, saw death but seldom. But a good physician, or a good G.P., kept an essential humility. The last enemy would beat him in the end, strive with him how he might.

She was happy, in these crowded months. Waking in the morning, she would lie gathering her thoughts together. Patients would flit before her, their faces, their expressions, their problems, and her plans for them. Then, like the brightness of the day blazing in at her window, the thought of Paul would come, and she would sit up, wondering how any day could be so bright or any thought so warm and comfortable. Going out, she would meet one person after another who knew her and gave her friendly greeting; and at some time, every day, she would see Paul striding towards the car, and stop and take him up, and they would kiss each other and talk. They were quite unconscious of faces at windows, and hidden smiles, and, "We'll be losing our lady doctor soon, I'm thinking," and, "Very devoted, aren't they?"

Paul persuaded her to go to the pictures sometimes, and to the local Repertory Company's plays, which were often very good. There seemed no end to the interests which opened out for them. She had fun, too, buying clothes, and wedding-presents began to come. She and Paul found they agreed very well about which of them they liked and which they laughed at. Only Paul would sweep away the laughable ones and never want to see them again, but Marion would take them out and smile over them because they represented some funny old woman or some strident platinumed girl.

A highlight was her first visit to Paul's home. His father had been "axed" from the Navy after the 1914 War and, having some money of his own, had bought a mixed farm in Sussex and was doing very well there, learning and applying new ideas.

Paul talked about it a good deal. "I'll retire there one day, p'raps," he said. "Would you like that, Marion?"

Marion said, "I don't know a thing about the country. I've always lived in towns. But I expect I'd like anything that you did."

On her first visit, that Christmas, she found a delightful little L-shaped house, once four fourteenth-century cottages, red brick, and roofed with golden slabs of Horsham stone. It was set in meadows and orchards, and watched over by a great evergreen oak, so beautifully shaped that it might have been a design for a tree etched against the winter sky.

Inside, her first impression was of cosy warmth and shining cleanliness.

"Central heating. We're completely modernized," Paul said proudly, laying his hand on a radiator which looked like part of the panelling. Marion loved it, but with some sinking of the heart because she could not imagine that Paul would be half so comfortable in any house which she might manage. She told herself that if one had always been very comfortable and was still young, it was rather an adventure to be less so.

In the dining-room there was a fire of great logs flaming against an Old Sussex iron fireback. A midday meal was ready, brought in by a shy, cheerful country girl. It was beautifully cooked and dainty. Mrs. Shepherd confessed to its cooking, and Marion's spirits fell still farther.

"Though cooking's easy, with our eggs and milk and cream. I'm fond of it, anyway."

"You must come out and see my Jersey cows," Mr. Shepherd said. "D'you like cows, Dr. Blake?"

"I'm a bit scared of them! And you must please call me Marion."

Paul's father seemed pleased by both sections of the remark. "A good name. Old English, sensible. Glad to hear you're scared of something – I rather pictured one of those intrepid females who would rush bald-headed at anything from a bull downwards!"

Mrs. Shepherd said, "Francis, really!"

Paul said, "She's intrepid enough in her own line of country!" and that led off to questions about riding, and Marion's willingness to be taught to do it.

"And you need not be scared of our cows," Mrs. Shepherd told her. "They're almost pets: handled from birth, washed all over – practically – twice a day before they're milked. They run after us to be fondled."

Marion said, "If they run after me I shall bolt!" and Paul said: "Not if you're with me!"

It was fun to be an ordinary young woman, to be loved and protected, instead of a doctor whose lightest word weighed as heavy as lead.

Afterwards, they walked in the sheltered garden, with fruit-trees all around it and laddering the walks; and went into the cow-sheds where the cows were standing, each in her named stall, slender, intelligent-looking creatures, more like deer than ordinary cows. Paul and his father entered into a learned discussion on feeds and yield of milk, and Marion looked and listened. And presently she and Paul went off together, through quaint Y-shaped stiles, across meadows, round the common to the windmill, and up behind it to the wide view of the fertile valley backed by the lovely curves of the south downs.

Paul said, "It's beautiful at any time of the year. I never know which time I like it best."

To-day the air was crystal clear, so that every tree in the clumps could be seen, and cloud shadows chased each other over the downland's velvet flanks, and the little half-timbered Sussex houses stood out like jewels in the valley. Sheltered from the north, the winter sun warmed their cold cheeks to a glow before it sank out of sight.

They walked back together arm in arm, almost in silence, the peace of the countryside upon them.

Later, they sat round the fire, the four of them, and talked. Marion found that these surprisingly young parents of Paul's talked like her own contemporaries, directly, neither misunderstanding nor laying down the law as parents, she had found, so often did.

On Christmas Day they went to church. "One does, in a village," Paul said, as though to silence Marion's possible objections. She made none, for none had occurred to her. It all fitted in with the country, and the people, and the need for thanksgiving, and Paul.

By the time the short holiday was over, she felt that she had absorbed Paul's background, almost that she was already part of the home life of the little farm-house. It was full of real goodwill and kindliness, happy and yet strong, as though, in spite of its present prosperity, it would be able to face hard times without flinching. The Shepherds' goodness was no milksop virtue, they were not the type who turned a blind eye to evil and, if they did meet it, often became its victims; they had keen brains and were not averse to criticism. Marion felt that they would fight evil, not pass it by: a parallel course, she felt, to her own, whose business was to fight disease.

One overwhelming impression which she carried away with her was that Paul was a rare person, to be prized and cherished, whose happiness was as porcelain in her hands. She wondered whether other women felt like that about their young men. She could not bring herself to speak about it even to Philippa, lest Philippa, by some matter-of-fact or trenchant comment should shatter something infinitely precious.

2

Her own people, Marion knew, were much more ordinary. Her father was a chartered accountant, shrewd, worldly, pleasant-mannered; her mother a suburban matron, full of her household and her bridge. Two younger sisters, one a librarian, one still a student in the University of London, were both mad about tennis, hiking, and, at the moment, Socialism; very modern, very opinionated. Their attitude towards their elders was "You don't understand!" Their elders' attitude to them was "You'll be more sensible when you're a bit older!"

Marion thought they would think Paul soft, which he was not, and be bored to tears or to ribaldry by his home.

They were, however, sufficiently thrilled by the fact of her engagement to think little, if at all; particularly as, to please both sets of parents, it had to be a full-dress wedding from their own Parish Church.

Marion had a week off to get ready, and lived in a most unaccustomed whirl of clothes and womanly conversation. She wished they could have just got themselves married, with no fuss at all, and announced it when it was over.

"We should do a whole lot of people out of their fun!" Paul protested when she put this forward as a serious proposition. "And I expect a rumour would go round that we were marrying because we'd got to, or that one of us had been divorced. Best to be public about these things, really."

"I believe you like the fuss," she teased him.

"Like it! I'm terrified!"

75

"Really?" she searched his grave face. "I believe you are."

"Of course I am!"

"I am too," she said. "Still, it's not so bad if we both are. We can wink at each other over the parson's head."

So they went through the business good-humouredly and allowed their healths to be drunk and made competent little speeches and were kissed by a surprising number of people. And then it was over, and the new way of life had begun.

3

They went to the Engadine for their honeymoon. On the journey across France they were guarded against emotion, against each other, good companions, as they had always been, on a new adventure. But when they found themselves alone, in their own room, in the chalet hotel above a great lake, in the magic of Switzerland's clear air and sweet distant sounds, they suddenly could not keep out of each other's arms; and when presently they wandered on to their balcony to look at the view, they could not bear to disentangle their fingers.

They ate largely of good Swiss food; walked a little in the crisp, cool evening along a flowery meadow-path; and turned in early, too tired by the excitement and the night in the train to do anything, yet, but sleep.

Out of some happy dream, Marion was awakened by tinkling elfin music, far away. The bed faced an open window, and she raised herself on an elbow, expecting, somehow, to see flickering lights. But there was nothing but infinite, indigo space, and stillness, and stars. The music, some five notes of it, in irregular cadence, came nearer, until she could hear also the patter of delicate feet.

Enchanted, she could not resist poking Paul, who was still asleep beside her. "Paul, listen! What is it?"

Paul, who had been in Switzerland often before, stuck his head up straight for an instant, then humped down again. "Cow-bells – confound them!"

She laughed. "But they're *lovely!*"

He grunted, then seemed to remember where he was, and flung an arm out, and pulled her down to him and kissed her; and when the bells had passed and faded they slept again.

Next time she woke it was early dawn. The mountains, a lovely grey compounded of all colours, stood sharp against a lemon sky, the misty lake quiet below them, a scene of unearthly beauty. This time Marion did not wake her husband, but just lay and absorbed it so that she might never forget.

When she woke again the sun was up, the mountains solid crags of rock and snow, the air full of lively noises of animals and men about their business, the magic gone.

There was coffee and rolls, butter and cherry jam; smiling Swiss maids, laughing attempts at conversation in English or German or French. And ahead, three weeks of this beauty, the excitement of new impressions – and Paul.

They started out after breakfast, and as they came into the pinewoods they saw a man, stooping among the tree-roots. He straightened up and smiled at them, and they recognized their rather stately host of the night before. With a child-like delight, he held out something to them in his hand.

"Morelles – I hunt morelles, to cook with my chicken for your supper!"

They peered at it, a little wrinkled fungus. "The most delicate flavour you can imagine," he assured them.

They went on, smiling. "Sweet," Marion said, "to think of that man, who owns a chain of hotels, grubbing about for fungi to improve his guests' supper!"

Paul said, "They're like that. Very thorough, and don't mind what they do."

In the pinewoods Marion found her first gentians, and crouched above the fat, upturned bells of brilliant blue which looked so different there from those she had seen cherished in English rock-gardens. There were sulphur-coloured anemones, downy like moths; and great ant-hills of pine needles, with convoys of big ants scurrying in and out and struggling with twigs ten times their size.

"I thought you'd like those," Paul said. "Remember that lace-wing?"

"They're quite fascinating," Marion said, and he took her hand and pulled her away from them at last.

Presently the path skirted a meadow, in which a stream gurgled among swaying golden bubbles of the trollius, forget-me-nots far bigger and more blue than those at home, pink ragged-robin, clumps of smaller, paler, more star-like gentians, a glorious patchwork of colour: and beyond the meadow, the green sward of foot-hills leading up to snowy peaks. Marion exclaimed with pleasure at almost every step, and Paul played strutting showman because he had brought her there.

They ate their lunch by the lakeside, enjoying not only the food but also the dainty way it was done up for them, and stayed there under a tree through the heat of the afternoon, undisturbed except by a few small parties of walkers on the path above them. Farther on, they found a chalet with tables outside it, and drank coffee and ate queer nutty cakes at one of them; and came back at last into the other end of their own village. They paused to watch a craftsman making a chair – a whole chair, not a bit of it or just a process in the making.

"He can be proud of it when it's done – and will be, judging by the care he's taking," Paul commented. "Which is more than our mass-producers can be of anything they turn out, with one to saw and another to plane, and a third to polish and a machine to fit the thing together."

"He looks so much more a person than they do," Marion said. "He would be, of course. He's creating, they're only earning their keep."

"I'm never quite sure," Paul said, "whether I really do like the Swiss. They're very admirable: individualists, industrious, kindly, not too money-grubbing, very honest, clean, gay – and yet, if you try to discuss anything with them they're as obstinate as mules, and most terribly pleased with themselves."

Marion said cautiously, "They look nice – and they must surely get their values right – put enough emphasis on material things yet not too much – with all this natural beauty round them and the dangers of the mountains as well."

Paul said, " 'M. Which is why, at bottom, one does like them, I suppose. And why they're so stable – no danger of war, and very little individual quarrelling, I should think."

Marion said, "One couldn't stay bad-tempered for long, with this to look at through one's windows."

They were gazing up the little street of white houses, heavy-eaved, green-painted, with gay gardens in front and dark swaying trees behind, to the remote, impassive beauty of the mountains, still snow-capped, reflecting in their shadows the blue sky above.

"And yet," Paul said, "their gaiety is like a child's, untried, and they have no sense of humour. So one would get bored with them sooner than with a Frenchman, whose gaiety is wit and who knows all about wickedness and discounts it, not from ignorance but from knowledge."

Marion, still entranced by what she saw, said, "With them, maybe. But with their country, never."

She was always a bit afraid, herself, of witty people. Paul wasn't witty, he was solid and quiet. But she knew that he could appreciate wit, perhaps even counter it, delightfully, certainly not be put out by it, as she might be. She said something to that effect.

Paul, glancing down at her affectionately, said, "You've been busy so long clearing up the messes people make of themselves – doing things, not talking about them – you haven't had time for playing with words."

She felt suddenly, securely, that he liked her as she was, that he didn't want her witty, or different in any way. She need not strive to be on her toes with him. Nor need she peer for the truth wrapped up in faltered phrases, the no that meant yes, the fear behind defiance. He was uncomplicated and true.

4

The hotel was entered by a flight of steps leading into a wide square hall, and here guests would congregate round about meal-times. Loitering there before dinner on that first evening, Marion noticed a woman of about her own age, staring at her. Marion stared back, mildly interested, at a plain, intelligent, very tanned face above a stocky body. Probably English, Marion thought, and hoped she was not another doctor, who would want to talk shop. It was so much pleasanter to remain an ordinary person, unidentified. Then Paul came in, and they moved into the dining-room and Marion forgot her.

But when the meal was over, the stranger placed herself near them, and presently spoke – the conventional question, did they know the district, had they had a good journey? She had a pleasing, educated voice, and Marion felt at home with her as they chatted. Paul was occupied with his pipe.

They must, Marion was told, do this expedition and that, and must not miss going up to Corviglia.

"Was that the one you said was specially good, Paul?" Marion tried to include him in the conversation. "My husband's been here several times before."

81

Paul said, "What was that?"

"Miss — ?"

"Brownlow."

"Miss Brownlow says we must go up to Corviglia."

"It's not," Paul said deliberately, "one of my favourites. It's one of those things everybody does who doesn't know the better ones. If you've done it once, that's enough."

"Then," Marion commented, "I must do it once, mustn't I?"

Paul, unsmiling, said, "Must you?"

After a few minutes' uneasy talk, Miss Brownlow excused herself. "I'm here with my friend, and she's staying upstairs with a dreadful headache. Perhaps I shall see you tomorrow."

Paul, to her departing back, said through his teeth, "Er-cher!"

Marion said, "Paul, you were awful to her!"

"I meant to be! Once let her get her talons into us, we should never have lost her." He frowned, ferociously and possessively, at his wife.

Marion said plaintively, "I rather liked her."

"Penny bun with a smear of lipstick across it!" he growled.

Marion said, "Probably better than if she'd had no lipstick at all. She had a nice voice and nice eyes."

"They gimmled," Paul objected. "Impossible not to be self-conscious, with that awful intense gaze bent upon one!"

"And being self-conscious makes one rude?"

"Perhaps. Anyway — " His own eyes crinkled at the

corners. "It's our honeymoon, not hers, and she's not butting into it. Come out!"

5

Days and nights passed deliciously. They walked by lakes and through villages, some little and wild, mere collections of herdsmen's huts, some set on heights, some laid out on little promontories, preening themselves somewhat for visitors. They climbed precipitous paths, sometimes above rushing torrents, and came out to still green uplands where quiet-faced peasants cut their hay with scythes and gathered it by hand, and the bright wild flowers were different from those at lower levels, as though it were spring here and summer down below. They went up in mountain railways and saw green inhuman glaciers above the snow-line, and bleak grey rocks where there were no flowers at all, only tough little grasses, and looked down at lakes and villages spread like a map below.

As the days passed, the precious blue gave place to the blush of alpenrose flaunted from every bush beside the lake, the golden trollius to moon-daisies, asters, and feathery polygonum, the sun grew hotter and the snow vanished from all but the highest peaks.

And all the time they talked; argued without rancour about abstract things, and found that Paul became ever more airy and far-away, while Marion returned, always, to the material and practical. Both were interested in 'ists and

83

'isms, but while Paul became emotionally involved in them, they left Marion quite cold. They told each other anecdotes of their childhood and found that their reactions to every experience had been entirely different.

"Rather alarming," Paul said when Marion remarked on this. "Who knows what rows and rumpuses it may lead to?"

Marion said, "Difficult, p'raps, but fun. I've always thought it must be a bit dull to run in harness with someone who's practically your double. Though lots of people do, I know."

They talked much to each other, but little to anyone else. There were few English staying so high at that time of year. The bun-faced lady had gone home, to Marion's secret regret. Paul was extravagantly glad to see her go.

"She got my goat, laying down the law as she did with a face like that!"

"You're not very tolerant, are you?" Marion teased him.

"No. I think tolerance is a sloppy virtue, and I've lost all the taste I may ever have had for the mediocre."

"But isn't half the interest in life," she said, wondering if he would think she were preaching, "in digging out the fine bits which are hidden in the mediocre? They're often quite rare and lovely — "

Paul, his eyes on her, said, "I like my rare and lovely things displayed for all to see. *You've* made me think that way — " and the conversation ended. They were sitting on a boulder in one of those high pastures which from afar look just a brilliant green, but prove to be a mosaic of waving grass and small sweet flowers. Children called in high Swiss voices round a chalet some distance away, their talk blending with the music of the cowbells, their pink-and-blue shirts with the cows' shaded fawn. Below, a river chuckled in a gorge, beyond it grey scree rose to snowy heights. It was one of those scenes whose memory lasts a lifetime and always brings back with it the emotion of its moment. Marion glanced round her, drinking in the beauty, then looked at Paul, lying at ease below her. She knew him so much better, now, than when they had started out together: his strong, lithe body, every fair hair, it seemed to her, on head and limbs, every expression of mouth and eyes and carriage: his likes and dislikes, his moods, his pouting frowns and gusts of laughter; his tenderness and care for her, his selfish arrogance. All these she knew or guessed at, and understood that there was still much more to know.

"And to-morrow," she said, "we go back."

Paul said, " 'M. Are you sorry?"

"Sorry and glad. This could go on for ever. But it isn't our real life. And that – our real life – is going to be marvellous, I think. We're different in all sorts of ways – I know that – but I think we're going to dovetail into a very good whole."

He squinted up at her and said nothing. They set off down the broad path hand in hand. But as it grew narrower and more difficult, each had to pick a way alone until some really precipitous obstacle gave them an excuse for a hand-clasp again by way of help. Marion, agile though she was, realized more than once his man's strength; and caught his eyes on her, in pleasure at her grace.

Coming back to the familiar house was queer, at first. Ethel, beaming, opened the door. Bill slithered along the hall – and back – and back again, barking, slobbering, his twittering tail almost in his mouth as he turned and twisted. But there was no Philippa, and for a little while everything seemed empty, for there had always been Philippa to come back to. But there was Paul bringing in suitcases, and later Philippa rang up chirpily, to welcome them without intruding, and ask when they were coming to see her flat, and telling how much better she liked the new job than the old one. After that the new pattern began to show itself and everything seemed better.

The next morning brought the usual litter of advertisements and samples in Marion's post. Paul, with one letter, from his people, looked across with interest at Marion's pile.

"What on earth do you do with them?"

"Take some myself, the good ones. The ointments I mostly try on Bill if he scratches or gets a bald patch."

Paul said, "Gosh, how awful! And if they work on him, you prescribe them to the next patient with an itch?"

"That's about right!" she acknowledged, and laughed at Paul's face of horror. "You'll learn a whole lot of things, I'm afraid, that the general public doesn't know!"

At nine, Eileen Roffey arrived, with lists and notes, and the waiting-room began to fill up. Paul disappeared, and Marion forgot all about him. His term did not begin for some weeks, and he intended doing some writing and research. And so the old life of her work and the newer one with Paul became for Marion blended, and because the whole was unbelievably harmonious at this time, and because of her capacity for living in the present, she had no regrets.

Paul worked partly in the room they had furnished for him upstairs, so as to be away from the comings and goings of patients, and from the telephone, and partly at the University Library. Sometimes he would stay there all day.

"I'll have my lunch at the Bay Tree," he said one day. "I often used to go there, and it takes up the best part of an hour coming and going, if I have it here."

Marion almost expostulated, she loved their meals together so much. Then she remembered several lunches, lately, which had been moth-eaten by telephone calls for her, or cut short at one end or the other by her appointments, and did not. Lunch, in the old days, had always been a scurried meal, not to be taken seriously. Paul went on, "Couldn't you join me there? The service is quite quick, and they give you a decent meal."

She looked up gratefully, glad beyond words that he had sensed her mood, and said, "Why not? I must lunch some-where, and I could give Ethel the 'phone number for anything that really mattered."

So that was settled, and she enjoyed the change of scene, and meeting with other people from the University. The cheerful clean little café saw them thereafter several times a week.

Marion quickly picked up her contacts with her patients – Mrs. Elroy and her baby, over a year old now, and beginning to stagger round on his own, a sunny, round-faced creature like his mother; other babies in various stages of development; Mrs. Gordon, who forgot as a rule that there was anything different about her and talked to her exactly as before; as indeed most of them did, having no interest at all in their doctor's private life except to resent it if it put her out of reach of their demands on her. A few smirked and inquired, "Well, and how do you like being married, Doctor?" To which Marion would reply politely, "Very much, thank you – and what can I do for you?" and the subject would be dropped.

Leaving her breakfast one morning for the telephone, Marion heard a male voice, amused, a little piqued. "Dr. Blake? Or should I say Dr. Shepherd?"

Marion said, "It doesn't matter, really. Most of my patients still call me Blake, because that's how they know me."

A chuckle. Then, "This is Dr. Dodds. I was sent for about four o'clock this morning by a Mrs. Scott in Elm Grove — "

Marion put in, "Good gracious, why?"

"You know them, of course. She had cardiac asthma, quite a nasty attack. The husband told me as soon as I got there – not before, unhappily – that you'd been looking after her for a long time. When I expostulated, he said they didn't like to call a *lady* doctor at night, and more particularly" – he chuckled again – "a *married* lady doctor!"

Marion snorted. "In that case they'd better make up their minds to have a man altogether, for *I* won't look after them on those conditions!"

He soothed her down. "Oh, I wouldn't say that, now! I

gave her some morphia and atropine, as I was there, and told them I'd ask you to call in the morning. I wouldn't dream of taking them off you, and I'm sure they wouldn't wish it. You know what people are."

"I shall tell them very definitely what I think of them," Marion grumbled, and he grunted little deprecatory grunts as she thanked him.

Paul, when she told him, choked over his coffee, and laughed until Bill came and stood up beside him and howled in sympathy.

Driving down the hill one day, she met Mrs. Bowen walking up it at tremendous speed, and stopped, surprised, and asked her how she was.

The woman scowled at her. "And how d'you think I am, with no husband and no home? How would you feel yerself? You ought to know, now, you ought!"

Startled, Marion parried, "I thought you were going to be much happier."

"You did, didn't you. You told me so, didn't you. Encouraged me to leave them. Didn't know no more about it than a sick headache, did you. Not that you knew much about sick headaches either, come to think of it. Well, let me tell you" – she stuck her angry face in at the window of the car – "I'm not happy at all, see? Not living in someone else's house and neither your soul nor your body yer own. You work, an' they scrimp and scrimp. That's all they're interested in, working you and scrimpin' you. If you have trouble of yer own, or if you're ill, they simply don't see it. If you stay ill, or even miserable, more than a day or two, they hint you better go back to yer own people. And if you

89

haven't any people, that's just too bad. You're not a person, you're just Mrs. So-and-so's domestic help. I hate it. I hate it so much" – she took a long breath, and Marion drew away from her –"I made up me mind I'd come back. And so – I came. This very afternoon, I came."

She stopped speaking, and her face began to work into puckers. She removed it, to Marion's relief, from the car window while she looked for her handkerchief.

"And now," she went on after a minute, "they don't want me. They're better off without me, they says. Me and me naggin', they says. Him and Florrie. Sittin' in his arm-chair at the back door, he was, as comfortable as you please. Florrie, she's got herself married, and they're all livin' there together. What they're livin' on I don't know. Florrie's husband's pay, I suppose. Poor devil, that's what he is, though I don't suppose he knows it yet. But there's no place there for me, no place at all. I might as well be dead."

She stood for a minute, forlorn, her anger faded. "For all I swallered me pride and asked him to forgive me. Him, forgive me!" She laughed, a bitter cackling laugh. "So I'll have to go and be Mrs. So-and-so's domestic help again, for always. Nor fish nor flesh nor fowl nor good red herring. Not single, not married, not a widow. Not even a friend." She had been looking away, at nothing, but now she turned on Marion again. "That's what you did to me, you batchelor-woman, you. Feels as though you'd cut a limb off me, cutting off me husband and children. Maybe the same thing'll happen to you, one day. Then you'll remember me!"

She stumped away, then, without a backward glance,

leaving Marion shaken.

"For it's quite true," she told herself, "I was rushing in on something I knew precious little about. Just as Mrs. Gordon said. And yet – it was only the end of a mess she'd got herself into already. A mess that was perhaps impossible to get out of any other way."

She did not tell Paul about that.

One evening, trying to collect a four for bridge, she rang up Miss Ferrers. "Come and play some bridge with us tonight?"

"With you and your husband? Thank you, no."

"Why on earth not? What's the matter with Paul?"

There was silence for so long that she thought she had been cut off. Then, very coldly, Miss Ferrers spoke again. "Nothing personally, I suppose. I just dislike most men. And" – her voice trembled – "I've looked on you for so long as a pattern of the woman who can stand on her own legs without becoming ungracious – that I can't bear to think of you as – just a spoilt pet."

Indignantly, Marion protested, "I'm not in the least spoilt! I'm working exactly the same as I did before I married!"

"All married women are spoilt!" came the hot, angry voice. "My husband says – my husband likes – my husband won't let me – I hate the lot of you!"

The 'phone clicked off, and Marion, puffing out her cheeks in exasperation, went back to her chair. Paul's comment on that, after his usual bark of laughter, was, "They are, of course! She's just jealous, poor lady! But they deserve spoiling – don't they – don't they?"

"Of course!" she agreed light-heartedly, and he went on, "I

91

suppose she's never been spoilt in her life. If she had, p'raps she wouldn't have got her arthritis, poor thing. Anyway she wouldn't have had to go about hating people. Or trying to turn perfectly good girl kids into bad imitations of boy kids!"

"D'you mean Guides?" Marion asked, surprised. "Because I think it's very good for them, myself. Makes them self-reliant, gives them interests and the idea of service – I was a Guide myself, when I was at school."

Paul surveyed her, his pipe in mid-air. "A good thing you stopped before it was too late!" was his opinion. "There are still traces of it – but they're mercifully submerged in your essential femininity!"

She laughed, because she could never help laughing at their disagreements. "But it's funny, isn't it, the one thing after another we do disagree about?"

"And it doesn't matter one hoot," he asserted, "because, underneath, there's only one of us, not two."

Sobered, she said, "I suppose that's true – bless you. It's fun to have such solid roots that we can let all our odd branches sway in the breeze and never be afraid we shall be blown over."

"You can share just minds with a person," he said, "as in friendship. Or just bodies, as in some marriages. But if two people share – spirits – I think the others give the best of themselves and differences make no trouble at all."

Dear Paul, she thought. She loved him when he bubbled and when he blustered, and perhaps best of all when these difficult profundities came to the surface. The bogey raised by Mrs. Bowen dissolved and was forgotten.

7

Very soon the nine days' wonder of her marriage ceased to trouble either the outside world or Marion herself. She managed the house, lightly, for Ethel and a daily woman did all the actual work of it.

How fortunate this was for her, she realized one evening a very few weeks after their return from Switzerland. It was Ethel's night off, the first she had consented to take, and she had left a cold supper more or less ready in the pantry. She could not set the table, because the dining-room was in use, as a waiting-room, during the evening surgery. This had always before been done by Philippa, who would throw open windows and whisk magazines away as soon as the last patient went into Marion's room so that everything was ready for a meal by the time Marion had finished and cleared up. And this evening, Marion just forgot that things were different. She had a long, absorbing consulting-hour. She had some tests to do and some syringes to boil, and it was not until these were done that she glanced at the clock.

"Half-past seven. I wonder what's for supper. I wonder if it's ready, or shall I stay and write some notes?"

She poked her head round the dining-room door, and there was the stuffy smell of patients' outdoor clothes, and open magazines and papers in a welter all over the table. Paul's face appeared from the sitting-room.

"Supper ready? Oh lord! Whatever's happened?"

"Ethel's out, and I just forgot!" She screwed up a smile at his raised eyebrows, and flew across the room to let in some air, and scooped up the papers and dumped them in a corner. "I won't be long!"

She heard the creak of Paul's arm-chair in the sitting-room as it received him.

She scrabbled in the sideboard cupboard for implements to eat with, and put out the minimum. The table looked a bit bare, but that didn't really matter. She scooted out to the kitchen.

Cold ham, covered up, waiting to be sliced. Paul could do that far better than she could. She shouted for him, and after a minute he came.

"Carve the ham for us, there's an angel. Put it on the plates, we can't have that great awful dish in there — "

He said nothing, but grinned at her, and found himself a big knife, and carried it and the ham into the kitchen, and cut thin, careful slices.

Marion said, "There's some salad, somewhere. She said she'd washed the lettuce and left it – oh, here it is!"

Lettuce draining in a colander, tomatoes in one bag, spring onions in another. She put the lettuce in a big bowl and dumped tomatoes and onions on top of it. It didn't look quite like Ethel's salads, but the essentials were the same, and there really wasn't time to mess about. She collected a Heinz salad cream, and carried them in.

Paul refused the spring onions, and spent a long time peeling his tomato. He also searched for bits of lettuce heart among the indiscriminate green leaves. Of the pudding, which was cold stewed cherries and custard, he took a small helping, and then said, "Shall I make the coffee? I'm not bad at that."

"She's left it mixed in the saucepan, I think. It just wants heating up."

He made no comment, but went out and heated it, and took it into the sitting-room. They drank it there, companionably, and then Marion got up. "I'd better clear the dirty things away. We can't leave food and platters all about."

"I'll help," he said amiably, and they cleared away, rapidly, together, and left everything in the sink and turned their backs on it.

Ethel's next half-day was wet and chilly, and Marion remembered in time to open a tin of soup and heat it up. Only the telephone rang in the middle of the heating, and when she rushed back to the kitchen Marion found the soup, all but a few teaspoonfuls, all over the gas-stove. She hurriedly poured some milk into what remained and boiled it up again—but it was very peculiar soup when they came to eat it. And after Ethel's return, punctually at ten, they went to investigate a queer noise in the kitchen and found her poking resentfully at the coke stove.

"Oh dear!" Marion said, "Is it out?"

"I'm afraid it is, Miss – Ma'am. There isn't a spark in it."

"I forgot all about it. I ought to have made it up."

Ethel stumped towards the scullery. "I'll have to put a kettle on for the washing-up."

"Oh Ethel, you're not going to do that to-night. Can't it be done with the breakfast things in the morning?"

"It would go against my conscience, Miss, to leave dirty pots overnight. And there'd be the smell of them to come down to in the morning. I never feel me best in the

95

morning, in any case." And she closed the door gently behind her, shutting Marion out.

Marion said ruefully to Paul, "I'm afraid I'm a rotten housekeeper! Not a housekeeper at all, in fact!"

"You don't really have to be, do you?" he returned, to her relief. "Can't we get Mrs. What's-her-name to come in the evening when Ethel's out? Instead of the morning, if she can't do both? It'll become more and more impossible for you, won't it, when the winter comes and surgeries take longer and we have to have hot meals."

"I wish," Marion said, still gloomily, "I'd thought of that myself."

Paul looked self-consciously pleased with his cleverness. And indeed, the idea, put into practice, worked well.

Medical work was not over-busy that summer, for which Marion was thankful. She delegated what she could to Eileen Roffey, to leave time to talk to Paul in the evenings and go about with him sometimes at week-ends. He liked, too, to take her to University functions, and she grew used to seeing groups of students poke each other and turn to look at them. She could not help knowing that they made a striking couple, he so big and fair and good-tempered-looking, with the hint of steel, which they more than anyone must have recognized, under his gentleness; and she tall and slim and dark, not beautiful exactly, but with the eager, questing look which so amused her when she caught it suddenly sometimes in her looking-glass.

There were indeed occasional rushes and contretemps, such as emergency anæsthetics in the evening which left Paul sitting rather grumpily alone, or an accident which arrived, dripping blood, in the middle of a dinner-party to one of the professors and his wife; and the confinements which got Marion out of bed at night. But all these were infrequent, and to Paul, who was new to them, mildly exciting.

As autumn drew on into winter and Marion grew busier, she found more difficulty in fitting her activities in with Paul's. She dropped several not-quite-necessary engagements, such as First-aid lectures to the Guides and the Red Cross, which had been more in the nature of publicity stunts than real interests. But even so, general practice was an irregular business, and smooth running never quite easy.

One day, coming in after a round of visits which had been prolonged by a call from a neighbour's window to "come and see my baby, she's lyin' like a little dead thing!" as she came out of a house, and by another household producing three patients instead of the expected one quick one, she found Paul walking up and down the dining-room like a caged lion. He stopped crossly in front of her and jerked his head at the clock.

"You're very late!"

Marion grinned, because she was sure that was just the way he would snap at a student who arrived for a coaching behind time. "I know. I'm sorry. They were tiresome this morning."

Paul resumed his walking. "Well, for Pete's sake let's have it now!"

"How late am I? Gosh, half an hour, that is a bit thick, isn't it!" and she bustled off to the kitchen, throwing over her shoulder, "You could have had yours, of course, and mine could've been kept hot."

She heard Paul bellow, "That's just what I apparently couldn't do!" before she was confronted by Ethel, flushed and flabbered. "It's omelettes!" she stated. "And I don't never start them until you're in, Doctor. To be sure they don't go leathery with being kept, but Mr. Paul wouldn't make up his mind what he did want, just kept saying you'd be in any minute, and so I waited, and now it seems it was the wrong thing!"

Marion said, "Well, it couldn't be helped, and there's no harm done," just as Paul came strolling after her. He remarked crisply, "There will be harm done if I'm late for this meeting I'm going to, I can tell you that!"

Marion snapped round at him, "How could I know you'd got a meeting? You didn't tell me!"

"There's always a Staff Meeting on the afternoon of the fourth Thursday, you know that quite well!"

She flared at him. "I don't even know it's the fourth Thursday without thinking about it – and I don't know your timetable by heart anyway!"

Ethel said, "The omelettes'll be ready in a minute. You'd better go and sit down," as though she simply couldn't bear another word. They grinned rather wryly at each other and went.

"I thought she was going to add, 'you naughty children, you!' " Marion giggled when they had shut the kitchen-door behind them.

Paul stood looking silently out of the window. The dog Bill, after a look at him, slunk behind a chair and lay down.

Marion busied herself cutting bread and pouring water.

"The trouble is," he said without turning round, "that the house does rather revolve about the practice, doesn't it?"

Marion, struck dumb for a moment, said, "Well, yes. It always has done, I suppose."

In a martyred voice, Paul complained, "It can be a great nuisance, if you don't happen to be part of the practice."

"But, Paul, it needn't be a nuisance at all! If you'd mentioned the meeting, you could've had your omelette, and I could have had mine later, and that would have been that."

"Or if you'd happened to say that you were going to be late."

"I didn't *know* I was going to be late! I told you, things just cropped up. They do, sometimes, in my job."

"And punctuality is sometimes important in mine! In any case," he went on icily, "I'll have my lunch in college next time I have to be back there early. Then you can have yours when it's convenient."

Marion laughed; more heartily than she felt inclined to, because Ethel was coming in just then with the omelettes, and she did not want Ethel to think they were really squabbling. But Paul did not play up. He scowled and began to gobble the meal, and burnt his tongue, and caught the unlucky, amused look in Marion's eye.

"I can't see anything funny about a late meal," he said.

She agreed with him. "Nor can I. They often are late in doctors' houses. We've been fortunate, so far, and they haven't been too bad. We must have a definite plan, I think, that the meal's to be punctual when you're in, and mine's to be kept hot. I'll tell Ethel."

Paul said grumpily, "I hate having meals alone!" and Marion all at once felt distracted by the sudden, silly storm. She must have shown what she felt, for Paul, sensitive in spite of himself to her mood, relented sufficiently to add, "and I like having them with you!"

He seemed to think that settled the matter. But Marion, irritated, somehow could not let the subject drop. She said, "It isn't a question of liking or not liking, or being convenient either. I have to do a whole lot of things I don't like, often most inconveniently. Doctors do. And doctors' houses get involved in it, that's all."

Paul, restored to good humour by his own magnanimity chuckled. "And if I marry a doctor, that's just too bad. All right, I'll take it!" And he swallowed his biscuits and cheese and gulped his coffee, and smothered any further speech from Marion with a hug and a kiss, and strode out; to be met in a flurry by his wife leaping into the car, barring his way and insisting, between laughter and tears, on driving him to his meeting lest he should get indigestion from too much haste.

"Medical to the end!" he teased her. "Anyone else would have said, 'Lest you should think your missus hadn't a heart and never come back to her!' "

8

Coming in at breakfast-time one morning after giving Bill his usual trot, Marion saw a grubby boy standing by a bicycle near her gate. He was sorting newspapers from a sack. She had often seen him before, and had noticed him because he had a funny long face like a horse's, and big glasses and a flapping, greasy, forelock. He was older than most of the paper-boys, who were urchins of twelve or so, and he had a look of fanatical intelligence. She could imagine him interrupting political meetings, or shouting slogans from a roadside platform. So ruminating about him, she bade him good morning, as an expression of interest, perhaps, or because she was so used to talking to all sorts of people. She was considerably surprised when he deliberately spat.

She stopped, and asked indignantly, "Now why did you do that?"

The boy reddened, but stood his ground. A low grumble escaped him, which Marion translated into, "Damn bourjoy proletariat!" Then, pulling himself together, he announced, "Because I don't see why yew should be able to walk round with your dawg while I sweats sellin' papers. An' why yew should live in luxury in that big 'ouse while I pig it in a tumbledown cottage down the 'ill! See?"

Marion's interest grew. Bill ambled back and squatted beside her, showing his great teeth until she dropped a hand to his head. She said, "I suppose – because I've got a bit farther on than you have?"

The boy tossed his forelock back and passed his hand over

it. "Ain't that just what I said? Why should yew get on –
and I stick where I am?"

Marion thrust her hands into her coat pockets. "Partly I'm
older than you are. And partly – I carried on where my
father left off."

The boy said, "Uh?"

"My father," she told him, "started as an office boy. He
went to evening classes, got a scholarship to the University
of London, went back to his old office as a clerk, and was so
good at his job that his boss took him in as a partner
without asking him to pay a premium as most partners do.
So he was able to give me a better start than I could have
had if he hadn't worked so hard."

The boy waited for her to go on.

"But I've paid for my own education since I was fourteen.
Junior county scholarship, then a senior one, at a secondary
school. Scholarship to Cambridge, and another to my
hospital. Put my plate up here and waited for patients to
come – and they came. What," she demanded, "is the
matter with that, for you to spit at?"

The boy scraped the damp patch on the pavement with
his shoe. "You're brainy," he mumbled. Then throwing his
head up, "But anyways, you bleed the poor!"

"I'm darned if I do! I treat them as panel patients, and
their wives and children for nothing or what they choose
to pay. And they get exactly the same time and care spent
on them as the rich man who pays me half a guinea a visit."

He stared at her, unbelieving, and she smiled and insisted,
"It's true. Ask them. You probably know some of my
patients."

"Your father bled 'em, anyways. Must 'ave, to get on like 'e did."

"I don't think he had much to do with the poor, directly. He's an accountant, checking up the money affairs of big firms. But I don't think he does anyone any harm."

The boy sniffed. "It still ain't fair," he shot out, "that I should be 'ere" – he spread his hand six inches from the ground, and drew it back when Bill sniffed at it – "an' yew – where yew are."

Marion said, "I think it's fair. My father worked hard and took the trouble to get on with people, and was successful. Yours evidently didn't. I've worked hard too – both of us in the service of other people, not just for ourselves, giving the best we can in return for the pay we get. If you did the same, you might get as far as my father did, and give your children the kick-off that I had."

"I should want eddication, for that," he said, dejectedly.

"You could get it, if you wanted it enough," she told him. "How old are you?"

"Fifteen. Errand boy for Finnie the grocer, an' this job in me orf time. My dad said I must earn money soon as I left school."

"And what's your name?"

"John Peachey. So what?"

"I'll think about it," Marion said, "and tell you another day. If you really want it."

"I do want it," he persisted. "I want to get on. I thought I might save a bit, doin' this job. But I'm blessed if I see how ter do it." He flung a leg over his bicycle and wobbled away, as though he was not quite sure what he had let himself in for.

Paul was already eating his porridge when she came in. He looked up, questioning, and she said, "Been gossiping to a young Bolshie," and told him about it. "I wondered," she finished up, "whether you could do anything for him?"

"Might do," Paul said, "if he's really keen and really intelligent. And if his dad agreed, which I should rather doubt."

"He struck me as a chappie who would get his own way," Marion said. "Very rough. But yes, I think intelligent."

Paul said, "Tell him to come in and see me one evening and I'll size him up. Don't promise him anything. The great trouble with people like that is that they're apt to turn into something so half-baked when you've done with them that you wish you'd let them alone."

Marion smiled assent, and added, "I often wonder what exactly one means by that. I know a half-baked person when I see him. But I couldn't define him, and I don't know the processes that go to make him."

Paul said at once, "The term defines itself. Half-baked. Cooked only on one side. Knowing a lot of facts about one thing – everything there is to know about one thing, often – and nothing at all about anything else, and so getting even the facts they do know all out of perspective. Quite a number of our academicals turn out like that, more's the pity."

Marion said, "That does describe them — "

Paul warmed up. "A very tiresome set of people. Another thing about them is that they never realize there's more to know than they know already. You can't bake them any

104

more, they won't take it. If you try, they go up in smoke. Your mathematician or your art teacher will treat you to puerile dissertations on law, medicine, philosophy, or anything under the sun, and think it's the last word. Can't open his mouth without arguing, if he's that type. I do my best to strangle it at birth by insisting that practically everyone goes to lectures on other subjects beside his own. Then they do know there's more to learn. And preach about going on learning after they've managed the minimum qualification for earning a living, which is all most of them are after."

Marion said, "I ought to be half-baked myself. Scientific education and nothing else. I wonder if I am?"

Paul threw her the glance of admiration which she occasionally surprised from him and which always made her gasp.

"You're *not* the type!" he informed her. "You're blessed with one of those broad intelligences which can learn from a hint – get the kernel of a subject from a very little observation. You perceive where a path leads to, even if you don't actually follow it, therefore you get your facts in the proper perspective even though you may know a great deal of one matter and only a very little of another. *And* you preserve a proper humility, you never think you've arrived at the end of any path at all. Gosh, I could make a lecture out of all that, couldn't I? D'you mind being lectured at so early in the morning? If I don't go I shan't catch my bus — "

Ruminating upon the boy and upon herself, Marion wondered what effect her own history had had upon her present state of mind. It was true that she had worked with her brain almost constantly since the age of fourteen, and had lived in a household where work was considered most important; far more important than personal relationships. If her young sisters were breaking away from this tradition, it was perhaps because their parents were now resting on their laurels. They had arrived. In Marion's childhood they were still climbing, educationally and socially, and they had projected their own aims into their eldest daughter. So then, and now, her work was her life and her god. Her engagement, and her marriage, had by the strength of the emotion behind them exploded this deep-founded pattern. The smoke of the explosion was a hardly realized sense of guilt. She could not contemplate the shattered pieces calmly. She could not let herself acknowledge that her relationship with Paul required of her as much consideration as her work did and every bit as rightly. Below the surface, the two loyalties struggled for first place. In consciousness, no antagonism was even thought of. As she meditated, she knew only that there was unease, and told herself that all work and no play had made, perhaps, a dull girl of her.

9

The next morning, she did not see the paper-boy at all. The following one, he passed her on his bicycle, pedalling furiously, his head down. On the third, he strolled across the path in front of her, elaborately not looking her way.

She called, "John! John Peachey!" and he stopped, as though surprised, as though he condescended in taking notice of her. Then, while she was wondering what, exactly, to say, he burst out: "Say – 'ave yew thought – Miss? Because – I've bin talkin' to my mum. And my mum says she'll 'elp me!"

Marion, a little taken aback, asked, "Help you?"

He nodded vigorously. "Says I can keep some of me wages to help pay for classes. Even if she 'as to go out to work a coupl'a mornin's to make it up!" He gulped, evidently overcome by his mother's generosity, and stood expectant.

"My husband," Marion told him, "is on the staff at the University. He thinks he might be able to tell you how to start. Can you come in and see him?"

"The University! Cor!" He turned his bicycle round at once to walk back with her and get the business settled, and Marion had to stop him.

"Not now. One evening – this evening, if you like. He has to go to work soon now – and he can't be late, any more than you can!"

He turned about again, philosophically. "O-ke-doke, Ma'am. I'll be there!" and he was gone, whistling shrilly, the bourjoy proletarian who bled the poor either banished from his calculations or ripe for bleeding by him. Who could tell?

Bill chased him hilariously for a few yards, then abandoned him to investigate a tuft of grass.

He came that evening. Old Ethel answered the bell, and when Marion looked up, as usual, to take her message, she said very disapprovingly, "It's a young boy. Rang the night-bell, 'e did, and when I told him of it, he said, 'Well, it's night, innut?' And when I explained the night-bell rang in your bedroom, he just stared and said, 'I don't want the lidy doctor, I want 'er old man!' "

Marion shouted, and Paul said, "Sounds hopeful. Send him in, Ethel, please."

He came, with a swagger. Marion welcomed him. "Hullo, John. Paul, this is John Peachey – I told you about him."

The boy just grinned at Paul shyly, a little reverently.

Marion, who had expected him to shoot out "Pleased ter meetcher!", was relieved. She said, "I'll leave you to talk," and went off to the consulting-room to write notes.

Writing notes was a problem, nowadays. Surgery hour was too busy for much of it. If it was not done at least the same day as a patient was seen, the less distinctive people became mixed up in the doctor's mind, and at some later interview Mrs. Jones, troubled with piles, would be asked sympathetically about the hacking cough which really belonged to Mrs. Williams, or at best Marion would spend precious minutes angling for clues to avoid being labelled forgetful, a fault no self-respecting patient ever forgives. She had been used to finishing her notes in the evenings, and Philippa, growing older with the practice and often having similar jobs to do herself, had taken this for granted. Paul, on the other hand, had a definite martyr reaction to it. He would offer her a cigarette, start some enthralling subject of conversation, and, when regretfully she stood up to go, would say, "Darling, aren't you being a thought too conscientious? Well – don't be long — " and she would feel

108

a brute. She tried taking her record cards into the lounge, and this he approved of. But he would never keep quiet, he would read her bits from the paper, or from his book, or chip in with an anecdote. Once, when she said good-humouredly, "Oh, shut up, Paul, I'm leaving out half this woman's symptoms, and, I haven't got her diagnosed yet, so it matters — " he looked so surprised and hurt, and said so crossly, "Sorry I'm being nuisance!" that she never had the heart to expostulate again.

So it wasn't a bad thing to have him occupied for an hour. She had nearly finished when she heard a movement in the hall, voices, and the front door shutting, and Paul going back into the lounge. She completed the card she was writing and went in to him.

He poked the fire up companionably.

"I've fixed him up for some evening classes," he said. "He's a funny lad. Very intelligent, as you said. And knows a whole lot more than you'd think to hear his ordinary conversation. Extremely observant, and done quite a bit of reading on his own, in the face of a lot of discouragement from his dad. He'll have to work like blazes and get his Matric; and then we can think about a grant for him, if he still wants to carry on. You seem to have fired him — " He smiled at her, amused by this odd enthusiasm.

"I didn't really – he was ready to be fired, I just happened to supply the spark."

"By being interested. Funny, I simply shouldn't have seen him, in your place — "

They sat, chatting, and Paul got up in a minute to turn on the news.

"I'll just wait for that," Marion said, "and then I've got to go out. A pneumonia that wants a shot of morphia to give her a night."

Paul made a face. "Can't young Eileen do it?"

"Physically, yes of course. Psychologically, no. She's really ill. It upsets them to have anyone but their own doctor, if that's so."

"It would me, I suppose," he allowed.

She put her face up to him as he passed behind her chair to his own, grateful for his understanding, the more because it was grudgingly given.

He grunted, comically, and said, "I'll drive you. I can give Bill his breath of fresh air while you're inside."

10

It was a few nights later that the telephone rang at four in the morning. Marion stretched out for it mechanically in the dark, subduing its screech to a series of hollow clicks.

A male voice announced sepulchrally, "Missis French's waters 'ave broke. The nurse says, 'Will the doctor come?' "

Marion smiled at the funny message, asked a few questions, and tumbled out. Paul flumped over and grumbled, "How you can laugh at anything that machine says at this time of night! I'd like to wring its neck!"

Marion had turned on the light in the passage outside, and stood silhouetted, slim and straight in her nightdress, looking down at him. "So would I, sometimes! Anyway, you haven't got to go out into the cold, cold night!"

He pulled the bedclothes round his chin. "Thank heaven, no. But I don't get the kick out of it, either!"

"So that's fair!" she declared.

She gathered up some garments and walked round to kiss him and tuck him in. "I won't come in again, then you can go to sleep." And she went across to the bathroom to dress.

In the morning, having tiptoed in without waking him, she slept late, and he let her, for it was Sunday. She had a bath, luxuriously, at half-past ten, and as she lay in it, the gobble-gobble of the re-filling tank stopped suddenly, leaving silence. Into it broke Paul's voice, conversing upon the hated 'phone.

"Yes, she's in. Can you give me a message? – No, I'm afraid you can't speak to her. She's in her bath. Yes, her bath. That's what I did say, in her bath. But good gracious, even the cleanest doctor needs a bath now and then!"

Marion, in the warm water, listened spellbound.

"Funny time to have it? I think it's an excellent time! So would you, I expect, if you'd been up half the night! – You never are up half the night? Of course you're not? Well, doctors are, often, of course, and sometimes other people as well, for one reason and another! Anyway, my good lady, the doctor *was* up half the night, working, not playing as it happens, and she *is* in her bath, and if you really won't give me a message you'll just have to ring up again in half an hour's time. Half an hour's too long? Well, she might be out in twenty minutes, I wouldn't know. Try twenty minutes, if you like. *Good-*bye."

Marion heard him replace the receiver and come out of

111

the bedroom, breathing heavily. She called to him. "Paul – who was it?"

"I haven't an earthly. She sounded dam-awful!"

Marion, through her laughter, said, "I don't know what she's thinking! You *can't* talk to patients like that!"

"I've been longing to," Paul said, "ever since I came to live here! She wouldn't take no for an answer, and she argued about every word I said!"

"They always do," Marion told him. "That sort. I'll be out in a minute."

They heard nothing more until they were having lunch, and then the 'phone rang again, and Paul sprang up to answer it. "You leave this to me!"

Then – "Oh, it's you again! I told you to ring in half an hour, didn't I, and you said it was too long. It's about two hours and a half now, and she's in the middle of a meal! Luckily it's a cold meal, so I'll fetch her. But" – his voice became admonitory – "you treat your doctor very badly, you know. She's got a body, the same as you have. It needs meals and sleep – yes, and baths – it isn't made of tin. Yes, yes, I'll fetch her, if you'll hold on!"

Marion shook her fist at him as they passed each other in the hall.

"Dr. Blake speaking — "

The voice which answered her was Mrs. Gordon's, old, authoritative, indignant. "Good afternoon, Doctor. Your messenger, if I may say so, is a trifle brusque."

Marion said a little breathlessly, "It was my husband."

A pause. Then, drily, "Standing up for his wife. Well . . . I rang you up about my foot. It's very painful to-day and I'd like you to see it."

"In the morning?" Marion suggested.

"To-day, if you please. I tried to get you this morning."

Marion hesitated. The painful foot was an old-standing affliction, and Mrs. Gordon would never see Eileen Roffey. And she and Paul had intended spending the afternoon together, leaving Eileen on duty.

She said gently, "Have you tried your tablets?"

"No, I have not. I dislike taking tablets as you know. Yes, they do the pain good when I do take them. You think I'm a selfish old woman, sending for you on a Sunday afternoon?"

"I didn't say that. But if I did come, I should tell you to raise it up on a pillow and take two of your tablets – and I can do that over the 'phone, can't I?"

Silence. Then, "Very well, I'll do that. And you'll come and see me early in the morning."

"I will," Marion assured her. "Good-bye, Mrs. Gordon."

"Was it a panel patient?" Paul asked pugnaciously when his wife came back.

"It was not. It was one of my few ten-and-sixpennies."

"And for that she thinks she owns you! Sunday visits for nothing at all, and long chats on the 'phone in the middle of lunch!"

Marion, getting on with her meal, said, "Oh well, that's what they pay for, isn't it? Amenities? Visits at a time convenient to them, twenty minutes' talk, the right to diagnose their own diseases and suggest their own treatment and to argue with you if you differ from them and put you at your wits' end, to convince them you're

113

working for their good! The comfort of a nursing home instead of the crudities of hospital. Attention to their fads and their feelings as well as to their illnesses. Apart from that, they get exactly the same as the panel patient does, with perhaps a fancy name and a spot of flavouring to their medicine!"

After lunch they had the telephone switched over to Eileen Roffey's number. Even Marion was in favour of an afternoon by the fire, to talk and listen to the wireless and read the papers undisturbed.

They talked of Marion's patients; of one whom she had been seeing much of recently – "She's a dreadful example of a little knowledge – one of your half-bakes who can't believe she doesn't know every single thing there is to know. Gives herself stomach wash-outs – actually swallows several feet of rubber tubing without turning a hair – and enemas – and has me in all in a hurry to tell me she must have a colostomy at once — "

"Permanent hole in your tum and a little box?" Paul put in, and she nodded.

"There's nothing the matter with her at all really – nothing of that kind, anyway – she's just one of those people who concentrates on all the feelings and digestive rumblings that most people take for granted and ignore."

"Hypochondriac?" murmured Paul.

" 'M. Before she took to the wash-outs, she went in for Christian Science. She really was the funniest sight. She had three very obvious wens on her head, and one of those awful red noses some middle-aged women get – no, she doesn't drink, it just comes like that, in some people – and

114

yet she would sit there intoning that her body was perfect and that anything that appeared to be wrong with it was only imagination. Then one of the wens got inflamed and she turned pettish and let me cut them out and cool her poor old nose with an ointment, and decided I did her more good than the Christian Science practitioner did with her helpful thoughts."

"Why did she call you in, in the first place?" Paul inquired.

"Thought the inflamed wen was a cancer, and didn't quite believe Christian Science was equal to that. They often do get the wind up, I find, if they're really ill – though sometimes not till they're nearly dead, poor things."

"I wonder," Paul said, "how much truth there is in it, really?"

"A germ," Marion suggested. "The truth of the power of spirit over matter, and of the accessibility of spiritual power."

"But can they cure disease, d'you think?"

Marion shook her head. "Organic disease, no, I'm sure they can't. Nervous disease, emphatically yes. And they can abolish the element of fear from any disease and hasten recovery if recovery's possible. That far, they do good. Where they do harm is in their refusal to act *with* doctors. They'll actually discourage someone with, say, an early cancer from going to a doctor, until the thing's become inoperable and all one can do is sign the death certificate. They're glad enough for one to do that, to escape an inquest and censure from the coroner. The churchmen who claim to heal by prayer are quite different. They say that the

Almighty uses every possible means to heal – doctor and parson alike – and that they should work together."

"It's difficult, isn't it?" Paul said. "Difficult for the ordinary layman to disentangle truth from charlatanry, willingness to serve from petty jealousy. Another instance of the half-baked, in most cases, I suppose."

Marion had yet another view of it a few nights later, when she was hunted out of bed by another husband – this time one who insisted that his wife was dying of hæmorrhage.

To an exasperated Paul, she explained, "One can't leave a hæmorrhage to die. Or even waste time getting hold of Eileen. It's one of the few things they *can* die of fairly quickly."

From the patient, when she arrived there, she inquired rather irritably, "Now where's this bleeding?" For there was no sign of it, and the young woman was very pink and quite obviously not dying of anything at all, although her teeth were chattering and her bed rattling against the wall.

"It's – int-int-internal!" she chammered.

Her pulse was strong and slow, she had no pain, and her temperature was normal. Marion was puzzled.

The husband, standing sourly by the hurriedly lit fire, said, " 'Ave you told the doctor where you've been to-night, and what time you came in?"

His wife screamed at him, "Go away! You go away!" and, sniffing with disapproval, he went.

The young woman and Marion looked at each other.

"You'd better tell me," Marion said. "There's nothing the matter with you except fright. What are you frightened of, and what's this nonsense about hæmorrhage?"

She began to sob, noisily. "I've done a bit of nursing. I knew hæmorrhage was a word which would get a doctor out. I had to have a doctor, I had to!"

"If you don't tell me why, I can't help you," Marion said.

Instead of the tale of matrimonial dispute and cruel husband which she had expected, there came a torrent of words about a spiritualist séance which the woman had attended that evening: messages and warnings, terrifying sounds and bizarre sights in semi-darkness. "They told me" – she spoke in a low monotone, just, Marion thought, as the medium must have spoken – "they told me some dreadful things that they wanted me to do. But if I don't do them – something will happen to me" – her voice rose shrilly and she peered into this corner and that – "something will – happen to me!"

Marion was beginning to ask what it was that she had to do, but she burst in, crying now, "I mustn't tell you! They said I mustn't tell anybody! I must just do it – and I can't – I can't!" She lay back on her pillow, shivering.

"I'm still wondering," Marion said conversationally, "why you thought you needed a doctor."

The young woman sat up and clutched her. "Don't you see? Don't you see? They'll make me do it, from pure fright. If I were asleep, I couldn't do it, could I? I thought you could give me something to make me sleep."

She leered in a queer, cunning way which made Marion doubt the whole story and wonder if she were perhaps out of her senses. There was, however, no doubt as to the need for a sedative. Marion stood over her while she swallowed

117

the two tablets, and went to find the husband and give directions as to a hot bottle, humouring, and tucking in.

He confirmed his wife's story, and added gloomily that she had wandered about the streets till midnight in her fright. "Or so she tells me. I've tried to stop her going to the place, but she's set on it. Got her by the short hairs, they have."

"P'raps this fright will put an end to it," Marion suggested, and he agreed, dispiritedly, perhaps it would.

"What was the matter with this one?" Paul asked when she came back.

"Fright!" she said briefly, and he commented, "Devil! To get you out for that!" and was sleeping again in an instant.

She told him the whole tale in the morning, and he snorted about sham and deception and silly women as he ate his breakfast. "The self-seeking canniness of some people! I'm sorry for the poor toad of a husband!"

"So am I, this time," she agreed. "It's generally," she smiled at him, "the wife's part I take. But not this time. However, people stop at nothing when they're frightened."

In the evening of that same day came another urgent call; this time from a guest-house for business-women. "One of my ladies is having a fit!" the proprietress gabbled. "She's just dashed out of the lounge, and she's sitting on the bed gasping and moaning most dreadfully!"

Marion was silent for a minute. Then she said, "Has she by any chance been going to the local spiritualist meetings?"

"Has she – what? Miss Smith, has she . . ." and a murmured conversation went on at the other end of the

118

telephone. Then, awestruck, "She has! How ever did you know?"

"Recognized the symptoms," Marion said drily. "Now look here. Sponge her face with cold water. Threaten to throw it over her, and really do so if she doesn't control herself. Then give her a cup of hot strong tea and two aspirins, and put her to bed. Good-bye."

Paul chuckled when she told him. "How was the other one when you saw her this morning?"

"Perfectly well. Doing her housework. Pretended she couldn't remember anything about it."

"I'm glad," he said, "you weren't caught the second time. The way people impose on you is unbelievable – or would be, to anyone who didn't live in a doctor's house. Each one of them thinks you do nothing but sit on your behind waiting for her personally to ring you up and blow off all her troubles. Nothing else matters."

"Did I tell you," Marion asked, "about the time when I took three days off to go to a post-graduate course? No? Phil was fairly free then, and it was before I was very busy, so she carried on for me. Someone rang up for a visit, and Phil explained and promised to go. Half an hour later, the lady rang up again to say she couldn't possibly employ a doctor who was still learning, she would never have become my patient had she known, and she had now made arrangements with one who knew his work thoroughly."

Paul laughed. "Just like them! I'm going to answer the 'phone myself whenever I'm in and educate them. Make 'em see you're as important as they are."

"I'm not, of course," Marion demurred. "Any more, as

119

Bernard Shaw put it, very properly, than the fireman is important, as an individual, when the house is on fire. It's only the fact that they're worried that makes them importunate and rude – they don't mean to be."

Unmoved, Paul said, "I shall try to educate them, nevertheless. Your job to treat them, mine to teach them manners. What's the matter with that?"

Marion, laughing, said, "Nothing. Except that you'll never succeed, and you'll probably annoy them very much."

"At present," Paul said, "they annoy me. And as for Philippa, when's she coming to see us? It's ages since she's been."

Marion looked distressed. "It is, isn't it? I'm always afraid she thinks we don't want her."

Paul said, "Honestly, we don't, much, do we? Philippa's all right – but I'd rather have us to ourselves – wouldn't you? I wondered at first whether she'd always be around."

Marion wondered suddenly whether he had said anything to Philippa, to put her off coming. She said slowly, "I don't know about that. I love – us to ourselves. But I love being together *with* people, too. Meeting your eye across a crowd when we've got separated at a University show — "

"Oh, that's different."

"Or hearing each other arguing with someone else — "

"Or" – Paul became more agreeable – "knowing that someone else is really an outsider even though we're trying to make him feel one of the family."

"Phil's not an outsider."

Paul grinned. "She's not one of the family, all the same."

11

The next time Marion heard Paul answer the 'phone, he began by being very courteous and good. "Yes, this is Dr. Blake's house. Yes, I'm sure she will. Can you give me any idea what's the matter?" Then a pause, then a snort, then another pause. Then, in a rush – "Well, there's no need to be so smart alick about it, is there? You must have some idea whether it's a cold in the nose or a broken leg!" Then, "Wouldn't you? Well, it does make a difference of course, she might want to bring a splint or something, mightn't she? Now will you please give me your name and address!"

To Marion's raised eyebrows, he retorted, "Yes, I know! And when I tried to get an idea whether it was urgent or not, entirely for your benefit – I suppose they realized that was what I was up to, and they hate not to be urgent, don't they – the reply was, 'Well, that's what we want the doctor to tell us!' and the most awful self-satisfied giggle at her own cleverness. No one could possibly go on being polite to them!"

Marion wagged her head. It wasn't any good arguing with him. She would tell Ethel to make a dash for the telephone as soon as it rang. It was nearer her kitchen than their sitting-room.

Paul was talking again. "I was telling the people at college about your spiritualists. And, do you know, several of them had been to those séances – they're apparently quite a feature of the town, and they were all upset when I trounced them."

Marion exploded, "Fancy University people going to

things like that!"

"Didn't I tell you some of them are half-baked? They were very indignant about the hæmorrhage story – and the other one too, that you diagnosed by black magic! Said they would have to find out who were the culprits who brought them so into disrepute! I told them there wasn't any question of that, they were in disrepute already!"

Marion sat up. "Paul – you didn't tell them the whole tale?"

"I certainly did – and a very good tale too! Why not? Didn't mention names! Didn't know them, anyway!"

"It's terribly likely to get back to them! I ought never to have told you, of course!"

"Good thing if it does, the silly blighters!" was Paul's opinion. "What's the matter? Professional secrecy?"

Marion said, "Of course!" and Paul said, "Pouf! I don't see that it comes into a case like that! They weren't ill!"

Marion lost her temper suddenly. "Paul, of course, it comes in! It was something I couldn't possibly have known if I hadn't been attending them professionally, and I ought not to have told you about it!"

"And as usual in such circumstances, you're cross with yourself and you take it out of me!" Paul countered.

"I'm far more cross with you! You marry a doctor and encourage her to talk, and then go and gossip like anybody's charlady! And what do you mean by 'as usual'? I hardly ever get cross – only under the very greatest provocation!"

Paul, whose fair skin had flushed at her taunt, laughed suddenly.

122

"I don't often provoke you, do I? Do I?"

She agreed, with a catch of the breath like putting on a brake. "Thank goodness, no, you don't. But I have got a temper – and seriously, Paul, you mustn't pass on tales I tell you – or we shall just have to sit mum – you have married a doctor, after all!"

Paul gave her a funny little look. "I know. I'll be a model of discretion. And – how about talking about my things sometimes for a change?"

She looked up quickly. "Paul – we do talk of your things!"

He said, "Not very often. Yours are more spectacular, after all! But never mind – we will. Just for a beginning, old Hughes has asked us both to tea with them on Sunday. His wife wants to meet you. Can do?"

Marion said at once, "Of course. As a matter of fact I'd been expecting some such gesture long ago. After all, he is your chief. What's she like, Paul?"

"Never seen her. He's a nice old boy. It'll probably be a party, on a Sunday."

But when they arrived, they found no one but themselves. Professor Hughes took Paul off to his room to see some papers, and Mrs. Hughes, surveying her guest, said, "This is nice. I told the others a later time to come, because I wanted to get to know you."

Marion said, "That was nice of you," and Mrs. Hughes blinked, as though she had expected less assurance.

"I think wives of staff should know each other," her hostess went on. "We're so dependent on each other for social life, aren't we? A body somewhat apart from the rest of the town. Do you play bridge?"

Marion allowed that both she and Paul were fond of it.

"Good. Good. Then you'll be able to join my Bridge Afternoons. Not your husband, he'll be busy, of course. We hold them definitely as hen-parties."

Marion said lightly, to hide her satisfaction with her excuses, "I should love to. But I'm afraid I'm busy every afternoon myself."

Mrs. Hughes pulled her large, pink chin down into her loose pink neck, her blue eyes bulging with such affront that Marion hurriedly explained. "I have a general practice at the other side of the town. I thought you knew."

The tension on Mrs. Hughes' cervical spine relaxed as though she were a jack-in-the-box. "Oh – that. But of course, you'll be giving that up now!" She ran on before Marion had time to agree or deny. "Now, the Women's Institute. You must give us some Health Lectures. The Health Visitor did it last year, a doctor would be a change. They meet in the afternoon too, of course – but one has one's responsibilities, hasn't one?"

Marion agreed that one had.

"Not," Mrs. Hughes changed the subject smartly, "that one's household isn't responsibility enough. Maids! Dreadful! I have a little hussy myself – always going out, insists on it, and on bringing her boy friend to the house and filling the kitchen with cigarette-smoke – she would fill my bedrooms with it too, herself, but I do draw the line there. Have you a maid, Mrs. Shepherd?"

Marion said, "Yes, I'm one of the lucky ones. I have an inherited one, of the old type, cap and apron and all. A darling." She added naughtily, "I couldn't do without one."

Mrs. Hughes sighed. "That's a thought which has come to all of us at one time or another. And then one learns. One learns."

She looked at Marion as one who would say, "I'd love to have the teaching of you, too!" Another couple fortunately arrived to divert her, and she swooped upon the wife. "My dear, how good of you to give us your Sunday afternoon! I want you to meet Mrs. Shepherd. She'll be so interested in your musical evenings!"

The new-comer, older than Marion but younger than Mrs. Hughes, smiled graciously. "That will be lovely of you. Real music-lovers are rare. What instrument do you play?"

"I'm afraid, none," Marion had to confess. "I'm just a good listener."

The other lady lost interest immediately. "Oh dear. Such a pity to have raised my hopes. Now just before I forget it – and before you're overwhelmed with other guests – I wonder if you could give me the recipe for that marvellous iced sponge I enjoyed so much last time I came to tea?"

Mrs. Hughes chuckled. "It was good, wasn't it? And I've got my recipe book right here!"

Over their bent heads, Marion caught the eye of the musical lady's husband, standing uncertainly behind. He smiled and moved over to her.

"Mrs. Shepherd, isn't it? So glad to meet you. I saw you both at the repertory show last week. What did you think of it?"

They pursued a pleasant conversation until Mrs. Hughes boomed at them. "I was telling my friend here that you have a really good maid, Mrs. Shepherd. Now she, poor dear, hasn't one at all!"

They watched accusingly to see what she would say.

Her mind running, as usual, to treatment rather than the endurance of any sort of trouble, Marion said, "Many people are having Austrians and such, aren't they? I believe they're very good workers, and most of them speak English."

"The question of language," the musical one said pettishly, "wouldn't worry me at all. I spent several years in various continental cities, including Vienna, studying music. But" – she leaned forward confidentially – "I wouldn't trust them! Not for an instant! German spies, practically every one of them! I assure you! We have inside knowledge, haven't we, Dick? And of course, a University town, a centre of all sorts of information, would be jam for them! Jam!"

Another couple came, and the talk lingered over maids for a few minutes and passed on to children.

"John's headmaster tells us his Maths are quite marvellous! So unusual in such a young boy, he's only just eleven!"

"But not surprising," Mrs. Hughes put in sweetly, "when you know who are his parents! You taught maths, too, Mrs. Dent, before you married, didn't you? And of course – your husband's one of the most talented young men we've ever had!"

"Stella," the first arrival said, "is no good at all at books. Games, yes. And she's a wonderful rider."

"And *very* pretty!" Mrs. Hughes supplied. "Brains don't really matter for a girl, do they, as long as she has a certain *savoir-faire*. And that she's sure to have, in your household! So interesting" – she turned benevolently to include Marion in the talk – "so very interesting to see one's family growing up! Grandchildren too, in my case. Three of them. Bill, the baby, is the dearest thing – so good – and so fond of me, I can do anything with him! Though my daughter Muriel is a wonderful little mother."

And so they went on, each, it seemed, trying to score over the other, even in the matter of their children's achievements. Marion listened, thankful that their attention had been distracted from herself.

Paul and the Professor came in, and Paul at once joined Marion, and the other men joined Paul. That was better. They had real things to talk about. She conversed with one or another of them throughout tea, the tea-trolley having come in while they were gathered in one group and the three other wives in another. They treated her, as men so often did, as one of themselves, and teatime made up for the afternoon's uncomfortable beginning.

Going home, they talked mostly of the conversation they had had with the three men – plays and places they had been to and the socialist outlook of one of them who had been in Russia – and little of the three wives. Marion thought with some discomfort that she had not clicked with them, and she didn't want Paul to realize it. She would have them to tea herself one day and draw them out about their children and their cooking and their good works and the brilliance of their husbands, and show them that she could be a good hostess.

Paul was remarking happily how well she had got on with his colleagues.

12

The boy John Peachey came now and then to see them. A friend of Paul's had found him a job in the University Bookshop, and he had spruced up enormously in both appearance and in speech. He was earning more money now, so he had given up the paper round, and they did not see him except for these visits.

"Every time he comes I think he's grown a bit more the typical Labour intellectual," Marion commented after one of them.

"Alas, yes. I always feel that he comes here snooping to see how educated people behave when they're at home."

"Partly. And a bit because he likes us and we welcome him."

"I do quite like him," Paul allowed. "I like his relentless way of pursuing the end he has set himself."

"And *I* like — " Marion frowned, searching for an exact meaning. "I like the mutual interest he gives us. You and me."

Paul said, " 'M?" and seemed to be waiting, ears cocked, for more.

"Does that sound funny? It does to me a bit," she said. "We have got the mutual interest of the home and the garden and the dog, I know, but that's not the chief interest for either of us. We're chiefly interested in our own work. In each other, of course, that goes without saying – and that's two separate interests, isn't it – woven together, but still separate . . . and it's fun to have some one pie in which we both have a finger – d'you see?"

Paul put his pipe down and said carefully, "Yes, I do see. I like it, too. Marion, wouldn't you like us to have a real mutual interest? A child?"

Marion cried out, "Oh, Paul – not yet! It would spoil so many things!" Then, at the look on his face, "Do you really want one?"

We are interested in each other, she was thinking. We do want to please each other. He's always making things easier for me, I ought to let him have what he wants.

He was speaking again, slowly. "I do want a family, some-time. A house in the country, too – there's some lovely country within travelling distance of here – a good-sized house, and several youngsters – and dogs – and ducks and hens."

He looked across at her, smiling, questioning, sure of himself, not quite sure of her.

"But that," she said presently, watching him, "would mean giving up the practice."

And he, at once, as though he had been thinking deeply upon the subject for a long time, agreed. "It would, for a while, wouldn't it? You could take it up again later on – part of it, anyway – couldn't you."

There was a long silence.

Marion was appalled at her own reaction. She longed to say, "The practice is my child, I made it!" But then, it wasn't Paul's child. She saw herself becoming like a professor's wife, clucking about children and maids, and later on about bridge, Women's Institutes, University Extension Lectures; boasting of the pre-eminence of her own husband above all the other professors; working in the background like Victorian women, like yeast, not going free, in the open, like she did, a person in her own right.

She said, "Couldn't we be looking for the house? And when we found it, I could plant Eileen here and come in, just as well as you could – and then think about the family a bit later on, when we're settled?"

Paul said, "That would be a beginning, anyway – bless you — " and bent his sweet, good-tempered smile upon her and left it at that.

13

They visited several houses – huge and dilapidated, with ten acres but no electric light, or modernized, but costing the earth to buy.

Then Eileen Roffey had a holiday, and several confinements fell due, and Marion was more tied than ever. She kept Paul hanging about for one whole Saturday when they had agreed to see yet another house, and then the baby did not arrive till one in the morning.

"Can't you *tell* when they're coming?" he asked her irritably.

"Would I waste time like this if I could?"

"Lord knows. You seem to like it. Can't you do something to hurry it up?"

"Not safe," she said tersely. "Anyway none of the houses seem much good, do they?"

And somehow the matter of houses was allowed to drop.

Paul, too, was extra busy himself very soon. He had written a play which the college dramatic society was to produce, and he pored over it every evening, polishing it up, unconscious of whether his wife was in the room or not. Then rehearsals began and he could talk of little else. The production was as much his child as the practice was Marion's, and for the present both were content.

They came in, almost simultaneously, late one evening. Paul, who had arrived a few minutes the earlier, flung himself into a chair and called, "Don't stay in that blinking surgery, come and sit down for a bit, can't you?"

Marion called back, "Shan't be a tick," and joined him after much longer than that. "Had to have a good wash," she excused herself. "Been to a dirty house. How's the play going?"

Paul said, "Pretty grim!" but with a hopeful air.

When Marion said, "Last rehearsals often are, aren't they?" he agreed, and launched into description of the various actors. It was only when this was talked out that he asked her, "What was your dirty place?"

Marion hunched herself forward, clasping her knees. "The most extraordinary scene. Would make a play itself. Like something out of Dickens. An urgent message, after supper. A boy. He sounded terrified, so I went."

"They always sound terrified – or some such thing," Paul put in. "And you always go!"

Marion went on as though she had not heard, as though she could not tear herself away from a memory. "It was a little house down the hill. People we know. The woman an old T.B. who has been dying for years. A big family, feckless and dead poor. The father, I knew, though I hadn't seen him, some sort of a cripple from an accident on the railway. He used to work on it. Well, this time she really had died – coughed up a lot of blood, which was simply all over the place. No attempt to clear it away – or anything away, for that matter. The sheet was grey and greasy, the pillows had nothing on but the original striped tick – you could just see there were stripes, but only just. There wasn't a space in the room where you could put anything down. Clothes and boots, all filthy, on the chairs, the floor, everywhere. And the stink! Windows shut up tight. And, lolling off the bed, the dead woman, black dusty hair hanging in lumps over her blue face. Mottled, blue and white, and her nightdress, what there was of it, stiff with blood, so much of it that it had dried almost black. Across the bottom of the bed, propped against the wall, was her husband. I couldn't think why he was there, immovable, until I saw that he had no legs – no legs below the middle of the thighs. A great big man with a bush of grey hair. And all round the bed their seven sons, great brawny creatures like the father, from about sixteen upwards, all struck motionless, looking at me as though they thought I'd come to do a miracle. When I said she was dead, the father dropped his face in his hands and began to sob – and the rest of them stood and stared and their faces crumpled and tears ran down their cheeks, and they sniffed and rubbed them away with their sleeves. Then I saw there was one woman there – a girl of seventeen, perhaps, in slacks. She would have been beautiful, I think, if she hadn't been so wild and so dirty. She suddenly came to life and hustled them all out – two of them picked up the father and carried him dandy-chair – and turned round to me and said, 'Tell me what I've got to do to 'er.'

"I told her I'd send the nurses, and she snarled like a bitch with puppies. 'No one else shan't touch 'er!' and she began to cry, too. Queer, how they all loved that woman who'd been nothing but a burden to them for years! So I stayed, and helped her tidy her mother up — "

Paul sat up suddenly. "*You* helped her?"

"I couldn't leave the girl to do it alone — "

He stared, as though he were visualizing the scene, and curled his nose. "I do wish you'd stop going to places like that! There's no need for it. Now, anyway, even if there was once."

"Need didn't come into it," she told him, "from my point of view, anyway. They're not people one could get a penny out of, at any time. From theirs, the need was tremendous. Ignorant, frightened people – they think of the doctor as a magician — "

"That must be most stimulating!" Paul said drily.

But Marion did not rise. She was still, in mind, in the little dirty room, watching the primitive emotions of love and fear, stripped stark by the fact of death.

14

As the University show drew nearer, Paul grew more and more absorbed in it. Old Ethel, who disapproved of everything connected with the theatre, remarked, "These

133

goings on don't suit Mr. Paul – he's as jumpy as a scalded cat!"

One evening he came in tired out, and Marion scolded him. "You look all in! Come and have a warm. That college hall is as cold as a church!"

"I am cold," he allowed. "And frightfully hungry. I didn't stop for any tea."

After he had warmed up by the fire and eaten ravenously a three-course supper, he seemed better. Relaxed in a chair, he talked again about the actors, the decor, and all the back-stage work which had gone to the making of the production. Marion, who had been anxious about him, was quite sure now that nothing was wrong except fatigue.

But when he wanted to get up, his face changed to one of agony and he clapped a hand to his back. "Gosh, I can hardly move! I must have got 'flu!"

Marion, looking him over with a seeing eye, said, "It looks more like lumbago, to me. If it were 'flu you'd have a temperature."

"You can't possibly know I haven't," he retorted. "I feel like fire!"

For reply, she propped him against the mantelpiece with a thermometer in his mouth. "No temperature. You can look for yourself if you don't believe me!"

"You know I can't read the damned thing!" he grumbled. "Doctors never tell their patients the truth!"

"I do. That's the truth, anyway. You've just got cold and tired and gone stiff. Go and get into a hot bath, and I'll see what I can find in my drawer."

He halted at the door. "Sample drawer? Things you try on

the dog?"

"They're not all things I try on the dog."

"Well, you're not going to try them on me!" He was through the door now, exuding injured dignity.

Exasperated, Marion called, "I mean, some of them are really good things that I would never go to the expense of buying!"

"Well, I don't want your mouldy samples," he said, decidedly and very crossly. "And I don't want to be told I'm only cold and tired when I'm perfectly certain I've got 'flu or perhaps pneumonia and I'm going to be really ill at the worst possible time."

He stumped off upstairs, pulling himself up by the banisters, and disappeared into the bathroom. Marion put a hot bottle into his bed and warned him not to lock the door in case he couldn't get out of the bath.

This brought indignant snorts and presently, on clouds of steam, thumps and groans of pain. When she offered to come in and help, he shouted, "You just keep out of here!" and next time she came upstairs he was in bed. He accepted a cup of hot milk with whisky in it, and, after due inspection of the bottle, two aspirins, with two more beside him in case he should wake up with pain.

"And I'd like you to ring up Dr. Dodds early in the morning. I don't believe in doctors treating their own families."

Marion said cheerfully, "Nor do I. It's far too much of a responsibility!"

He scowled at her in such a way that she knew he had meant to hurt her feelings and was disappointed that he hadn't.

In the morning, the extra aspirins were still by the bedside, the back better, and Paul himself very jaunty.

"I did get the wind up!" he confessed. "Silly of me, but it really would be the last straw to be ill now. I was simply tired out, nothing more."

Marion refrained from saying, "What did I tell you?" but chuckled to herself none the less.

He went on, "It matters so much, this play. I feel it's a test of all sorts of things. Ability as a writer and producer, of course. Influence over the students – popularity – being able to get things done as one wants them – all the oddments which make for getting on in the world."

"It's a very good play as one reads it," Marion assured him. "And your stock's always pretty high with the students, isn't it?"

He grinned the little-boy grin. "High enough, with them. But not always with the senior staff. I'm not – somehow – quite their sort. Not solemn and academic enough."

Marion said, "Just as I'm not quite their wives' sort either."

Paul waved that away. It was not what he was talking about. "I must prove that I'm outstanding in my own way, even if I'm not in theirs."

Marion, her eyes on him, said seriously, "I shouldn't think that needs any proof – it shouts — " and their eyes met and they broke into laughter, with relief that last night's alarm was over.

Paul said presently, "The Vice-Chancellor has invited us to dinner before the first show. Awful bind, I'd far rather be prowling round the stage. Ought to be, really. But we

136

shall have to go."

"I suppose we shall. I wonder what I'd better wear."

"You'll look all right," he said handsomely. "Only don't be too knowing – Mrs. Shepherd, not Dr. Blake, see?"

She said, "Paul, I never push Dr. Blake in ordinary company, now do I? I'm glad not to – glad just to *be* ordinary."

"Never ordinary. Far from it!"

She giggled. "Now you're being gallant husband. A bit heavily. I'll be good — "

She hardly saw him during the next few days. She was less busy herself, because Eileen Roffey was back. But on the day before the college show, the telephone shrilled its warning note.

"Dr. Blake? This is Mrs. Tuson speaking. I think I've started — " A mingling of relief and apprehension, fear and hope – this is *it.*

Marion contributed her usual encouraging, "That's good. A few days early is always a few days gained. I'll be along presently to see how you're doing."

But to herself she was swearing mildly, "Confound these babies, one has only to arrange something – I do hope to goodness she'll get it over!"

By the next day it was apparent that Mrs. Tuson's labour would be a long drawn-out one. When Paul came in at tea-time, Marion blurted out, "Paul – it's the most awful pest – but I just simply shan't be able to come to the dinner!"

Paul stopped in his tracks and stared at her. "What did you say?"

"Mrs. Tuson's baby. It's been going on all day, and it'll be born, I should think, about eight o'clock."

Paul sat down. "So what?" he asked amiably.

"So – so I shall have to be there instead of with you at the Vice-Chancellor's dinner."

They sat in their two chairs looking at each other; Marion all anxiety and big-eyed contrition, but confident of understanding; which was, however, the last quality which Paul's unbelief, passing into anger, could contain.

He said, "I'm damned if you will!"

She watched him in silence for a minute, then began, patiently, to explain. "She's in her late thirties, and she's had two miscarriages. This may be her last chance – it matters frightfully that this baby shall be all right. I simply must be there."

"I don't care," Paul said through his teeth, "if she's in her early nineties and has been having miscarriages all her life. This dinner matters frightfully, too – the impression I make at it. It may matter the difference between staying a junior lecturer all my life – or going on to be, ultimately, a Vice-Chancellor."

Marion said feebly, "I don't see what difference my being there makes – to your impression."

"Which only shows you don't know anything about the internals of Universities. If you're a bachelor, there's still hope for you. Though a bachelor isn't generally the favourite for the highest posts. Anyway, I'm not one and everyone knows it. They like one best with a nice, intelligent, circumspect wife who'll be good for the students."

Marion waited for his eyes to crinkle up to tell her that

138

she would meet the bill, but they did not.

"If there's anything wrong with your wife – or between you and your wife – you're finito. Definitely and hopelessly. I've seen it happen. The best man for the job, with a dud wife, passed over for the second best man, whose wife is suitable."

Marion cried out, "But, Paul, I'm not a dud wife, and there isn't anything wrong between us!"

Paul frowned at her. "No. But what would those old fossils think when I turned up without you to a dinner at which we're practically guests of honour? They can't imagine there could be anything more important in the world than their functions. Whatever we said you were doing they'd be sure it was only an excuse. That for some reason you didn't want to come. Someone would invent a reason – a horrid one with the tiniest grain of truth in it – and pass it round – and the thing would be done!"

His brow was wrinkled, his eyes popping out of his head. They stared into a vista of dull, shoddy houses, poverty, pot-boiling, a slum doctor's husband delivering medicines for her and cleaning the steps.

Marion shook herself. "I don't believe anybody of intelligent people could be so petty! Anyhow, why not tell them the true reason and done with it?"

"They'd have a fit! Things like that simply aren't spoken of, except as a statement of fact after it's all over, in their circles."

Marion put in crisply, "Don't you believe it!"

That stopped him, for an instant only. He spread out his hands in despair. "I tell you, I've seen it happen. The

139

rumours, the pettiness!"

"You don't seem to realize I've a duty to my patients!"

"What *you* don't seem to realize," Paul shot out, "is that you're married to me!"

Marion deflated all at once. I suppose I shouldn't have married him, she was thinking. I should have stuck to my job, not tried to grab the best of both worlds. But when one's – enchanted – one doesn't think, one can't.

Paul, swift to perceive an advantage, said, "What on earth's the matter with sending Eileen? She's qualified in that sort of thing, isn't she?"

Mechanically, Marion replied, "Yes. Yes, of course she is. But she's young – and Mrs. Tuson doesn't know her – and the psychological side, having someone you trust and all that – is so important in these cases– I must go, Paul, I really must!"

Paul, his hands unsteady with his pipe, said, "Oh, well. If this woman means more to you than I do, I suppose you must."

Marion stamped her foot. "Oh, Paul, don't be so childish. – and so *personal!* You know it isn't that at all!"

Paul said, "There's no point in discussing it any more, is there?"

He looked so dejected that Marion suddenly could stand out no longer. She said, "I expect I'm making a silly fuss. There's no reason to suppose the baby won't be born normally, really, even if she is a bit more frightened than she need be. I'll ring up Eileen and tell her exactly what to do."

Paul's face cleared ecstatically and he held out his arms.

Marion evaded them, but could not help kissing the top of his head as she passed behind him. He caught her hand and nibbled at her fingers.

15

The dinner was certainly a function. The Vice-Chancellor and his wife were ancient and well born. Their house was conventionally beautiful, their approach to life conventionally formal. Marion felt on the very doorstep that here were unwritten laws, stretched like gossamer, all about her, which she, untutored, must perceive and not break.

She was glad she had only put on the faintest smudge of lipstick and had not had time to pink her nails.

The butler was announcing them – "Dr. Shepherd — " How annoyed Paul would be – why should they put her first?

"Mrs. Shepherd — "

Of course, Paul was a Doctor of Philosophy. How idiotic of her. That was all right.

The Vice-Chancellor had trotted three steps forward, and his ancient face was wrinkled into a smile. He had taken Paul's hand and was leading him to his thin, once-beautiful, grey-haired wife, whose darting glance travelled up and down. Marion trailed after them.

"My dear, here is our brilliant young friend – the author of the play we are going to enjoy – Dr. Paul Shepherd – and

141

his charming wife!"

The old lady's smile was conventionally sweet. It thawed a little into real pleasure as Paul pressed her hand, and stiffened again as her glance passed over Marion. The Vice-Chancellor patted Paul's arm and murmured, "We'll see you later," and turned to the next arrivals.

Marion thought, "Golly! And he wants us to grow old like that!"

She was staring, across the crowd, at the solemn face of one of the husbands she had met at the Hughes' tea party. It crinkled suddenly into a most understanding wink, then froze again. Marion's own eyes twinkled. She felt better.

The other guests were mostly people she already knew or had heard of: University staff and their wives. One man who was a stranger was, she learned, a dramatic critic. He was paired off with the only woman who was there in her own right, a lecturer in art who had been responsible for much of the scenery. They were soon deep in conversation. Another couple who did not seem quite to fit the mannered picture were a London producer on the look-out for talent and a lady who was surmised to be his wife.

Marion realized almost at once that Paul was right – that it would have been the most dreadful breach of good manners for her to have stayed away.

At the table she found herself between an elderly professor of archæology and the theatrical producer. She lost herself for a moment in an imaginary conversation with one of them —

"I ought not to be here at all, really."

"Indeed? What ought you to be doing instead?"

142

"Having a baby!"

"I *say!*' the poor man's eyes would sweep in horrified apprehension over her figure and away. "Is there anything I can do?"

He would think, of course, that she was due for a lunatic asylum rather than for motherhood.

She caught Paul's glance on her, appreciative, a little questioning, and flung herself into the business of being an intelligent, circumspect wife. She was really interested in the theatre, and knew something about it from contact with a woman playwright who had been at Cambridge with her, and from Paul; and a Hellenic tour, before she had settled down in practice, gave her a superficial acquaintance with archæology. Listening to case-histories was not very different from leading people on to talk of their own shops and hobbies, and she and the good dinner left her neighbours beaming and gave her quite a good conceit of herself as well. Paul grinned at her in evident content from the other end of the room as she went out.

In the College Hall, she had to sit prominently with her hosts in the front row, instead of with the families of the younger staff as she would have liked to do. She must remember, she told herself, not to guffaw at the funny bits, but to smile gently or even look innocent. Then it occurred to her that, in such a company, there would surely be nothing to guffaw or look innocent about. The situations which had amused her in Paul's manuscript would surely have been watered down, beyond recognition, to please such an audience.

But she was wrong. The play was entrancingly funny.

143

The audience, quick with intelligence under the convention, barked with laughter nearly all the time, sat tense for minutes together, and sighed with delighted relief when, by a clever twirk, all came right in the end. It was a topical play, fitted together like a jigsaw, and played with the greatest verve by a talented and well-coached collection of youngsters, whom Paul had picked himself.

The producer from London bustled up to Paul the minute it was over. No University customs were going to keep him from pursuing his own ends. Catching from Paul the worried look of one whose interests are divided, Marion put herself into the position to receive the compliments which would have been better paid directly to her husband.

And they were many. Apt topical allusions pleased the politically minded; classical tags delighted the academic; the characterization was good, to satisfy the psychological, and the jokes and some clowning with comic situations had kept the students in good humour. If Paul had been out for acclamation, he had certainly scooped in every possible bit of it. His many-sidedness once again took Marion by surprise. She was proud and happy in her association with him.

When, presently, he strode up to her and demanded, "Did you like it?" as though her approval mattered more than anything else, she was immensely pleased with him and replied with enthusiasm, "It's the sort of play I would spend a night in London specially to see at a West End theatre, and it wouldn't be acted any better there than it was here."

The people round them laughed and murmured

agreement. Paul beamed at her. All seemed set fair, she told herself ruefully, for a Vice-Chancellorship. Though she refused to envisage herself, at seventy, sucked dry and cut off from all enlivening contact with life and death, with suffering and joy.

In the car going home, she told Paul, "A lovely evening. I enjoyed every minute of it."

His eyes paid tribute to her. "You were marvellous. I heard a lot of admiration showering round you."

She teased him. "A good second to the Guest of Honour?"

He sobered down a little and answered her, "Very good indeed!"

16

On the table when they came in was a message. Marion pounced on it, and Paul grumbled, "Why didn't you leave that switched over to Eileen for the night?"

Marion was reading the message. "Couldn't do that," she said absently. "I wanted to know what had happened. And" – she raised a worried face – "I wonder what has. Eileen says, will I ring up Mrs. Tuson's house as soon as I come in."

She moved along to the telephone, hardly hearing Paul's complaint that he wanted to celebrate. When she did hear it, she threw over her shoulder, "I won't be a minute!"

But what Eileen Roffey told her put celebrations right out of her head. She dashed upstairs to change her dress, and when Paul barred her way as she came down, she brushed past him. "I've got to go along there right away. You'd better get to bed."

Unlocking the garage seemed to take half an hour. She only just missed taking a wrong turning, only just didn't crash another car at a cross-roads. When she came to Mrs. Tuson's, the house was silent; no light shone out of an open door to guide her, no baby's cry told her even that all was safely over. Mr. Tuson let her in grimly and nodded the way upstairs.

Mrs. Tuson was quiet, anæsthetised. Eileen Roffey, dishevelled, looked at Marion over her mask. The nurse was busying herself at a table.

"Not born yet?" Marion asked softly. And the young assistant answered as softly, "Yes, it was born half an hour ago," and mouthed, lest Mrs. Tuson should hear, "Dead."

Marion felt all the colour drain from her face as she looked at the still little bundle in the cot. "Have you given it Lobeline? And CO_2? There's one of those little cylinders in the bag" – she made a dive for it – "and done artificial respiration?" She could not believe that the baby could not be brought to life.

But Eileen Roffey took up the CO_2 cylinder and a used ampoule of Lobeline from the table near by. She said sombrely, "Yes. We did all those things – of course. But it had been dead some time. The prolapsed cord had stopped pulsating – Oh, an hour ago now."

When they had finished the whole business and given Mrs. Tuson a shot of morphia so that she should not wake up to the bad news before she had had a rest, the two women doctors went into the bathroom together and shut the door, and Eileen Roffey gave Marion details of what had happened.

"I did everything I could think of – all the things they tell you in the books – but it just wasn't any good. It hardly ever *is* any good, is it? Isn't there an almost 100 per cent mortality? I've never seen one before – a prolapsed cord —"

Marion nodded. "I'm sure you did everything it was possible to do. I'm not blaming you the least bit, please believe that."

But Mrs. Tuson's husband, when she told him his son was stillborn, said heavily, "I don't think it would have happened, Doctor, if you'd been there."

17

Paul had taken her advice and gone to bed. Marion dawdled about the surgery when she came in, too tired to think coherently, disliking the idea of bed for herself. When she did lie down, in the little room she kept for busy nights, she fell asleep at once from sheer fatigue, and when she awoke, at about five, her thoughts had that cold clarity of early dawn which never recurs during the day-time bombardment of cares and pleasures.

I don't think it would have happened, Doctor, if you'd been there.

Nothing's much good in those cases – there's a 100 per cent mortality – almost.

Almost, but not quite. They're avoidable, with proper forethought.

The doctor was out at a dinner party, and didn't get there until too late.

If Mrs. Tuson had had the thought she had a right to expect, it might never have happened. Your thoughts have been a bit divided lately, haven't they? And if you'd been there, with your skill and experience, with your small, strong hands which are better than any other sort of hands for manipulations of that kind, you might have averted disaster even at the last minute.

From him to whom much is given, much is also expected.

It matters the difference between staying a junior lecturer all my life and going on to becoming a Vice-Chancellor.

Paul's life and happiness. Mrs. Tuson's happiness and her baby's life.

I must never let myself be landed in a predicament like that again.

Never – but how?

Paul was his jauntiest self at breakfast. He did not mention the night before – Marion's part of it, anyway. He talked about the affability of the London producer, who wanted that play, just as it was, for his Repertory Company, and perhaps, if it did well, for the West End, and perhaps other plays too.

Marion said recklessly, "It would be more fun to write successful plays than to be a Vice-Chancellor!"

Paul said he didn't see why one shouldn't combine the two. Nothing seemed impossible to him that morning. He bounded away through the November mist to catch his bus.

The telephone rang several times with requests for visits. Bill had his piece of toast and his brush. Ethel asked for suggestions for the day's meals. Patients began to drift in for morning surgery.

Some of them were just routine things, repeat prescriptions, certificates.

One was a woman who needed an operation. She had to be coaxed to the idea carefully, like a nervous horse to a jump. When she had at last been persuaded, she pressed Marion's hand in gratitude. "I'll take your advice, Doctor. You give me such confidence!"

A spoilt little boy came with a sore throat. At first he hid behind his mother and whined. But a little patience, a little firmness, and he stood still and "made a big mouth" like any singing angel. "You're so good with children, Doctor!" his mother sighed as, clutching the prescription, they made off.

Another caller was a man, inclined to bully, insisting that his wife's fatigue and depression must be something more than mere nerves and that something must be done about it, who left, presently, understanding that the healing of the "nerves" lay largely in his own hands.

Yes, there was no doubt that she could manage people, Marion said to herself.

The rest of the morning was spent at the hospital, giving gases for dental extractions; a horrid, brutal business with no time for finesse with patients' feelings, only stertorous breathing, spattering blood, teeth all over the floor. But at the end of it the dentist, a brisk young man, said, "I'm always glad when it's your morning for this, Dr. Blake. No

149

alarms and excursions, no one asphyxiated, but everyone deep enough for me to do as much as I want to. It's astonishing how few people can give a good gas."

Marion bowed elaborately and laughed. It seemed easy enough to her. All her work was easy to her when she gave her mind to it.

The first visit after lunch was to Mrs. Tuson, so as to be there before she settled down for her afternoon rest. No need to dodge the baby's feed-time, Marion realized with a catch of the breath.

She came to the point at once, for she was not one to shirk an issue. "My dear – I'm so very sorry — "

Mrs. Tuson surveyed her mournfully, then managed a smile. "I knew you'd be nearly as disappointed as I was, Doctor. It was just too bad that the other case kept you away. She was – just luckier than I was. Though Dr. Roffey was very sweet. She did everything she possibly could. I guess – I'm not built for breeding – am I?"

Marion said, "Perhaps not quite — "

"I'm going to adopt one," Mrs. Tuson went on. "Right away, if I can find one. Nurse thinks she knows of a little girl, born last week, whose mother doesn't want her – fancy not wanting her, when you've had her – and if you want one as badly as I do, you just can't get it!"

Marion, her voice lighter than her thoughts, said, "Contrary creatures, aren't we? Yes, I know about that little girl. She's a dear little baby. Dark, like you."

"I do hope I can have her," Mrs. Tuson said, and presently waved good-bye almost gaily from the bed.

She bore no grudge, blamed no one, Marion realized. And

Eileen Roffey, or the nurse, or both, had invented "that other case" which had saved a reputation. Perhaps they thought that a reputation built up over years did not really deserve to be damned by one lapse from its usual rigidly high standards.

Marion went on to a Mrs. Manners, a sharp-tongued, newly-rich little north-country woman, who lived in a very fine, modern, over-decorated house a few miles out of the town. Marion always felt that she had to walk delicately with her, that they never quite trusted each other, although the family had been faithful patients ever since the daughter, Daphne, whimpering with tummy-ache and dosed with castor oil by a robust father, had been snatched back from peritonitis and the gates of death by Marion's timely diagnosis of appendicitis. Daphne had been a leggy schoolgirl then. She was grown up and married now, to a young man who was starting in the world at the same level at which her father was leaving off, rich, responsible, and respected. Mrs. Manners' thoughts, nowadays, were divided between her daughter's prospects and her own ailments, which last were mainly the result of unaccustomed leisure.

Mrs. Manners was more than usually off-hand in her behaviour to-day, Marion thought. Then she wondered if perhaps she were a little touchy herself after last night, and recalled that in the past Mrs. Manners' off-handedness had often been a prelude to a gift, a sponge sandwich lavishly spread with lemon curd, or a bunch of dusty purple grapes from the green-house. She dealt carefully with Mrs. Manners' troubles one by one, and Mrs. Manners answered each of her suggestions with a grudging, "Umph. Maybe."

At last, disconcerted, she rose to go, and Mrs. Manners went with her to the door. Here she planted her short, square self directly in the way.

"My daughter Daphne," she announced, "is going to have a baby."

Marion looked down at her, interested. "How nice. When is she coming to see me?"

Breathing heavily, Mrs. Manners said, "She's going to have it at the hospital. Private Block, of course. We think it better."

Surprised, more at the manner of the information than with this news itself, Marion commented, "Well, she can." And was more surprised when Mrs. Manners snapped: "She's going to. It's all settled. I took her to Sir Alan Forster myself. She's not coming to you."

They stared at each other, Mrs. Manners suddenly, inexplicably hostile. Then Marion said mildly, "I should be glad to know why?" Impossible, surely, that this could be so soon the result of last night's tragedy.

Mrs. Manners began to talk rapidly. "It's the way I'm treated on the 'phone. I ring up and ask if I can speak to you, and they say you're out."

Marion interposed, "I generally am, except at meal-times and during surgery hours."

Mrs. Manners gave her a dirty look. "So you say. I ring again, and I'm told you're having your lunch, and if I persist, that even doctors must have time to eat. Well, if I'm ill I have a right to speak to my doctor, haven't I? And if you don't choose to make it convenient for your patients to speak to you, I take it you don't want patients. Not that you need them, now, I suppose. Anyway, I don't like to think of Daphne being treated as though she were a nuisance – so I'm taking her – elsewhere."

She shut her mouth with a snap.

Marion, suddenly tired, opened the door. At her unmoved, "Thank you. Good afternoon," Mrs. Manners drew in her breath with a hiss and took herself indoors without another word.

The rest of the patients on the list were chronics who could be seen any day. Marion felt an overwhelming urge to get away and think quietly. At the end of Mrs. Manners' drive (I suppose I shan't be coming here again, she told herself) she turned out towards the country instead of going back to the town. Bill, sensing the possibility of a walk, put his paws on the back of her seat and his nose out of the window.

She parked the car at the opening of a cart-track, and he leapt out, sure that the expedition had been arranged for him, and raced away across the fields. Marion kept to the path, and in a few minutes was climbing rapidly up towards the top of the chalk downs. When she was high enough to command a spacious view, she turned and sat down, facing it, in the stillness of the late November afternoon. The dog came and gave her an interrogative poke, and when she took no notice of him, wandered off among the bushes.

She sat among dry grass which curved away or stuck up at all angles round her, with here and there a late knapweed flower or a yellow hawkbit. At her side a hedgerow straggled: strong stems of bramble, maroon, with

153

thorns of pearl and an occasional crimson leaf, bright haws and shining bryony balls, sign of some fairy pawnbroker, were cobwebbed with old man's beard. The skeletons of fennel plants formed a ghostly, rustling frieze. Below her stretched the fertile fields of the river valley, rich brown earth or golden stubble, with little haystacks picked out clearly, like a child's bricks, by the sun's low beams, their shadows twice their own length. The trees threw long shadows too: elms with scattered leaves of lemon yellow, birches like little mounting flames, and between them the red roofs of the town, church spires and the new University buildings; and beyond, another line of downs, some tawny to the very top, the higher hills grey green with wintry grass. A dog barked, far away, small sounds of hens and ducks came floating up. Mist hung in the distance, the sky above was muted blue.

For some minutes Marion sat still, letting the peace encompass her. Then, with difficulty, she tugged her thoughts back from this breadth and clarity, formed, even this, of Nature's small things each harmoniously in its own place, to the small but very urgent problems of her own life.

She reviewed her week's work. Visits to old ladies to save their families the trouble of an inquest should they die suddenly of nothing but old age. Other old ladies, in so-called nursing homes because their families did not want them, just not dying of neglect, but reeking of urine, intent on nothing but their food and the actions of their bowels, disgusted by both, whimpering at the rudeness of chits of untrained nurses to women who had carried authority,

154

many of them, in their day; herself powerless to improve their lot because whatever she might say could not, nowadays, get a nurse even a reprimand, much less the sack, and they knew it. Visits to other people, too: to young Mrs. Turner, a fit young woman to all appearances, who had married an equally fit young cousin with Marion's professional blessing, and had produced two idiot boys one after the other who weren't even going to die and leave her free. And I ought to have warned her that there was that one in a thousand chance, and I didn't. To Mrs. Lord, who had attended every week for rheumatism in her knees for years and only disclosed the cancer of her breast when it was stinking and inoperable. "I didn't want to bother you, Doctor," she had said. "I knew it would make a lot of work for you if I did." I expect I was short with her – rheumatic knees are boring things to treat, one knows one can do so little for them. I ought to have made her feel that nothing was a bother.

Miss Ferrers – she had had news of Miss Ferrers only yesterday – that she had taken a new job elsewhere and had died, suddenly, at work, of her failing heart. I did warn her, but I wasn't firm enough, I ought to have made her retire, I ought never to have let her lose touch with me, who knew her.

And then the baby last night, at a time when almost every stillbirth could be prevented.

A G.P.'s most important job is to keep watch and ward – not to make lightning diagnoses and spectacular cures – and I haven't been doing it, I've been letting them all down, when they trusted me.

155

And now, there are people who won't call me out at night because I'm married, and people who are so put out by Paul's naughtiness on the 'phone that they must go off to someone else.

Those are nothing but excuses, of course. They would have, called me out at night, and they wouldn't have let Paul put them off, if they'd really wanted me. But they sense, as people in need will, that they're not my first interest any more. That Paul is competing with them – and winning.

Her thoughts paused there, as though they could go no farther: then bubbled up heavily, one by one, in answer to the insistent question, what shall I do?

I shall have to give up the practice. Better give it up than spoil it. But I can't, I simply can't, it isn't all failures even now, and there were hardly any failures before. I shall have to give up Paul, then. It isn't fair to spoil his life with this continual conflict. Then, in a panic, I shall spoil it even more if I do leave him – anything wrong between you and your wife, and you're sunk.

Her mind went back to her life before she had married Paul, the full, contented life she had shared with Philippa, and she recognized it for the arid thing it was, full of bustle and importance to fill an emotional void. She lingered fleetingly on the thought of Mrs. Bowen, who had left her rogue of a husband and regretted even him; and on old Mrs. Gordon, who had brushed away her spinsterish plans for Mrs. Bowen's future as the merest unwisdom. They had known more than she did, then. But not now. She knew, now, that you could not leave someone you were joined to

156

with almost every fibre of your being just because there were still some few fibres flying loose and the someone wanted to gather them up too and control them along with the rest of you.

She sat up straight, her hands gripped round her knees. She must make some treaty between these two claims she had allowed on her. And Paul must help her. If she must not spoil the life he was building for himself, neither must he be allowed to spoil hers. Perhaps – her practical mind sought round at once for plans which could be laid hold on – perhaps he would be satisfied if they could get moving over this matter of a new house.

A flight of rooks went over, so near the hillside that she could hear the beating of their wings, and settled chattily, with much changing of places, into a clump of elms. There were starlings too, flying round as though in formation, joined by echelons of three or four more at every turn; until the sun disappeared behind the far hills, and they, too, as though at a signal, dropped sheer among the bushes below.

Marion shivered a little; stood up and stretched, and whistled for Bill. As she walked briskly back across the field he trotted up and followed behind her, and they made together for the car, and tea.

18

Paul was very sweet to Marion in those days after the still-birth. He did not grumble about the hurried meals, the odd visits she had to do when she might have been with him. He coaxed her to a good film on her half-day instead of leaving her to her own devices, and brought in to coffee people whom he knew she liked: people who were appreciative of her as well as of him, and did not push his own type of conversation; although she was glad, with them, to forget her doctoring and talk as an ordinary citizen.

He rang up Philippa, and she came to supper after an interval of many months, and while she was there he took himself off to his own room and the two friends had a glorious pow-wow. It was mostly about Philippa's concerns, though, not Marion's. Marion was fiercely anxious to dispel any suspicions that she was not conducting a life successful in every particular. That was the Marion whom Philippa knew, she would not easily recognize any other.

Another evening, Paul produced John Peachey, spruce in his bookshop dress of morning coat and striped trousers, with pronunciation and turn of speech modified by much reading into almost B.B.C. correctness. He seemed on the straight road for his particular brand of success.

"The most extraordinary change!" Paul commented when they had shut the door behind him.

Marion said lightly, "It's because he's doing the thing on which his heart is set, don't you think? Nothing to put the

158

brake on him."

She was not thinking consciously of herself as she spoke, but Paul surveyed her seriously for a minute before he agreed. "Yes. Yes, I suppose that's it."

She hugged his arm and laughed as they passed into the lounge, because she was happy, and it seemed as though her treaty was being made by Paul's volition even more than by her own, and this tiresome situation resolving itself.

Then the telephone rang, and Paul, with a twinkle in his eye, went to answer it, and all Marion's fears and doubts flooded back again, and she knew that this was only a pool of sunlight, shadow-bordered, in which she was basking, and that she would have to talk to Paul after all as she had planned.

He began the telephone encounter very cautiously, little boy Paul resolving to be good.

"Yes, this is Dr. Blake's house – Yes, she's in. Can I give her a message? – She will if it's necessary. Are you sure it won't wait until to-morrow?"

A long pause, then patiently, "I quite understand that."

Another pause. Then Paul, clipped, angry, his irritability after all so little beneath the surface, "I'll ask her to speak to you. Is there any need to be quite so rude?"

Marion sprang up. She passed Paul in the hall, his face white, contorted, furious beyond all proportion to the provocation. He hissed at her, "Some devil wants a visit! At this time of night!"

Marion soothed the ruffled messenger, suppressed an inclination to say, "Give the little blighter an aspirin and

I'll come in the morning!" and promised a visit before she went to bed.

The telephone had been placed near the kitchen to save old Ethel's legs when she had often been left to answer it alone. Opening the door as Marion put the receiver down, the old woman, on her way upstairs, came face to face with her, gave a look, and burst softly into speech.

"Mr. Paul, he don't understand that you get fond of your patients, Doctor. Nor that you make your living out of them. Nor yet, that it's only fright that makes them demanding and rude — "

Marion said, "No. No, he doesn't. Sometimes, I think, he doesn't want to — "

Ethel had become again the inscrutable elderly maid. She murmured, "Maybe, maybe," and lumbered on her way.

Marion waited a minute before going back to the lounge. Then, impelled by curiosity, she compressed her lips into a smile – Paul was always amused by these encounters, once they were over – and went in.

"Paul, what did she say?"

But Paul would not play. "The usual nonsense. I tried to find out what was wrong – she spat back at me, 'we shouldn't send for the doctor if we knew that, should we?' and then fairly ticked me off – 'if Dr. Blake doesn't want to attend my child I'm sure we can find somebody else who does!' I do think your patients are the rudest, most uncouth, ignorant lot of morons one could find in one place!"

Sitting on the arm of a chair looking at him, Marion said, "You do hate my work, Paul, don't you?"

160

Paul bit on his pipe, then laid it carefully aside. He said, "Yes. I do hate it. I thought I wasn't going to. But I do."

Marion slid down into the chair and sat looking into the fire, wondering what, exactly, it was best to say next.

After some minutes, Paul stirred. He began to justify himself.

"It isn't that I don't – approve of it, in any way. I do, of course. It's a job worth doing, and you're good at it, and I knew from the first that you wouldn't want to give it up. I haven't any right at all to hate it. I think the trouble is – primitively – that it takes you where I can't follow you – in thought as well as in deed – and I resent that."

He looked up to see what she thought of his reasoning. She said at once, "But, Paul, I don't follow you into yours."

He asked her curiously, "Don't you want to? I've wondered, sometimes — "

She shook her head. "Not a bit. I'm interested in the out-skirts of it, but not in the details at all. And it just wouldn't occur to me to make suggestions – how you were to do it, or when, or anything like that — "

Paul said, "Well, you couldn't, could you? I mean, you don't really know much about it, do you? It just isn't your cup of tea!" When she was silent, he fidgeted and presently exploded, "I suppose you mean, I do make suggestions about your work to you! Not knowing much about it?"

Marion pitched her voice lightly, not to make these petty things seem too important. "Well there is the telephone business. You hate the patients. You don't attempt to see their point of view. It would really be much better to keep out of it altogether."

161

Resentment, injured dignity, and unbelief chased each other across Paul's face. "D'you mean my efforts at educating the patients in good manners is a hindrance, not a help?"

Exasperated, Marion said, "Of course it's a hindrance! We're not here to teach them manners, however much they may need it; we're here to look after their health! And the sort of things that happen if you do try to educate them, as you call it, is – what happened just now – or this…" and she told him about the defection of the Manners household.

"I thought," she finished, diffidently, for she hated lecturing Paul – would never have presumed to lecture him on any subject less important to her than this one – "I thought perhaps you were *trying* to be a hindrance. Trying to show me what a nuisance it all is. Bust it up altogether, perhaps, so that I should have to give it up. P'raps not consciously trying – but trying none the less."

Paul opened his mouth and shut it again; rumpled up his hair, clapped both hands down on the arms of his chair and sat there staring into space; and finally burst out, "Hang it all, Marion, how can I possibly know what my subconscious does? It wouldn't be subconscious if I could! I suppose under my educated, civilized skin I'm a primitive man who wants his wife for himself and himself alone, whether his rival's another man whom he can clop and be done with, or some vocation which he doesn't quite know how to attack except with childish or even primitive methods. I *do* want you just for myself, Marion. You're so beautiful. You're like a tall, lovely tree. It's awful – *awful* –

to see you wasting yourself on these sick, selfish people! Most of them'll never get better whatever you do for them, a lot of them don't even want to, and the rest would get better if you did nothing at all. Isn't that true? I just want to love you and work for you and have you – that's true, anyway – all your thoughts and preoccupations – for myself alone."

He came over to her quickly and squatted beside her, and then with one swift movement scooped her up on to his knees and sat in the chair with her.

She said weakly, "Love me and work for me and have me spend all my time telling you how wonderful you are!"

He kissed her ear, her chin, her collar-bone. "If you think so!" he agreed. "And I rather hoped you might, in time! Marion, we mustn't quarrel!"

She was so comfortable, lightly held in his arms. "I'm unhappy when we even disagree. But I'm unhappy, too, if I think of giving up my work. Paul, people do manage these things, why not us? I should have to kow-tow to your work, if you were the doctor."

He said immediately, "That's quite different!"

She countered, "That's what you say! And why?"

He hoisted himself a little, and put on what Marion called his lecturing face, and she tapped his lips warningly with one finger. "No," he said, "this isn't a dissertation, it's a plain statement of fact. The thing's entirely economic. If I were the doctor, I should be the breadwinner, and that's why you would of necessity kow-tow. You're not the breadwinner, and so if I kow-tow it's by courtesy. See?"

"We can have more fun if we're both earning."

163

"More money, but not necessarily more fun. We could have both if — " He held her away from him and looked at her seriously.

"If?"

"If you would pursue your profession in a milder way. Some way that would avoid all these emergency calls. Something you could do by appointment."

She cried out, "But, Paul, there isn't anything! Only consultants work by appointment, not G.P.s, and I haven't the qualifications or the hospital posts for a consultant. The only other thing is just baby clinics and such – and – well, you've no idea how dull they are!"

He said rather wistfully, "Well, if you can't, I suppose you can't. I just wondered if it mightn't be a way out. I know there's a lot of excitement you'd miss. Only – Marion, darling, don't forget I'm here — "

19

Thereafter, Paul kept away from the telephone. Marion gave him every minute of her spare time, and he made the best of it and did not demand more. If the practice was often time-consuming, it was often also possible to unload much of it on to Eileen Roffey, who was a whale for work, and some sort of equilibrium seemed to be attainable.

Christmas came, and they left her in charge and went to the Sussex farmhouse again. Here, Marion's work was ignored completely, not disapproved of, simply ignored.

164

The only point about her of interest to Paul's parents was that she was Paul's very presentable, entirely devoted wife.

She left them re-infected with their belief that Paul's happiness was the only thing in the world which really mattered. Only she knew, now, that it had a certain toughness about it.

The after-Christmas epidemics of catarrhal illnesses began. Influenza, and several pneumonias, kept Marion busy and worried. She saw little of Paul for weeks together, and when she was with him she would find his eyes on her, and she would smile across at him and say, "I'm sorry, my dear, about this rush, but it won't last for ever. We'll have fun again when the spring comes – start looking for a house in real earnest." And Paul would nod and say, "I'm putting in a lot of time on the new play," and they would settle into their two chairs, because she was too tired or had too little time just then for doing anything else, like a couple who had been married for years and years and whose life was a contented routine.

How far below the surface Paul's contentment reached, Marion did not know. They had small disagreements, of course; and she was conscious sometimes, when she gave her feelings a thought, that her own nerves were not entirely composed. Matters of housekeeping, particularly, bothered her. Old Ethel really was very old, and had to be jacked up out of ruts in the way she fed them, and, when Marion had no time to attend to them herself, of decorations. Paul was fussy about flowers, and had very definite ideas about them. One evening after a specially annoying day – I'm tired, that's all, Marion told herself crossly – they bickered because he would not say he liked those on the dining-table.

"Snowdrops in a ginger-jar! All things bright and beautiful!" he complained. "Sort of thing you might find on a schoolmarm's desk."

Marion blinked at him. "They were absolutely all I could get. I hadn't a minute. And Ethel always snatches the first vase she lays her hand on."

Paul went on grumbling, "Colourless! Dull! Like under-clothing on a line!"

"*Paul!*"

"They'd have looked a bit better if she'd decorated them with a pink frill, like a ham!"

"P'raps they are a bit dull," she agreed good-humouredly. "I'll see what else I can find, to-morrow. But — " She fingered the snowdrops tenderly, "I love them. They're innocent and virginal — "

Paul said, "*Virginal!* Huh!" and went off into a hoot of laughter, which, as it so often did for them, ended the dispute. But somehow this time the laughter did not heal; the unease was too deep. Marion was frankly glad when she was haled off to the hospital to give an emergency anæsthetic.

The young house surgeon – not young Furnivall but a different one, they changed every six months, but each one soon came to welcome Marion with pleasure – was full of excitement. "Perforated Gastric. Only happened an hour ago. His G.P. spotted it at once. Not that he could help it, the thing was absolutely text-book. We ought to be able to sew him up without a tube, getting it so early, don't you

166

think?"

Marion settled into the routine as though into a childhood home, single-hearted. She induced anæsthesia carefully, sensitive to the slightest change in the man's breathing, increasing the strength of her vapour almost imperceptibly so that he should not struggle; herself poised over him, intent on nothing except his well-being.

In the theatre, there was a sense of urgency, because this was one of the rare cases in which minutes counted; silence, a wordless teamwork, the surgeon's instruments in his hand before the hand was stretched for them, blood staunched before it had time to flow; a breath of relief, more felt than heard, when the rent had been closed and the laconic word, "stitches", signalled that the operation was almost done.

It was only then, when she could relax a little, that Marion became conscious of a most peculiar sensation; as though every object in the theatre were infinitely far away; pin-points, each one revolving furiously where it stood, buzzing, booming; herself immovable and very cold. Amazed, she thought, I can't be going to faint? She pulled herself together by a great effort. You've never fainted in your life. Stop thinking about yourself, anyway. You're not here to think about yourself– yourself – yourself . . .

Sweat stood on her forehead and ran down her nose inside her mask. But that was not unusual in a hot theatre. What a blessing a mask could be. It hid things. The patient was breathing quietly – in – out – in – out. Concentrate on breathing like that yourself. No, concentrate on the patient. She slid her finger along his jaw to feel his pulse, then planted her elbows firmly on the table and leaned on them. That was better. She eased her mask below her nose, the better to breathe. Unorthodox to do so, but very helpful, and the stitching up was nearly finished.

Quite finished, now. Deliberately, with a sense that her hands were wooden and might not obey her, she divested the man of his trappings and turned his face on its side, not having to think because she had done all this so often that it was automatic. Then she set herself carefully to walk across the open space between the table and the door.

No one was looking at her, which was a good thing, because she was sure her face was green. She attained the lavatory and was very sick.

When she felt better, she found the rest of them gathered in Sister's room drinking tea. Someone pushed a cup towards her, and the smell of it nearly turned her up again.

"No thanks. Keeps me awake."

Sister said, "Horlicks?" and a pro went off to fetch it. Doctors were temperamental people who were allowed their fads.

She drank the Horlicks resolutely and did not stay to gossip.

In the car, she thought her symptoms over. Nausea, now she came to think about it, and irritability, for several days. Faintness, sickness and a distaste for tea. She made a rapid calculation. Last week-end – the one before – the one before that – and before that again however far back was it? So it *was* that!

She sat quite still, sorting out her reactions. First came fury with Paul, because she was sure it hadn't been an accident. Then despair, because now she would have to give up her work. One couldn't give anæsthetics in a fainting condition, and even if she got on top of that, which she would, of course, the division of loyalties would be too great. And welling up, stronger than all else, was a normal female exultation that she was bearing a child. But that was purely an affair of the body. With her mind, she didn't want a child yet, if at all. She was not going to tell Paul about it until she simply had to.

PART THREE
*
Philippa

1

MARION'S first action was to transfer from her drug cupboard to her own bag a supply of phenobarbitone tablets to guard against a repetition of her faintness in the theatre.

Her second was to take Eileen Roffey into her confidence and to ask her if she would like to buy the practice.

The younger woman demurred at first. "Can't I just carry on for you until you feel inclined to come back?"

Marion shook her head. "I don't want to be tied to it. I'm a whole-hogger, at heart, and that's been part of the trouble. I shall sell it in any case, and I'm giving you the first chance. You can pay for it in any way you like – in a lump or in bits. You could easily afford to do it in bits, out of the income it would bring you. And it seems a pity for you not to have it, if you're happy here."

Eileen Roffey flushed and mumbled that she was very happy, but that a good deal of the happiness was due to her relations with her chief.

Marion was not to be put off. She threw over her shoulder, "Well, think about it. You'll have to be your own boss some day, so why not now? The house you can buy or rent as you think best. And let me know as soon as you can."

Her third was to get seriously down to house-hunting. She looked at several by herself, and then dragged a surprised and gratified Paul at her chariot-wheel to the three she thought most likely.

None was their dream house, but one was very pleasant,

Georgian, with a garden already full of perennials, vegetables, and fruit-trees. Wandering round it, Paul said, "There's room for a tennis court. That would be very good for College parties. Funny, I've never seen you play tennis, have I?"

Marion thought, there won't be any tennis for me for a while, but you don't know that. Aloud, she said, "I haven't played any for years and years. Not since Cambridge. I wasn't bad, then. Only I'd learnt to play with an underhand service, and I've never cultivated an overhand one."

Horrified, Paul said, "Good lord! No one but a Methuselah serves underhand now! You'll have to keep out of the parties until you've learnt better, if you don't want to be dated!"

Marion grinned, and said to herself, you're telling me!

The drawback of the house was that it was fifteen miles out of the town.

"D'you think you can manage that?" Marion asked, when the pros had been weighed and found more than the opposing cons. "There won't be any bobbing in for lunch."

"I'm just as happy getting lunch at college or at the Bay Tree. You know that. But what about you? A good half-hour's drive to every confinement won't be any fun, specially in the winter, will it?"

Marion examined minutely the cupboard accommodation of the kitchen before she spoke; so minutely that Paul repeated the end of his question. It was as though she could not quite bring herself to burn her boats. But at length she looked up at him in a bored sort of way, as if to say, how silly you are, I expected you to see for yourself the way the

174

wind is blowing.

"It won't matter to me. I'm packing up the practice and going in for a family."

"You're – Marion, you don't mean that?"

Marion's dimples came. He looked so astonished, almost frightened.

"It's all signed, sealed, and settled. Eileen is buying the practice and renting the house. And the baby's due in early October."

Paul stared at her; caught her by both hands and hugged her to him; held her away and remarked suspiciously that he couldn't see any difference in her.

"Of course you can't, yet. You will, soon enough."

"It's wonderful. You're wonderful. Doing – all this – because you knew I wanted it!"

Marion said drily, "I wouldn't rate it as high as that. One can't arrange these things alone, even if one wanted to, which I didn't."

Paul said with apparent irrelevance, "Won't the parents be pleased!" which strengthened Marion's belief that it hadn't been an accident and that, moreover, Paul had not plotted all alone. However, her course was charted, and, that being so, it was no good to thresh around and make things unpleasant, and, whatever her mind might say, there was this odd little thrill of animal enjoyment that she couldn't get away from.

She said firmly, "I think it's going to be fun. Now, as it seems to be settled that we're going to have this house, let's go all over it again and see exactly what we want to do with every room."

175

They linked arms amicably and set off; argued here, barked with laughter there, and came back to the car in a state of hilarious excitement, largely induced by Paul, but played up to very cheerfully by Marion, whose gift for living in the present helped greatly to banish regrets and determine her that the new way of life should be a success.

In their own garage, presently, she turned to Paul. "Now look. Not a word of this – my own private part of it – to anyone. Anyone, Paul, please."

He looked abashed, a little, like a schoolboy caught poised above a plate of cakes, and she persisted, "I'm serious. I don't want the annoyance of the hundreds of people I know asking questions. And, more important than that, it isn't fair to Eileen to give the patients too long to think about it and p'raps go off to another doctor. Promise?"

He agreed soberly enough. "All right. Not till you say the word."

They went into the house, Marion in front, feeling, oddly, it seemed to her, more mistress of the situation than at any time since her marriage.

2

Moving out, moving in; arranging for ante-natal care and confinement, getting together baby clothes; handing over, unobtrusively, patients to Eileen Roffey, helping to find and approve a new assistant; finding and installing domestic staff, for old Ethel did not like the country and was sure the practice could not get on without her; all these, combined with an increasing slowness of movement, made mincemeat of the spring and summer. The house was big enough for them to employ a man and wife, the man to look after the garden and the car, the wife to do the housework. They found a couple in their early fifties who seemed to suit their needs well. If Marion did not take to the woman, she felt she must not be too choosey, since it was difficult to get domestic help at all.

The baby arrived one early morning when the hunter's moon was almost full.

"Such a relief to a husband," commented the brisk colleague in whose care Marion had placed herself, "when his wife can do this business competently and without a lot of fuss!"

Marion, exhilarated now it was over, agreed. "Though a person who knows as much about it as I do surely ought to do it better than most people!"

"Doctors are frightful patients, usually," the other said. "They think they ought to be allowed to manage the whole thing themselves. You were pretty good."

Marion had found her labour tiresome and undignified, but, lacking the element of fear and having made excellent arrangements, less unpleasant than she had expected. She was surprisingly touched by the baby, the warm, silken vitality of its skin, the perfection of its little hands and feet, the butterfly softness of its fair upstanding hair, the queer, painful satisfaction of its grip on her breast. It was a girl, and she called it Joan.

During convalescence, the days seemed to fly; with her

own meals, rest periods and exercises, the baby's feeds, letters to read and write, and later, visitors to talk to, she had hardly a minute of real leisure. Paul strutted in and out, beaming, and made faces of horrified unbelief when he was told that the baby was like him. He could not, however, be kept away from her, and spent hours simply watching her as she lay asleep.

Before her three weeks in the nursing home were over, Marion was bored and clamouring to have the baby under her own control. She cajoled the elder of her two sisters to go home with her, and went.

After that, it soon became evident that, so far from having given up work, she had only exchanged one form of busy-ness for another. She wondered often how old Ethel and a sporadic woman had managed to accomplish so smoothly what she and the gardener's wife and an energetic young country woman for several hours a day found difficulty in keeping upsides with time. True, this was a bigger house and there was the baby, and the gardener's wife made a great point of having to look after her own husband and of generous time off, but Ethel had been at the mercy of the telephone and could never put her feet up and leave the front door unanswered.

Marion read her *Lancet* and her *B.M.J.* and, after some hesitation, accepted the charge of the Antenatal and Infant Welfare Clinic which was only now being started to serve her own village. Apart from this, she did not give medicine a thought. It could not, she held, be tinkered with. And she had quite enough of her own concerns to occupy her.

The baby was an ever-present joy. Healthy and good-tempered like Paul, she did everything she should do, and hardly gave them a bad night.

"She's such fun!" was their smiling comment to anyone who asked questions about her.

It was fun, too, to have enough room to ask people to stay with them whenever they liked. Paul's people came seldom, because the farm could not be left easily; Marion's more often, in ones and twos, becoming more her friends than they had ever been; Philippa very often, and sometimes other, older friends of Marion's with whom, during the rushing life as a G.P., she had almost lost touch; University students, past and present, whom Paul wanted to know better, came in their vacations.

Marion enjoyed having more time to spend on her own looks, to take more care of her clothes and hair and make-up, and to smock dresses for baby Joan and embroider cushion-covers in bright colours to scatter about the house; to read all sorts of books, to entertain her own acquaintances and Paul's to meals. She had to acknowledge that there was something in this purely feminine life which gave contentment, and that the running of a household could call for quite some exercise of brain-power.

It called also for common sense and tact. She had never taken to the gardener's wife who lived and worked with her; she seemed an amiable slattern, and although Paul liked the one side of her, Marion could not abide the other, did not, even, trust the apparent amiability. One evening, while she was still trying to make up her mind to tell Paul the couple must go, the situation resolved itself.

They had been out for the evening to a friend's house,

179

leaving, as they often did, the baby in the woman's care. They came home a good hour earlier than usual, because Paul had some work to finish, and heard her crying as they walked from the garage to the house.

"Funny. She doesn't often yell like that. Why on earth doesn't someone go and look at her?" Marion champed while Paul was feeling for his key.

As he found it, he said, "There's another funny thing. Why are all these lights on?"

In the lounge, the hall, and the dining-room lights showed through the drawn curtains. Marion said uncertainly, "They're tidying up – putting things away."

Paul said, "We'll see," and opened the door quietly and went in. Voices – a number of voices – could be heard in the lounge. Somebody laughed. Through the open door of the dining-room a decanter and glasses showed, not in their usual position but out on the table.

Paul made a dive for the lounge, Marion close behind him. The gardener and his wife, two other men and two women, sprawled or perched on the cretonne-covered armchairs. The air was full of the smell of smoke and drink. For an instant no one saw them. Then, uneasily, the talk and laughter died, and all six heads turned in their direction.

Paul, his blue eyes frosty under his thick brows, remarked, "I'm sorry we were not at home when you called, gentlemen."

The gardener's wife, a hand on her hip, answered mincingly in his own idiom. "Cousins of mine, Mr. Shepherd. Just looked in for a drink."

"So I see. And now, we shall be glad to have the use of

180

our own room, if you please."

Marion had hurried upstairs to quiet the baby. From the landing she saw a subdued procession file out to the kitchen. When Paul came up presently, he said, "I told them to get out of the house to-morrow."

Marion nodded over the baby's head. "You had to. I never liked them, from the first."

"Nor did I. It just seemed so difficult to find anyone at all, and there was nothing against them that one could put a finger on."

Marion agreed. "I know. Next time, we'll have the guts to say we just don't like a person and – just not have him."

Next day, when they had gone, the absence of hidden friction made a great feeling of peace in the house. But when, after days of inquiry, no one could be found to take their place, and Paul had to wrestle with coke-stoves and clean the shoes, while all Marion's time was taken up with the baby, cooking, shopping, and housework, a new strain began to develop. There was no time and little energy for the pursuits that they were fond of, and they could never go out together. They did go out to bridge one evening at the house of some of Paul's friends, taking baby Joan in her carry-cot. But she did not approve of such treatment, and cried nearly all the time. They left, regretfully, much sooner than they had intended.

"The best hands I've had for ages," Marion lamented, "and I just couldn't concentrate on them!"

"I thought we'd got free of things that butted in and prevented us doing what we wanted to do," Paul grumbled. "And now we have to spend half our lives doing things we

181

don't want to do at all!"

"We shall have," they agreed, "to look into this question of foreign maids."

And so, in another few weeks, they acquired two stolid, stocky sisters, Jewish refugees from Austria, they said, willing to work and thankful for a home. One cooked and the other cleaned, and both became quickly devoted to baby Joan, and Paul and Marion began to enjoy life again.

When Joan was nearly two, a delicious sturdy, staggering creature full of chuckles and curiosity, Marion, in her own phrase, "started another." He, when in due course he arrived, was a totally different type of child, thin, dark, and jumpy. He yelled in the night, vomited his feeds for no evident reason, and hardly ever slept. Paul, who was the best possible friends with his daughter, treated young Martin with caution, sometimes almost with dislike. But Marion, bending her brain and her acquired knowledge to this new baby's difficult happiness, found her own happiness bound up with him far more than with the easier child.

By the time he was four, she had steered him into fairly calm seas, in which, however, he would stay only as long as he knew her to be near him. He would sleep the night through if his bedroom door was left open so that he could hear her about. If she were going out for an evening with Paul, she must slink away after Martin was asleep. And if any whisper of such a plan leaked out beforehand, Martin did not go to sleep, but lay conversing affably with anyone who passed. Marion would harden her heart then, and go out in spite of him. But when she came back, she would find him in an exhausted sleep, his hair and pillow damp, his eyes dark-ringed, his hands flung despairingly above his head. The Austrians, left in charge, would tell how he had called and called – "Mummy, Mummy!" and sobbed until he could sob no longer; how Joan had stood beside him in her nightie, insisting, "Don't be silly, Martin, she's coming back, they *always* come back!" and had ultimately gone off to bed, and at once to sleep; how they themselves had stayed with him because they did not know what he might do, they thought he might perhaps take a fit. The next day he would be fretful, sick, perhaps.

"Kid looks awful!" Paul would say with distaste when Martin turned up his nose at porridge and refused bacon and wailed when Marion threatened to leave him behind when she took Joan to school. It soon became agreed that Paul should drop Joan on his way to college to leave Martin more time for body-building.

Paul at this time had a foot in two camps. His position at the University had stabilized, perhaps, but had not changed, simply because none of his seniors had left. His first play had been a moderate success, and he had written two more, both of which had run for a season in London and one been filmed He was not as constantly occupied as might have been expected, because he was a quick writer and he did most of his writing in the long holidays.

Marion liked his plays; they were clever and entertaining. "Though I don't know," she teased him, "whether they're compatible with this Vice-Chancellorship you're chasing!"

Paul was serious that day. He said, "They bring in a nice little something for the present, and I enjoy doing them. As

183

to the future – well, it doesn't seem much good making plans, to me."

Neither he nor she was politically minded, nor had they given much thought, at that time, to international affairs. Marion had fiercely resented Munich; Paul had hoped that the respite it gave might lead to peace, not war. But this was the spring of 1939, and the hopes of even Paul and his fellow-ostriches were growing shaky.

They had been shaken still more, that very week, by the sight of one of their Austrians in earnest converse, first, with a soldier from a Territorial camp on the downs, and later with a policeman; and a few days later by the sudden departure of the two sisters for home, "because their mother was ill." The ominous words of the Professor's wife about spies had come seeping back.

Marion said, "You'll get exemption easily enough, even if war does come. Not that I think it will; surely we learnt a bit of common sense before about the good it does – *good!* But education, for the next generation, has to go on, doesn't it, whatever happens."

But Paul looked past her, past the children playing elaborately among the welter of toys on the floor.

"The first thing is to ensure that there *is* a next generation. I know there are all sorts of arguments about keeping out of it, if war does come. But somehow – I don't think I could." He looked at Marion straightly, to see what she thought.

She almost cried out, "But you *must* keep out of it – with your brain, your gifts, your peaceful, happy temper, you're not just an ordinary person! It isn't only that you're mine

184

and the children's and that you *could* keep out if you would
– England – the world, perhaps – would be the loser if you
went and got killed just as one of a crowd!" Then the
principle by which she had always steered, that one
mustn't prevent another person from living his own life as
he wills it, though one may, even must, resist his efforts to
infringe that law, floated into consciousness and steadied
her.

She heard herself say, "Which service would you go
into?" She knew he would say, "The Air Force," and he did.

They did not like to be apart, during the next few weeks.
They made excuses to be in the same room or the same
corner of the garden. If Paul went into the town, Marion
and the children would go too, to shop, or even without
bothering to provide a reason. Better to shut up the house
now and then, they said, now there was no maid in it, and
have a meal out, all of them. Even when they found a
pleasant mother and daughter to live in and relieve Marion
of the housework again, they still piled, all four of them
together, into the car whenever it was feasible to do so.

The actual declaration of war did not, however, find
them rebellious or unprepared.

When Paul came back from his interviews and said he
would be in training not too far away and could come
home for weekends, it was almost an anti-climax, though a
blessed one, and except for his absence at evening and
night-time through the week, life went on much as it had
done before. But not for long.

The new gardener was called up, and since no other could
be found and the garden could not be left wild, Marion

began to spend many hours working in it, which soothed her mind and did her body good. Then the maid joined the A.T.S., and her mother decided to go and live with her sister and make munitions. And finally, an ordnance factory came into being close at hand, and the casual woman drifted into that.

Paul's week-end after this last defection was a hurry and a rush. Family and fowls must be fed, and a certain minimum of shopping, washing up, and tidying must be done. On Sunday they sat down to discuss the immediate future.

Marion's people could not come to their help. Her father's office had been evacuated to Wales, and he and her mother were going with it. The two young sisters had joined the W.R.N.S.

Farming was far too important for the farm to be left, even if the older Shepherds had wanted to leave it. And Paul would almost certainly be posted somewhere miles away very soon.

So, weighing the possibilities as best they could, they let the house to the manager of the ordnance factory and packed up, all of them, and went to the Sussex farm. No one thought much about invasion in those early days, and country was a less likely target for bombers than town. If invasion did take place, they argued, the whole island would be over-run, and one place was as good as another.

The grandparents welcomed them gladly. Paul wangled ten days' leave to help them settle in. And Marion registered, with all the smoothness that she could, another change in the gear of her life.

3

Sussex in autumn was beautiful. The gardens were filled with Michaelmas daisies of all possible shades of purple and pink, asters, and regal, velvety dahlias. The apple trees still bore bright clusters of fruit; the corn had been cut and harvested. Some of the fields which had carried root crops or cabbages were being ploughed, a tractor chugging here, a team of strong, slow horses there, followed by swooping gulls, or rooks and jackdaws which rose and fell like black leaves carried by the wind.

Marion, with some inward misgiving, took the advice of Paul's father about the children. "Dress them up in something that doesn't matter, and turn them out."

"Won't they get into mischief – damage things – or wander off and fall into ponds or something? I've always kept them with me nearly all the time, when we've been here before."

"You were here for such short times that it didn't matter," their grandfather said. "Now, if they're going to be country children, they ought to learn country ways. Much less trouble for you, and good for them. I'll give them some broad rules. Children are pretty sensible."

He inspected their boiler-suits and stout shoes. "That'll do, fine. Now listen, you two — "

They stood solemnly before him.

"You can go anywhere you like on the farm except into the cowsheds. If I catch you in there" – he scowled and shook a ferocious fist, and Martin jumped and Joan thrust her hands deep into her pockets and stood square – "off

187

come your heads and on go two coco-nuts! See?"

Marion expected a yell of terror from Martin, but instead he flung up his chin and laughed out loud.

His grandfather eyed him seriously. "That isn't funny!"

"I've seen a coco-nut," Martin bubbled. "It's got hair on it!"

"Exactly. It would make a good head. Except that there'd be nothing inside."

Martin dissolved into giggles again, and Joan, after a questioning look at her mother, joined in on a deeper note.

Mr. Shepherd gave up the attempt to impress them, the more so because the small boy was now leaning, warm and intent, against his knee.

"All right. You're not to go into the cowsheds, and you're not to go off the farm. That means you must stay inside the black gates and the hedges."

Marion said hastily, "I'll show them — "

But their grandfather contradicted, "No. I'll do that," and they trotted off with him, without a backward look.

Marion did not know whether to be pleased or exasperated by this transfer of affection. Martin still came to her for all his material wants, and did not like to be parted from her at bedtime. But during the day, and particularly out of doors, he followed his grandfather round like a little dog and soon came to be treated rather like one and taken almost everywhere as a matter of course.

Joan, on the other hand, poked about the farm on her own, talking to all the animals and to any human she might meet.

For the first time in her life, Marion found herself with

time on her hands. She tidied her own room and the children's, mended their clothes, hounded them in to meals, insisted on the midday rest, and that was all. They would look for her when they came in; Joan, with a basket of mushrooms, perhaps, which she had gathered in one of the meadows. "I know which is mushrooms," she would explain patiently when Marion, in doubt, turned them over. "Gardener showed me." And, according to her grandmother, who looked after the cooking of them, she was always right.

"I've been picking apples for the market – or helping to pack them or riding on a tractor – or feeding the chickens – with Grand-fa'," Martin would announce.

Or they would both rush in together, brandishing big sticks, having been playing Red Indians among the stooks of corn.

But if Marion suggested that she should join in these activities, she was quite firmly put in her place. "I'm going with Grand-fa'," from Martin, and, "I can manage, thank you, Mummy," from Joan. They were finding their own feet.

"And a good thing too," she told herself. "The best possible place for them to do it."

She busied herself looking for a school for Joan, but that did not take long, for there was little choice. She did some fruit-picking, and some weeding in the garden, and helped to cut up apples for bottling and made some blackberrying expeditions. But all these were jobs she had to ask for, and carried out under supervision. She realized very soon that she would have to find some definite occupation. She must be there, because of the children. But she had not the temperament to do nothing for long.

Mr. Shepherd turned down her offer to work as a land-girl. "I shall have to have one. But she'll have to work regular hours, and the farm will be her first – her only – call. You couldn't do that, with the children."

Regretfully, she agreed. He went on, "I believe the A.R.P. people in the village could use you. We've got to have a First Aid Post, and there'll be lectures and training to be done. I'll put you on to Tickner – he was a city man of some reputation before he retired here, and they've made him Head Warden."

Mr. Tickner received her doubtfully. "I've got a mixed bag of people who think they know something about First Aid. Could you sort them out for me? Put them through one of the Red Cross Exams? They've had a few lectures —"

She did not add to her popularity by failing the lot of them except for a man and a boy. "But you've killed your patient!" she exclaimed to one after another during their attempts at bandaging, staunching blood, and setting fractures. To one irritating woman who insisted, "Well, that's my way, anyway!" after every mistake she made, she said at length, "You'd better write a book yourself and send it to the Red Cross Headquarters. I'm examining you on the book they publish now."

"Oh, that old thing! We never look at it," she was told.

The Head Warden sighed at her complaints. "That was the lady who's been teaching them. She's supposed to be very good. You'd better give them some lectures yourself, more orthodox ones."

So, through the winter, she taught an audience of village people, from big houses, shops, and labourers' cottages, to treat shock and stop bleeding, to immobilize fractures and to carry stretchers, in the light and in the dark, with gas-masks and without. And by the spring they had acknowledged her efficiency, and she was confident that her First Aid Post could deal with any injury and that its personnel had got on top of its prickly class distinctions and its petty jealousies and would work loyally together if air raid, gas attack, or parachute invasion came to test them.

But nothing did.

The only other way in which she could be specially useful was in driving people round in her car, which she had refused to give up, and this she did. The older Mrs. Shepherd loved to be taken into Brighton or Horsham or even to London, to shop or to visit friends or go to a theatre.

It was on the way home from one of these expeditions, driving along a narrow, curly lane, that some extra sense – a burr of raised voices, hardly heard, perhaps, but unusual in such a place – warned Marion to slow up, and, rounding a corner, she stopped behind a big car, turned sideways a bit and obstructing the road. The queer sound which had warned her came from a boy, groaning on the ground between the ruins of his bicycle and a motor-bike, thrust into the hedge while its owner, white-faced, bent over him.

The car had evidently not been involved in the accident, for a man was only now descending from it. A well-dressed woman, leaning over from the passenger's seat, was, it seemed, trying to dissuade him from interfering.

191

Marion, who had been aiming at getting home in time to give the children their supper, turned a vexed face to her mother-in-law. "Oh *dear!* I'm afraid I shall simply have to go and see if I can help!"

"Of course you will. And let me know if there's anything I can do." Mrs. Shepherd senior had all the layman's morbid interest in an accident.

"Anyway," Marion added, "we can't get by."

The woman in the car had got hold of the man's sleeve, and he was evidently arguing with her. Marion took the easiest route, on the inner side of them, to get to the boy.

The motor cyclist turned an anguished face to her. "Come straight out of the gate across the road, he did. I wasn't going fast – I didn't have a chance!"

The boy was jerking his head to and fro in pain. "My leg!" he was crying, "Oh – oh – oh my leg!"

Marion said, "All right, let me have a look." And to the motor cyclist, "You were at the First Aid lectures, weren't you?"

He nodded. " 'M. But I didn't want something like this to practise on! Broke it, hasn't he?"

The bullet-headed little country boy sat cautiously bolt upright, easing himself off the damaged leg and watching Marion anxiously as she felt along the bone. He said nothing more until her fingers came to the tender spot. Then he shot out, "Oo – ah! Broke, I should think it *was* broke!"

Marion said, "I'm afraid it is."

Something from his recent lessons evidently clicked in the motor cyclist's brain. He murmured, "Fractured tib and fib? First treat for shock," and hurriedly flung off his haversack and pushed the boy down gently until his head rested on it, and covered him with his coat and tucked it in.

"That right, Doctor? Shall we want a splint?"

A deep voice behind Marion said, "There's one in my car, if you'd care to have it."

Glancing up, she saw a man in his late fifties, perhaps a little over-weight, a kindly, humorous face, brown eyes, a forehead wrinkled by many cares. Sitting back on her heels, she said, "Thank you very much. I'm sorry if I'm butting in."

His mouth tightened a little as he assured her, "Not at all. I only happened along, the same as you did, and you were quicker off the mark."

He moved back to his car, and the woman's voice floated from it shrilly, "Well, they don't need two doctors, do they? Give her the splints and let's get on. You did promise to take me to this dinner, it just isn't fair to make me late. And you know perfectly well that accidents always make me feel sick!"

The man retorted testily, "If you thought a bit more about the poor devil of a boy and less about yourself, you wouldn't feel sick – only sorry!" He came back to the group by the roadside, accompanied by her indignant, "*Ohhohh!*"

"Splint – wool – bandages. And, if I'm not mistaken, a strong arm – and that's all you need."

He gave no directions, just waited until Marion had laid the splints alongside the leg and secured them, then, evidently trusting to her to hold it firmly, lifted the boy free of his tangled bicycle and sat him on the bank.

193

Marion said, "Thank you, that was marvellous. But what now?"

The big man flung a glance over his shoulder, a funny, furtive glance. Then he looked at her again, like an anxious, apologetic old dog.

"I'd cart him home in my car," he said. "But I'm taking my wife to a dinner-party, and she's – she's afraid she's going to be late. That's no excuse really, I know. The boy's a patient of mine, and I ought to take him. But you know," He looked her up and down and his eyes twinkled and he continued his sentence, "You know what women are!"

Marion, her lips twitching, said, "Home? Or hospital?"

"The nearest hospital's Brighton, nineteen miles away. The leg looked good and straight when you'd finished with it. It should be manageable at home."

"I'll take him, of course," Marion said. "If we can get him in."

"I'll do that for you," he told her cheerily, and picked the boy up again as though he had been a doll, with Marion holding the leg out straight, and they sidled along to Marion's car.

Mrs. Shepherd was out on the road by the time they reached it. "Good gracious, it's Dr. Hawkes. Good afternoon. I didn't recognize you till my daughter-in-law had taken control, or we'd have driven on and left you to it!"

He said absently, "Good afternoon. You'd have had a job, with my car where it is." He edged the boy carefully into the back seat, and Marion ran round to the other side and leaned in to help him. He said, "There – that'll do, I think

It's most kind of you." Turning to Mrs. Shepherd, he added, with a slow, charming smile, which had somehow a mischievous twirk in it, "You can't think what a relief it is to shift one's responsibilities now and then!"

His wife's white face was looking out at them, angry impatience in the very tilt of it. He said no more, but raised his hat and strode away, a curious mixture of courtly manners and bluntness, a strength gone flabby yet still capable of use, a solid worth yet pleading for recognition.

The motor cyclist was heaving his machine out of the hedge and preparing to leave. "I know where the boy lives," he said. "I'll go ahead and guide you."

When Marion arrived, he had told his tale already to the boy's father, who was on the doorstep of the cottage. His mother, who had also attended Marion's lectures, had a hot bottle in the bed and the bedclothes rolled back, and was standing by almost at attention.

"All ready to receive casualties!" Marion smiled at her.

"I'd just as soon it was that old doll we used to practise on," she shot back, "and not my Jimmy – you wicked silly boy!"

Marion said, "Tuck him up warm and give him a cup of tea and two aspirins." She extricated herself with difficulty from joining them at a meal and went back to the car.

"I do like these people," she said. "They're so sturdy and sensible, not a bit spoonfed like my town patients. What sort of a person is Dr. Hawkes, Grannie?"

" 'Old Salt-and-water', they call him in the village," Mrs. Shepherd told her. "Why? Because he's always telling them to soak their various injuries in it, and gargle with it, and

195

douche with it. They like Lysol better, because it has a good clean smell. He's very much liked – loved, one might say, I think. He's a bit casual and lazy, but they put up with that because he's so kindly. They don't like his wife, though. I don't myself. She's one of those people who must always be in the centre of the picture."

4

They found the children waiting for them, a little reproachfully, at the black gate which was their boundary. Marion stopped, and Joan scrambled in, and Martin dashed away with a mongrel puppy which had become his constant companion, shouting that he would be at the house before they were.

"He's a different boy since he's been down here," Marion said, and her mother-in-law smiled and remarked that a farm was the right place for a child to grow up in.

Joan startled them by butting in. "He likes people to like him, and they do, here. He didn't see many people at home, did he, except us, and we like him when he's good, but we don't much when he's ill and cross, do we?"

Marion said, "I don't know about that. We're sorry for him, aren't we?"

"I'm not. I just don't like him," Joan insisted. "He likes bossing people, too, and he can boss Waggers like anything."

Marion said, "It's good for dogs to be bossed," and Joan

196

chuckled and said, "I know. That's why it's a good thing he's got a dog. I don't let him boss me."

She hung about until Marion had put the car away, and then said, "Mummy, I want to show you something. Can we go the long way in?"

They passed the bird-bath as they went, a great shell held up by a moss-covered cherub. In the water a single little bird was splashing. They stopped to watch him, and he looked at them with black beady eyes and went on with his bath quite unafraid.

"A robin," Marion said. "Isn't he up late – it's almost dark."

Joan twirled suddenly on one toe and hopped away as though she were a robin herself. "He's the last bird to go to bed and the first one to get up," she said.

"Did they tell you that at school?" Marion inquired.

Joan looked scornful. "Goodness, no! They don't tell us things like that at school. I seed it for myself. He sings outside my window every morning and wakes me up, and he has his bath every night just before it's dark."

"Do you go to sleep again after he wakes you up?" Marion asked.

Joan said, "Sometimes I do," in a withdrawn sort of way, as though she would discourage further questions. Queer, Marion thought, how a child demanded its own privacies as it grew up. And difficult, for a parent, to know what you ought to know and yet not to probe.

"That wasn't what I wanted to show you," Joan was saying. "It was this – see?"

They turned the corner of the house and saw, in a little-

197

used nook, the old, beautiful evergreen oak, and under it, a drift of snowdrops, newly born, their white heads still hanging unawakened among their defending spikes of green.

Joan was on her knees beside them. "They're so delicate, and the earth's so hard – only just stopped being frosty – and yet here they are."

Marion was thinking that this daughter of hers might be going to enjoy life very richly, with her vivid perceptions, her honesty, and her power of taking all that she saw to herself and loving it.

"They're darling things," she agreed. "little and delicate and very brave."

Joan looked up with shining eyes. "That's just right. Very brave."

She jumped to her feet and leaped towards the house. "Do you think someone will have got our supper ready, Mummy? Do you? Or shall we have to wait ever so long for it while you do?"

A little funny echo came into Marion's mind of herself touching softly some snowdrops in a bowl, and Paul snorting, "Virginal! Huh!" This child had, all unknown to her, been already, then, formed in her womb.

5

When Paul came, as he did, infrequently, Joan would seize him by the hand and drag him everywhere, to see everything, animals, birds' nests, flowers, the farm-hands and their wives and children. Martin, on the other hand, was always missing, and, if he were forestalled, would be ready with some plan which he put forward most importantly. "Granfa' wants me to go with him to this — " or "I've got to do that with gardener."

Paul, seeing him so much sturdier and more self-reliant than he had been, only laughed and said, "That's just what I used to do when we went to my grandparents' farm for holidays. Couldn't bear to be out of farm things for a minute." It did not seem to occur to him that he was being avoided; and perhaps, Marion reproached herself, indeed he was not, any more than any other grown-up who might have intruded on a child's own ploys.

She found herself longing more and more for Paul's visits. For although she got on well with the older Shepherds, their talk was all of the farm, of Paul's childhood, and of her own children; and with the First Aiders, but they were not, even the best of them, quite her sort of people. She missed the parry and thrust of informed conversation, even more than the excitement of the old "Quick, quick, Doctor!" way of life. The urgency of that, so long ago it seemed now, had given place to the urgencies of the children's needs, but there was nothing in this quiet country life which took the place of talking with mental equals. The village library could not cope at all with her demands, and the books from The Times Book Club came all too seldom.

When Paul came, they would talk and talk, for his lack in that respect was, she found, much the same as her own. He was not over-happy in the Air Force, mainly because the authorities would not make a pilot of him.

Marion, secretly relieved, could understand this better than he could. He lacked the crackling devilment which could swoop and dive, the alternative of steady endurance to carry through a gruelling task. His quiet good humour had its fires so far beneath the surface that to emerge they must attain a dangerous heat; a heat which could warp judgment at its most urgent need. Probing deeper, she saw why it was that such unexpectedly primitive things kindled the fires in her civilized, intellectual husband. He had been so little thwarted that he had thrown up no defences, his oyster had made no pearl because it had not been troubled with an irritant. At home, at school, at college, and in his chosen career, his success and his popularity had been unbroken. He was resenting now, with bewilderment, that he was not in the highest class as he had always been. Marion's love for him, at first adoring, lately itself resentful at his demands on her, became infused with the same tenderness that she felt towards the children.

He had been learning to become a wireless operator, but was not, it seemed, to be one of a regular air-crew. He was older than most of them and obviously used to authority. He very soon acquired stripes and an administrative job, but on the ground. Marion hugged herself with relief and would have hugged his C.O. too if she could have got at

200

him.

At the end of one of his leaves, she travelled with him to London and saw him off. She was turning away from the barrier when a young man hailed her – a horse-faced young man in glasses, well-dressed in mufti. With a shock, she recognized John Peachey.

He was beaming at her and shaking her hand, confident, equal to equal.

She said, "Hullo, John. Not called up yet?"

His smile grew wider. "Not me. A pal of mine put me into a job in the M.O.I., and there I am for the duration, if I behave myself!"

"I've just been seeing my husband off to his R.A.F. station," she told him.

"That's tough! However did they get their claws into him? I should have thought he was safe, if anyone was."

"He volunteered, on the very first day."

John's eyelids flickered for an instant behind his glasses. "Oh well – there's no accounting, is there? Seems to me I've got a flair for getting to know the right people at the right minute, don't you think? I'll never forget you, putting me in the way of getting on in life. And I don't mind telling you, if I was your man nothing would get *me* into the forces to leave you alone! P'raps I'll be able to pay you back one day, who knows! So long, Doc – I can't tell you where I'm going, it's hush-hush!"

He swaggered away, leaving Marion wishing savagely that she had set Bill to tear his trousers off him instead of inviting him in to meet Paul, that morning when he had spat at her.

She went on to a meeting of the Medical Women's Federation, mainly with the idea of linking up with people she had known, a little of stimulating her brain by listening to a lecture. She had not advertised her coming, and stood blinking in the doorway of the big room in B.M.A. House, trying to pick out a friend. She was surprised by the number of uniforms, for although she knew vaguely that many medical women had joined the forces, she had lost touch with nearly all her fellow-students during the last few years.

It was Philippa who sprang upon her: Philippa now a pathologist in the R.A.M.C. with the rank of Major.

"What do I do exactly? Well," she said in answer to Marion's questions, "at present I mostly sit at a desk, and the only evidence there is that I work at all is my blotting-paper, covered with little P.M.S.s in red ink, upside down – every one of them a signed report based on someone else's observations. Like it? No, I detest it, but I have to do as I'm told."

The crowd contained lots of khaki, a sprinkling of Air Force blue, none of the Navy yet; but most, even now, older women in ordinary clothes, talking of the E.M.S., of iron rations, of petrol coupons in sealed envelopes for use in grave emergency, of special labels to let their cars go through roads closed by the police, of carrying on practices for men who had been called up.

Philippa brought the coffee they were all drinking before the lecture started, and stayed by Marion, and a group formed, as it always did round Philippa, and there was quick, shrewd talk and laughter.

"What are you doing?" someone asked.

"A.R.P.," Marion answered firmly, and the questioner was satisfied and left her alone.

But others wanted to know more than that. "Full time? I didn't know there were any full timers in A.R.P." Then, on Marion's admission that A.R.P., now took practically no time at all, they nodded. "Oh, of course, you've got young, haven't you? And no nursemaid, I suppose. Doesn't it feel awful, to have gone all domestic now there's such a shortage of doctors?"

Marion said, "There doesn't seem to be any shortage where I am."

Philippa cut in, "She did enough work for three when she was in practice. Now she's living, instead – give her a chance!" And they shrugged, and talked of other things.

It was Philippa Marion was concerned with. She had changed in some indefinable way. Perhaps, she thought, it was just the uniform, being in the forces instead of an individual, spending so much time with people swarming round her, giving and obeying orders. She was thinner, sharper in her speech, a little shrill and brittle in her laughter, her glance, always before direct and kindly, brooding now, almost suspicious.

They sat side by side through the lecture, so all that Marion could see of her friend was the restless movements of her hands. When it was over, Marion turned quickly to her. "Phil – is anything the matter? You're different — "

But Philippa laughed and took her hand and swung it. "Aren't we all different, with this blinking war? You're different yourself – tremendously! We can't stay still, can

203

we? We have to grow!"

Other people came up, to say good-bye, and Marion waved to them and went home to her village by a late train, puzzled, a little, and disgruntled with herself for being "all domestic".

6

When she came down to breakfast the next morning everyone was before her. Martin, very cock-a-hoop, announced, "I dressed myself all myself, except Grannie did up the buttons on my pants!"

"She did my pigtails, too," Joan supplied.

Mrs. Shepherd senior laughed good-humouredly. "We thought we'd let you sleep, as you came in so late to bed. I told them not to come in to you, and they actually remembered."

"We acksherly remembered!" they chorused, pleased with themselves.

Someone asked Marion, "Did you have a good night?"

"Not very," Marion said. "I took ages to go to sleep, and when it was just beginning to get light an awful bird came and shouted through the window, 'Hee-oo, hee-oo, hee-oo! Get some air!' Over and over again. I nearly threw a boot through the glass at him and shouted, 'There, is that enough air for you? Go away!' And then, of course, I went to sleep just when I ought to have been getting up."

Martin, very matter-of-fact, corrected her, "Mummy, I

don't believe you've got any boots."

Joan and her grandfather were looking at each other and cocking their ears. "What did you say he said?"

"A bubbly bit that I couldn't really interpret, and then, very clearly, 'Get some air'."

They repeated it – "Ee-oo, ee-oo, ee-oo – get some air!" Then Joan squeaked with delight. "A chaffinch – that's what it is – a chaffinch!"

Mr. Shepherd agreed, more soberly. "I've never heard it put like that, but it does say something very similar. You didn't see the bird?"

"I didn't. I kept my eyes tight shut and tried to go to sleep."

Joan chuckled to herself between every mouthful, "Get some air! Get some air!"

Marion suddenly liked them all, and the sunny room, and the smell of wood smoke, very much indeed. She said so. "I do love it here. It's so normal and healthy, this kind of life. I've lost my taste for towns."

Mr. Shepherd asked, "What do they think of the war, your friends in London?"

"They don't think it's going to end very soon."

He agreed. "Nor do I. One almost wishes it would get a move on – and then, one doesn't dare to wish any such thing."

Mrs. Shepherd asked, "How did the meeting go? Interesting?"

"So-so. They all seem very busy. I put" – she might as well tell them – "I put my name down for some part-time work if they could find me any."

"In London?"

She nodded. "I suppose it would be in London."

"But you've just said you don't like towns!"

They all looked at her, not understanding how she felt.

Joan said, "Would you have to go to London every day, then, like you did yesterday?"

"I don't suppose it would be every day. Some days."

Martin looked out of the window, then straight at her, as though he had been thinking deeply. He said, "You can't do that, Mummy. You've got your children to look after."

They shouted with laughter, and Martin, after one quick glance round, put his head in Marion's lap. Joan said, "I can go to school by myself." Mr. Shepherd said, "Impudent monkey," and Mrs. Shepherd said, "I'm sure we could manage, Marion, if you feel you ought to!"

Martin, over-ruled, climbed into his chair again and sat obstinately mum. Joan addressed him. "The evacuated children don't have their mummies with them, Martin, and they get on all right!"

Martin looked suddenly as though he were going to cry. Marion went over to him and rumpled his hair. "It's all right, old billy. Nothing's settled yet. By the time it is, you'll be going to school all day yourself, I expect, and you won't miss me at all."

He smiled up at her, his sweet, fleeting smile, and seemed to be placated.

In the middle of the morning, Marion went out to fetch him in for milk and biscuits. The spring wind caught at her skirts and ruffled the robin's feathers as he twittered at her from the fence. Three young silver birches, green-veiled, swayed like Botticelli maidens. The little round, rosy-throated chaffinches warned her from the tree-tops – "Get some air – get some air!" Martin came racing and whooping, his puppy at his heels.

But he had one of his attacks that night, and lay languidly being waited on all the next day. "You've got your children to look after," he had said. Yes, Marion admitted with exasperation, she had. And even if doing so had interrupted her serious work, surely her medical training had helped her to guard against some ills for them and treat others more adequately than an ordinary mother would be able to? Perhaps an ordinary mother would not have reared Martin at all, tiresome, difficult baby as he had been.

7

It was soon after this that the war did begin to get a move on. The invasion of Denmark and Norway, of Holland, Belgium, France, set people boasting, "We'll get at them now, anyway!" And then, with a horrid bewilderment, saying, "Nothing seems to stop him! Why can't it rain?"

Dunkirk brought tears of thankfulness. Mr. Churchill's fighting speeches set racing pulses steady and strong again, The early summer was more beautiful than ever before with sunshine and blossoming trees. There were a few air-raids, sirens and silver planes in formation, sailing inland, very high in the blue, and darting back in ones and twos. And, shot through everything, however it might be beaten down, the thought of invasion.

Men were recruited for the L.D.V., and in the village one met them, marching, or creeping in ditches, grotesquely, on boy scout games which might be rehearsals for something real and deadly. It was after getting mixed up with one of these that Marion one day came upon a car which was still held up by them, and sitting in it Dr. Hawkes, with whom she had done no more than pass the time of day since the incident of the boy with the broken leg.

He saluted her. "They seem to think I've nothing to do but attend to their imaginary wounds!"

"Have you?" she teased him.

"Have I? My assistant's been called up, didn't you know? Went off this very Monday, and left me to carry on the whole show, evacs and all!" He slumped in his seat in a comical attitude of despair. To Marion's gesture of sympathy, he went on, "The great headache is this maternity place in the old Manor House. Forty expectant mothers from the slums of London, and the top floor – why the top floor I have never been able to discover – made into a labour room and so on. Mallory – the assistant – had agreed to act as M.O. – and now I see no way of backing out of it . . . I detest midder . . . most of mine seem to miscarry, thank God, and the rest of them the Queens' nurses do and I just blow in and say 'there, there' when it's all over . . . "

Marion was really shocked. A miscarriage, in her practice, had been a tragedy and a reproach. But Dr. Hawkes sat there, smiling benignly, quite impenitent. Then the same idea seemed to spring into both their minds at once. Marion opened her mouth and shut it again.

Dr. Hawkes heaved himself upright. "Did you do any work of that sort before you were married?" he asked.

"I did six months at the Mothers' Hospital. Then I was in general practice for six years. I squatted, but it grew very quickly: there wasn't another woman within miles. I did more midder than most G.P.s. I liked it, and they get to know."

They looked at each other speculatively.

"I don't really approve of lady doctors," he said. "But – in extremis – would you?"

"Would I what?"

"Take on that Maternity Home, to help me out?"

Marion said, "Nothing would give me greater pleasure. I've been aching for a job!"

He put out a big, soft hand, and shook hers solemnly. "O.K., partner. I'll put you in touch with the matron."

It was not long before this was done, and after some cautious fencing with the matron, Marion started a regular ante-natal clinic. The mothers were a mixed crowd, philosophical cockneys, most of them, who trailed in boredom about the village with cigarettes glued to their lower lips, grumbled at the lack of cinemas and Woolworth's, and squabbled about the chores of the Manor House, which they were supposed to share. The clinic was something they understood, and Marion a voice from the outer world, which they welcomed.

They welcomed her still more when they realized she had children of her own. One ponderous lady expressed the general feeling in the wink with which she answered a question about her imminent fifth labour. "Worried about it? Did you have easy times with your other babies?"

"Well." Her rough hands tried to smoothe her ungainly stomach, toothless gums and an occasional tusk showed in her smile, and then came the wink. "Well, the best of labours ain't a picnic, is it, dearie? The nurse called them normal – normal, they called 'em, see?"

Marion knew something of the talk which went on behind the scenes, shocking talk, frightening, encouraging, obscene. But they were polite enough to her, especially when they realized she was not a spinster. They disliked spinsters, laughed at them. The matron was a spinster.

There was one of them who had a letter pinned to her notes, sent on from the clinic in London. "Dear Doctor, my daughter has unfortunately got herself into a pregnant condition . . ." Looking up from it, Marion saw a pair of eager, innocent eyes, a child aged eighteen whose every gesture expressed giving. A pity, she would have made someone a sweet little wife.

Another, whose eyes snapped warily in a thin face, whose tight lips minced with a borrowed gentility, expressed nothing but grab and greed. She was respectably married to a master baker. A pity, too.

Another, a sharp little Londoner, shook her head when she was offered a printed feeding-chart. "I'd ruther you told me yerself what ter give 'im, Doctor!"

"Why? Can't you read?"

She flushed. "Yus, I c'n read. But that" – she poked the chart – "that's for just *any* baby. I want advice for *my* baby, special, see?"

Marion laughed, and did as she asked. Individualism, and therefore good? Or bone laziness, which would not adapt the printed word to her own use?

The matron, after several wary encounters, was kind enough to approve of her new M.O. "Though I couldn't stand the last lady doctor I had to work with. Didn't seem to know whether she was a doctor or a nurse. Started sponging the patient's face after she'd had her baby, and told me she ought to have a clean pillow-case. I walked out, and sent back a message that she could wash the woman all over and make her bed if she didn't think my nurses were capable of it!"

"And did she?" Marion asked.

"She walked out too, and told me I was insolent. And the patient didn't get a clean pillow-case for three days, although she had been sick on it. Not very sick, mind you. But she would have got one, if I'd been left alone!"

Marion, who privately agreed with the unhappy doctor, said lightly, "I promise I'll stick to my proper business and leave you to yours!" And the matron laughed and produced a cup of coffee. Marion had seen enough of matrons and sisters to know that they had very tender toes and to mind her step accordingly, and they got on together well enough. It was fun, to be working again, using one's knowledge and experience which it was such a pity to waste, managing people. Gratifying one's lust for power? Perhaps, but where was the harm, if you knew what you were doing and used the power to a good end? Why did power give one pleasure, anyway, if it was not meant to be used?

8

One morning when she was occupied with the children's washing, Marion was startled by the arrival of a telegram. Telegrams meant only one thing during a war – but an impossible thing, for her surely – no, not impossible, for lately the air-raids had been aimed increasingly at air-fields, and Paul was at an air-field, of course, even though he was, relatively safely, on the ground. She tore it open.

It was reply-paid, from Philippa, and it read, "Can you put me up to-morrow night? Must see you."

A mixture of relief and apprehension flooded Marion's mind. Then there *had* been something wrong about Philippa. She went to find Mrs. Shepherd.

She took the children in the car to meet her friend, and they were all over her, interested in her uniform, in the fact that Marion had known her before they were born, talking all the time, Marion thought at their most engaging. But Philippa watched them sourly and was monosyllabic in her replies. Marion caught sight of Martin, back to front in the seat beside herself, glowering at the visitor when they were half-way home. She made the rest of the journey as swift as possible, afraid he might burst into some shattering personality.

At lunch, Philippa made visible and successful efforts to be sociable, which were soon made unnecessary by Martin. Having decided that he did not like Philippa, he must become himself the centre of attention. He prodded the contents of his plate. "What is it?"

"Fish. Eat it up."

"Don't want fish. Want rabbit."

"There isn't any rabbit. We've all got fish."

Martin laid down his knife and fork carefully. "Don't want fish!"

Marion treated him rough. "All right. Don't eat it. But you'll be very hungry by teatime."

He looked at her under his eyebrows, and then across at Philippa, appraisingly. Philippa was talking, rather painstakingly, to Mr. Shepherd, not noticing Martin at all. He put his head on one side and curled his lip at his fish and did not touch it. Joan was going steadily through hers; it took real illness to put her off her feed. Martin grabbed her roll, half-finished, put it in the middle of his plate, and began to build a castle round it.

Joan let out a yell. "Mummy, he's got my bread!"

"Then you'd better have his!" Marion was beginning, when Martin seized his own and took a big bite out of it, then threw it on the floor, where it was at once pounced upon by Waggers.

"Martin, you're being very naughty! And you're making Waggers naughty too, you know he isn't allowed food in here!"

Martin was out of his chair in an instant. "If you touch Waggers, I'll – I'll shoot you!"

"I'm not going to touch Waggers. If you throw him food, of course he'll pick it up. But if you don't behave yourself, you'll have to go to bed."

Martin, having captured his mother's ear and, for the moment, everyone else's, went back to his chair.

"*In*to bed?"

"Yes. Into bed, and stay there."

He threw a roguey look at his grandfather, who was, to his annoyance, watching something out of the window.

"What'll happen if I get up again?"

"I should think you would deserve a whacking," his mother told him.

With no experience of any punishment so drastic, Martin addressed the company. "If I was sent to bed, I should wait until I was all alone, and then I should get up and go out and never come back again!"

But the company did not play up. Philippa simply was not interested, and the grandparents kept strictly to their principle of non-interference between Marion and the children.

Marion said matter-of-factly, "You're being a very silly boy," and Martin, after a moment's pause, swept his plate and all its contents on to the floor with an angry movement of his arm. Waggers, too much frightened by the commotion to profit by this added largesse, retreated into a corner.

Marion, suddenly stung beyond endurance, flung an arm round the small boy and bore him, kicking and protesting, out of the room. She heaved him into the little morning-room, and there, imprisoning one of his arms, she dealt him three smart slaps on his hand before she released him. He sprang away from her, such a welter of resentment, pain, and hurt pride on his face that she nearly cried out. Then he flung himself into a chair and howled.

His mother leaned out of the window until his sobs had died down; then, having got herself under control also, she turned to him. "Are you coming back now, to eat your pudding?"

He eyed her, and must have caught the affection struggling through her exasperation, for he scrambled up and gulped, "Yes!" and went before her back to the dining-room.

"You'd better," she told him when they arrived there, "say you're sorry to Grannie for making such a scene."

He looked such a little seraph as he stood, white-faced, that she longed to hug him. He said very meekly, "I'm sorry, Grannie," and climbed into his chair and ate his second course without a murmur. Marion felt that he had somehow got a kick out of the whole business, but she was too thankful to have it over to worry much about that.

"You can go out now," she told him when his plate was empty, and added to Joan, who was again showing interest in Philippa, "You'd better go too, and keep an eye on him. He's in a wicked mood."

Mr. Shepherd got up. "They can come with me. I'm going to put the calves out in the field."

When they had gone, Marion turned to Philippa. "It isn't all jam, you see, coping with children."

Philippa said politely, "No. No, I suppose it isn't."

She was so painfully polite, so queerly uninterested in anything. When Marion asked her what she would like to do, be shown the farm, or go out in the car, or walk, she chose to walk, and they set out in silence. It was a lovely summer day, warm with a cool wind, and the country was looking beautiful. Marion, who had grown used to looking for its beauties, sniffed the air and glanced around with

215

enjoyment, but Philippa strode on, looking at nothing but her own feet. Long before they had reached the viewpoint which Marion had aimed at, the windmill with the wide sweep of valley and down behind it, she said abruptly, "Can't we sit down somewhere? I want to talk to you."

So, on a grass bank above a rabbit warren, with bluebells springing round them and catkins hanging like raindrops from the oak tree above, and across the meadow a drift of apple blossom, they sat facing each other, and Philippa began to speak.

"Marion, we haven't seen a lot of each other lately, we may have grown away from each other. Do you still think of me as – your very good friend?"

Marion looked away at the apple-trees and back into time; when she and Philippa, more interested in each other than in anyone else, had refused, tacitly, to call each other, "Dearest", because comparisons were distasteful and relationships like theirs, their clear sight told them, did not last for ever, and one couldn't have more than a single "dearest" in one's life. She turned to Philippa, dainty, fastidious, feminine even in her uniform, as she had been, somehow, even in a white overall in that grim haunt of hers, the hospital post-mortem room.

"Always, my very dear friend, of course," she said. "And even if we've grown away a bit – I expect we have – we've got some roots which are pretty close together."

Philippa smiled, on and off like an electric light. "Then you'll help me? Promise? No, that isn't fair. Marion, I've done the silliest, unutterable, idiotic, thing. I've landed myself with a baby!"

Having said it, she flamed suddenly scarlet, and ran on before Marion, taken right off her guard by such an unexpected dilemma, could say a word. "You'll condemn me, I suppose, now. We never judged each other before, did we? – just accepted. But there's such a gulf between married and unmarried – bond and free – you resent our freedom, and we despise your safety and envy your privileges – no, we won't argue about that, I'll get on – but don't judge, Marion, don't judge, please, for you can't, fairly. Just help me. We should have got married, I think, though it didn't seem to matter. And now – he's been – killed."

There was silence. A bird chirped, a cow lowed in the meadow, a car passed along the lane.

Marion stretched a hand to her friend's and cried out, "My dear – Oh, my dear!" and so they sat, gripping each other.

Marion pulled herself together presently. She said, "Are you quite sure, Phil?"

For answer, Philippa stood up. "Yes. It's three and a half months."

A quick look this way and that, a hand run over Philippa's slim front, and Marion nodded. "You're right, of course. What do you want me to do?"

Philippa shook her skirt and sat down again. She said shrilly, "Get rid of it, of course! I can't keep it, can I, now?"

Marion cried out, "But Phil, I can't do that! You know I can't!"

They had talked about this problem so often in the old days. So many women, of so many types, turned up at a woman doctor's surgery with this same demand: and went away dejected, throwing over the shoulder as they went, "I did think a *lady* doctor would have enough sympathy to help me!" because the law of England, and medical ethics, forbade such help, however strong the sympathy, great the apparent need, or tempting the promised reward. Philippa had always said the same thing when Marion told her about them – "Don't get yourself involved in their messes. They've had their fun, they must pay for it!" But now —

Philippa was running on, urgently. "I thought – you could let me stay here – and just do it – and nobody need know a thing – we could think of something plausible to tell your in-laws – they'd never suspect, nice ordinary people like that — "

When Marion did not reply, she said, "You could, Marion – couldn't you?"

Marion began to speak, carefully. "Phil, there's more in it than that. To begin with, leave — "

Philippa cut in, "I can get a few days, quite easily — "

"You wouldn't be fit to go back after a few days."

"I don't do anything to exert myself – only sit at a desk or a microscope — "

"And supposing it didn't go well – if you bled, or went septic – it's an awful risk — "

"I'd take it, with you to look after me," Philippa said, so magnificently that Marion could not help but smile.

She tried another angle. "Were you fond of him – really fond of him? Not just something sudden and over?"

Philippa shot a look of horror at her and hid her face in her hands and shivered. Marion could see that she was struggling to control her sobs. She continued steadfastly nevertheless. "It's his child. Won't you be glad of it, presently, to remind you? It could be brought up here, with my couple, if you couldn't manage it yourself. It would still be yours. They're such fun, Phil, there's something about children that gets you even when they're being demons like Martin was. You can't really want me to kill a child which might grow up like him?"

Philippa was sitting up very straight now, turned away a little, drying her eyes. When Marion's words tailed away she waited a minute, and then said simply, "I should hate it. For ever. It would remind me, not of him, but of how far we'd both fallen below our own standards. It would spoil his reputation as well as mine, and I should hate it. Don't argue, there's a pal. Just tell me what you think of my plan."

Marion said, "I think it's frightful. I think a procured abortion is wrong in itself. It's killing something that ought to live. It's avoiding a natural consequence."

Philippa shot out, "As though any treatment for any disease isn't doing that! Every time you operate on an appendix you're dragging back to life someone Nature has decided to kill off. There's no rational argument against it, none at all. It's just nonsense to talk about killing something that has never lived! My body's my own, and I don't want to use it to nourish an illegitimate brat, and why should I be made to?"

"If you must look at it that way," Marion said, "just because it's illegal. D'you want to get me struck off?"

"That's exactly why I came to you," Philippa said. "That,

and because I thought you'd take care of me for old times' sake. It wouldn't matter to you if you were struck off, really, would it? You don't need to practise, you're independent of it."

"It might not harm me much," Marion said slowly. "Although, of course, I should hate the disgrace of it. It would do a lot of damage to medical women as a whole."

"As though they couldn't stand it!" Philippa snorted. "It isn't fifty years ago! There's no prejudice against medical women now."

Marion thought suddenly of Paul. She had forgotten him entirely in this argument with her old friend. Now he appeared as a saviour. She said firmly, "It would wreck Paul's whole career. University people have to be most frightfully proper."

Philippa abandoned her persuasions. "We're silly to be talking like this. If we carry out my plan, no one can ever possibly know. It's being done every day. Anyone who's lived in the world, the real world, knows that. It's only because you're stuck away down here that you look at it as you do."

Marion took her by the shoulders and plumped her upright. "Listen to me," she said. "It's no good your pretending I'm an innocent young girl. I'm not. I know these things go on. I see women who've – been through them – not infrequently. I was talking to one not long ago. An intelligent woman who had had an illegal operation done on her by an old nurse, for a reason that seemed to her a good one: that her husband was an incurable drunkard and his father had been the same before him. She

220

said she had never felt so degraded in her life. She'd done something right against her nature, and she would never lose the scar. It seemed to alter her whole outlook. From being a courageous, happy person, she became a bitter, sneering one. And I know another woman who's brought up illegitimate twin boys. Worked for them, loved them, never been ashamed of them. She's a happy, useful person herself, and they're going to be the same. Phil, take my advice, please take it. Go through with the thing. I'll help you all the way with it. You'll never be sorry, I'm sure."

Philippa's face was withdrawn. "You're talking to me as you talk to any little slut who comes to your surgery, aren't you? As the Hippocratic oath and the B.M.A. and the laws of England tell you to talk. Not to me, your friend, whose point of view you ought to understand."

"I'm talking to you from my deepest depths, my dear! Isn't it true that one must do the right as one sees it, and leave the issue – on the lap of the gods? And that two wrongs can't possibly make a right?"

"Platitudes!" Philippa said scornfully.

"Principles!" Marion corrected. "Things one holds on to at dangerous corners. I'm trying to peer round such a corner to your ultimate happiness."

"Happiness! Why use that word – to me?"

"I'm sorry."

They sat silent. Then Philippa said bitterly, "You won't help me? You're all tied up in convention, aren't you? Won't take a risk – such a little one – to save a friend?"

"I won't help you that way. I'll do anything in the world for you, and for the child, if you go ahead and have it.

People treat these things kindly, during a war, Phil, they realize the stress. Sleep on it, and we'll talk again in the morning."

Philippa shook her head. They walked back very soon, hardly speaking. They were glad when Joan came out to meet them and chattered all the rest of the way.

Marion spent a horrid night. She was desperately sorry for Philippa and wished with all her heart that she could set her mind at rest. But even setting aside her professional teaching, the Hippocratic Oath – "I will not produce abortion" – even disregarding the damage she might do to Paul's future, to her own, there was still, behind these, perhaps conditioning them, the deep distaste for a crime against nature, for the destruction of life by one of a profession dedicated to its saving, by a woman designed for its nurture.

She took Philippa an early cup of tea, and found her, with her eyes dark-ringed, her bed awry, already awake. She pulled her friend's blankets straight and took her hand. "No good asking if you've had a good night — "

Philippa managed a smile. "Nor you. I'm a pest and a nuisance!"

"And now you're going to be sensible – please, Phil?"

"Not your way," Philippa said. "I'm a bad girl, and I must arrange things after my own pattern. Put me out of your life!"

Marion grinned and said, "Never!" and Philippa said, "Bless you, anyway. We've had fun — " and on that note they parted, later in the morning, at the station.

9

The next weeks were a nightmare of anxiety. Marion did not know what Philippa might do, and did not hear from her. Air-raids were becoming more frequent, and Philippa's telegram, although it had in fact nothing to do with Paul, had brought home the possibility of his danger.

Their own danger, too, became apparent. Dog-fights between British fighters and German bombers might be staged anywhere along the bombers' route, and several times children, and villagers came rushing out to stare up at the silver insects which darted and swooped so excitingly in the sky; until a day when one of the downward swoops was not arrested, one of the insects became a visible 'plane, its hum became a screech, louder and louder until it ended in a tremendous crash – and silence – and a mushroom of black smoke rising slowly from a meadow.

Marion bundled the children indoors, ran for her car, collected half a dozen of her First Aiders from their homes, and zoomed along a lane to the nearest point she could reach to the wreckage. They all hurtled out of the car and dashed across the rough grass. But all they found was a heap of twisted metal, so hot they could not get near it, and, sticking out from it, a heavy boot. There was a bit of a swastika still visible on the biggest fragment of the plane.

Someone said, "Thank goodness it isn't one of ours!"

A man suggested uncertainly, "D'you think we ought to try and get him out?"

They all looked at Marion, for a decision. "Can he be alive?"

She shook her head. "Not possibly, in that. It's as hot as Tophet and still smouldering. No job for us here, I'm afraid."

They turned and clumped back towards the gate, and then two of them clutched each other and pointed. "*What's that?*" It was a brown hillock, motionless, a little distance off. They went to it, quickly, in a straggling line. It was a cow, lying dead, with a queer-looking seared wound in its head, where a lump of hot metal had struck it. They stood round it, sobered even more than they had been. A farmer had lost a good cow. And it might so easily have been a man, going quietly on with his work in the fields.

Marion wondered if the children had been frightened, but she found them not in the least perturbed. Joan said excitedly, "Mummy, wasn't it a good thing it was a German? Because now it won't be able to come back and bomb some place again, will it?"

Martin, after a long silence, delivered himself of one of his odd questions. "Mummy, if people can shoot down aeroplanes, why can't someone shoot down an angel? Then we could see what they're like!"

Joan said breathlessly, "Martin, you're wicked! It would be awful to *want* to shoot down an angel, even! And anyway no one can see angels, so they couldn't possibly shoot them down!"

He persisted. "Why not, Mummy?"

His grandmother cut in serenely. "Angels aren't made of solid bone and muscle, like we are. If you tried to hit one – which I hope you wouldn't – you'd find you were hitting air. And a shot would go right through him without

224

hurting him. You can't hurt an angel – except his feelings, by being bad."

Foreseeing a moral, Martin hurriedly said, "Oh. Mummy, when can we go and look at the bits of that 'plane?"

10

One day when she came in after an outing with the children, Marion found an urgent message waiting for her from the Maternity Home. Dr. Hawkes was there, would she come at once? When she arrived, she found him dressed up in gown and mask and gloves, preparing to put on forceps while the Matron, under his direction, gave the patient chloroform.

She smiled at him and asked, "What's the hurry?"

He growled, "Long labour. Matron says we shall lose the baby if we don't get it out. Don't ask me! They couldn't get hold of you, so they dragged me in."

"Shall I get her anæsthetized for you? Then Matron can help at your end?"

The Matron gave up the bottle of chloroform. Instead of it, Marion used the more modern weapons from her own bag, and watched a little anxiously, knowing what harm ill judgment and inexperience could do, and not certain whether the village doctor had been exaggerating when he had spoken of his dislike for and avoidance of midwifery.

He grunted and grew red in the face and let out explosive damns and blasts; but his big hands were deft enough, and

225

slowness was no bad thing in such a case; and in a little while he had produced a squawking boy and the mother was coming back to consciousness and all was well.

Marion said, "You do swear a lot, don't you?"

He looked at her benignly as he pulled off his gloves. "It lets off a lot of steam and does no one any harm."

"I suppose so," she agreed.

And somehow, in her anxieties during the next few days, she found it catching, and some of her own tenseness found vent in "Hell's bells!" and "Damn and blast the thing!"

She encountered Dr. Hawkes another day, when her car had developed a punctured tyre in a little turning off the High Street. She was struggling to undo a tight nut, and, her feelings and her language rising in a crescendo of intensity, shouted loudly, "Hell take the whole concern and burn it!" when he appeared, walking.

"Tchk, tchk! I thought you didn't like my swearing!"

"You've infected me," she told him crossly, "and now I can't stop!"

He grinned delightedly. "Get rid of some of your repressions for you! Anyway, if you persist in doing a man's job, why shouldn't you swear like a man?"

"If you mean doctoring," she said, "I don't agree that it's a man's job. I could give you a lot of historical evidence for that."

"Don't trouble," he assured her. "I believe you."

"And if you mean changing a wheel on this car, it undoubtedly *is* a man's job, and I can't do it!"

He took the wheel-brace from her. "Pff – it is a tough one – there — " They finished the business between them, helping each other very amicably, and then stood up, dusting their grimy hands.

Dr. Hawkes said, "Come in and wash. My house is round the corner."

Marion went with him; in through the old country garden, heavy with fruit trees, untidy, cared for only just enough to be productive: up some dilapidated steps into a dim passage, at the other end of which was the front door, an impression of yellow-and-green stained glass.

"There's running water in the dispensary," Dr. Hawkes said, and guided her into a box of a room, like a house-maid's pantry, with shelves of bottles and an old apothecary's balance.

"I never did my own dispensing," Marion said. "Isn't it an awful job?"

"One almost has to do it, in the country. I keep some stock mixtures in Winchester quarts – pink bromides – brown cough stuff – white pepperminty digestives or yellow bitter ones – wait, I'll give you a clean towel – there – one makes a lot of money, selling tuppenny bottles of medicine for one and sixpence, you know, and it does them much more good if the doctor makes it up himself!" He made a comical face at her as she dried her hands. "Come and see my funny old surgery. It was my father's and my grandfather's before me."

The waiting-room was a dingy place of brown linoleum and wooden benches. They passed through it into a room only a degree less depressing, carpeted and curtained in an ugly blue-green, with a couch and a desk and a swivel chair. It was so different from her own bright little consulting-room, with flowers always about, and its screen embroidered in panels of them for patients to look at as they lay on the couch, that Marion checked at the entrance. Dr. Hawkes seemed unconscious of anything wrong with it. He said, "I'll show you my treasure – my grandfather's chest for precious drugs – a hundred and fifty years old, and still has its crystal bottles and a secret cupboard at the back – see?"

It was a little mahogany cabinet, eighteen inches or so in every dimension, beautifully made, with tiny white-knobbed drawers which ran with silken smoothness. "I still use it," he said, and they were bending over it when a face appeared, looking in at the open window.

"Who – Oh, it's you, Bob. I heard a noise, and I thought you were out."

"A good thing I wasn't examining a patient,"

"One wouldn't expect you to be, at this hour of the after-noon – even you!"

"Come in," he said, "and meet Dr. Marion Shepherd."

"You'd better come into the drawing-room," and the face withdrew.

"My wife," Dr. Hawkes explained, "won't come in here at any price. She thinks medicine is black magic, and patients are pests."

Not knowing quite what to say, Marion merely followed him into a room where ancient and modern rubbed unsympathetic jowls, a steel table, glass-topped, with a green Lalique glass lady dancing on it, beside a Sheraton cabinet. With a shock, she recognized the doctor's wife as the lady whom she had so firmly failed in her First-Aid examination, the argumentative one who had taught all the others and knew less than any of them. She had not turned up to Marion's own lectures, and she had never consciously seen her again. She was looking at Marion now as though she had never seen her before, a gracious, if somewhat haughty hostess, of an undoubted though faded beauty, spoilt by an expression of chronic indignation.

She said, "I expect you find the country very dull."

A hardly audible, "Tchk — " from the doctor beside her imposed caution on Marion. She said, "It's very different from town. But I was only saying the other day I thought I liked it better. I haven't been here long, of course."

Mrs. Hawkes said, "Not long enough to find it out!"

"Your husband," Marion interposed, "very kindly helped me with a flat tyre."

"He spends his life helping people," she said dully. "And expecting his household to help him. That's all they're here for."

Scenting trouble, Marion said lightly, "Well, I was very grateful to him for helping me!"

She was dismayed to have this capped smartly with, "That's more than most people are!"

She excused herself, soon, and drove home with an idle curiosity about the village doctor's home life uppermost in her mind.

Looking back, weeks later, she marked that day as the last on which she was free to do anything idly at all, even think; the last on which events did not crowd her so thickly that she almost could not deal with them; or perhaps, the first on which they did.

11

The next day, Paul arrived, unheralded, very pleased with himself, in a new uniform. He was now, all of a sudden, a Squadron Leader, in charge of a large section of the newly expanded Education Department of the Air Force. This was good. What was not so good, Marion thought, though Paul himself seemed excited by it, was that he was going abroad, probably to India, perhaps for two or more years. This was embarkation leave – a whole ten days of it. Tacitly, they made it a holiday, planned outings, with the children and without, enjoyed each other's company to the full and showed it; and did not talk, or even think, too much about what might be coming.

And then, when he had been at home four days, came their old enemy, the telephone. Paul jumped, and sighed, but Marion said, "It's all right, it can't be for me now. Some farm thing for your father, I expect. I've told old Salt-and-Water I'm having this ten days off, evacuee mothers and all."

Paul watched her amiably as she plaited Joan's pigtails. A voice floated up from below. "Hold on a minute, will you? I'll see." Footsteps began to climb the stairs.

Paul said, "It's for one of us. There's always the possibility, I suppose, of an early call back for me — " His brow wrinkled as he went to open the bedroom door.

The rosy-faced country maid who stood there said, "It's a trunk call for Dr. Marion."

Marion said, "Here, tie this bow like a good parent!" and fled down the stairs. The Medical Women's Federation,

230

offering her belated work? Her father or mother sick? She arrived at the telephone and took it up. "Marion Shepherd here — "

"This is the Hospital of St. Severs, East London. We have been asked to contact you for a Mrs. — " She could imagine the little girl clerk breathing heavily over her message pad, " – a Mrs. Spencer. Mrs. Philippa Spencer."

Marion stiffened. "Yes? Yes, I know her, of course."

The girl said, "I'm to put you through to Dr. Munro." The next minute an older woman's voice came through, a pleasant, calm, slightly Scottish voice. Thank goodness for that, anyway.

It said, "Good morning. We have a Mrs. Philippa Mary Spencer here. She came in as an air-raid casualty last night. She's very ill. Too ill to tell us anything about herself. However, she perked up a little after a blood-transfusion, and she gave us your name as the only person she wanted to see."

Marion said, "Is she on the danger list?"

"Emphatically yes. She's asked to see you several times. Can you come?"

"Of course I'll come. At once."

"Any time. I'm glad. I'd like to see you myself — " and the 'phone clicked off.

Marion stood there, trying to get things into focus again. Philippa, at death's door, in East London in the middle of the night, when she lived on the south-west fringe. What was she doing there? It was possible to make a guess. Philippa, her friend since they were both eighteen, dying, perhaps, for lack of help from her – calling now for help

231

again. Paul, on embarkation leave, his claim on her undisputed. The bowl of her life cracking round her into little pieces. She pushed that thought away, it was not she who was the sufferer. She went upstairs in search of Paul.

"Who was the devil?"

"Philippa," she said, and sat down on a chair which was already full of clothes.

Paul threw a look at her. He got rid of the children and came back to her.

"She's in hospital," she said, and briefly told him the whole tale, briefly, and a little fearfully, because she thought he would be hurt at her going, and yet she must go. She finished up, "I feel a bit responsible."

"You shouldn't do that," he said at once. "It was her headache to start with, the cuckoo. You think she went to the docks, or some such place, on a moonlight night, in the hope of a bomb finishing her off without any fuss?"

Marion nodded. "It's the only explanation I can think of."

"It's a possible one," he agreed. Then, with a grin which made Marion catch her breath, it was so conspiratorial, "We'll go together, shall we? I'll be finding us a place to sleep while you're seeing her. They won't want you there long at a time, if she's as ill as all that, will they? We can go to some shows."

Marion was so grateful as to be speechless. She felt tears, most unusually, pricking her eyelids as she looked at him, and he came across to her, and she clung to him for a minute and felt his lips on her hair.

He said presently, "I'll go and tackle Mother about looking after the kids."

12

Philippa was in a little side-ward, in normal times for one only, but now shared with two others. It was the sort of little room, Marion well knew (and probably Philippa knew too) which was reserved for people who were either septic or were going to die. Philippa looked dreadfully ill, pinched, and waxy white; and was in fact too weak to do anything but smile at Marion and answer, fleetingly, the pressure of her hand.

The ward sister said, "She's pretty well doped," and Marion nodded, and watched until Philippa opened her eyes again, and then bent over her because she seemed to want to speak.

She said, "Don't – tell them," and that was all. In a minute she was fast asleep, a peaceful, morphia sleep in which nothing mattered.

"What are her injuries?" Marion asked the sister. The discreet, watchful face became guarded at once. "I think you'd better see Dr. Munro," she said, and Marion agreed, "I'd like to."

Dr. Munro proved to be a middle-aged, kindly, competent woman, more concerned with getting Philippa better than with tracing her relatives, which was worrying the ward sister very much, and in which Marion gave no help at all. "Her husband," she said firmly, "was killed a few weeks ago. I don't know any other relatives at all, although she and I lived together for several years."

Dr. Munro seemed to be summing her up. Then she said, "I'd better tell you about her. She isn't injured at all, any

233

where. But she's bled practically to death from a miscarriage, and she's running a temperature."

The two doctors looked at each other. "I knew she was pregnant," Marion said. No use denying that, with things as they were. "And she was terribly upset, of course, about – her husband's death." That much of loyalty to Philippa she could and would persist in. She went on, "What do you think of her chances?"

Dr. Munro spread out her hands. "You know what these cases do – loss of blood – sepsis – no resistance – not much will to live. But I think now, with blood transfusions and these new M. and B. drugs, the sulphonamides – there is a chance for her. But she's very ill."

"I'll ring up late to-night, if I may, and come again either then or to-morrow," Marion said, and the other waved a hand and said, "Any time. You don't happen to know where she lived?"

"I do, of course. Not anywhere near here. I can't think what she was doing here."

They watched each other for a minute again, and then Dr. Munro turned away. "It doesn't matter, really. We'll treat you as her next of kin, if we need you, and leave you to cope."

Marion was grateful to find Paul waiting for her at the University Women's Club, which had seemed a convenient meeting place. He was jubilant because he had fixed up a place for them to stay in; one of those hotels, not far from there, which consists of tiers of service flats.

Marion objected, "It'll cost the earth!"

"It may. Why not? We've got it. We'll have dinner there,

234

and go on to a show. I've got some tickets for the Coliseum, it'll be lively, anyway. Everything provided for. Our bags have gone up. Come along and see."

He piloted her, a hand under her elbow, and hardly paused in his talk until a breathless passage along some small streets, through a flower-filled foyer, quite unwarlike, and up in a lift, brought them into the quiet of a little suite such as Marion had only seen before on the pictures.

She said so, and Paul agreed. " 'M. I didn't believe they really existed, did you? Except perhaps in America. It was the only thing I could get and, when you come to think of it, it's just what we want. Privacy, and a place down below where we can have meals, even to supper after the theatre, and dancing!"

Marion said, "It's a good thing I flung in an evening-dress!"

It was only when they had explored the flat and were unpacking that Paul said, "Is Philippa all right? I didn't like to ask — "

Marion's thoughts came back from this film-star existence to reality. "She's alive, and they say she's got a chance. That's about all. Paul, ought we to tell the Army? Won't they post her as a deserter or something?"

Paul considered. "There's no harm in telling them she's an air-raid casualty, is there? That may happen to anyone. D'you know where she works?"

"Fulton Emergency Hospital, at Wimbledon. Why?"

"Couldn't you ring them up and ask to speak to her? That'll tell you whether she's on leave or not. If she is, you needn't say anything, it's no business of theirs where she is. If not, you can ring again later and tell them you've discovered she's been hurt."

"That's a good idea." Marion nodded. "If they do have to know, I shall just say she's too bad to be visited. That's true enough."

"I can't imagine Philippa being so idiotic," Paul said. "She always seemed so sure of herself, so poised."

"She was," Marion said slowly, "until you came along. — No," she added, smiling at Paul's sudden startled lift of the head, "I don't mean that. I mean, our getting married shook her. She was envious of us, a bit — "

"And quite right too," Paul said positively. "It's a good show, ours."

Marion agreed, in the same idiom. "I'll say it is — " And they laughed, and kissed, and forgot Philippa for the rest of the evening.

In the morning they explored London; the parks full of troops, balloon-sites, and trenches, the skeleton, still acrid with smoke, of John Lewis's, the ruins strewn about St. Paul's, which stood majestic, miraculous, in their midst.

Marion said, "I suppose we're idiots to be sleeping up here."

Paul said, "There's a good concrete shelter under those flats. I found out about that before I fixed up with them." When Marion said she had never given the matter a thought and had had no idea how bad it was, he added: "I've seen more raids than you have, and it's pretty well drummed into us that while a live airman's an asset, a dead one's a loss and a wounded one's a liability." He grinned affectionately at her. "Foolhardiness isn't any more popular than cowardice – perhaps they're only two sides of the same medal."

"I've wondered sometimes," Marion said, "whether we ought to have sent the children to America. Lots of people I know have done – some few are still waiting for them to go."

Paul became explosive. "And teach 'em the proper thing to do about danger is to run away from it? Not on your life! Keep them in their own place, take the best possible care of them and preach courage, courage, courage, all the time!"

Marion sighed ecstatically. "I do like it when I've formed an opinion of my own, on my own, and then the same one bubbles up out of you without any discussion or contact about it whatsoever – don't you?"

He looked lovingly down at her as they strolled along the battered London street. "I do. It brings home with a bang that we are, really, in an incomprehensible sort of way, one."

She hugged his arm. "Incomprehensible," she said, "because we're both such headstrong, individual sort of persons — "

"Are we?" he said, and so they went on, walking, looking, talking.

13

Philippa, when Marion saw her in the afternoon, was a little better. She had been given another transfusion, and she was able to talk. When Marion asked her, "Whatever were you doing down there by the docks? You must have known the danger!" she gave the ghost of a smile.

"I didn't mind about it. I'd lost such a lot of blood – from the other business – I knew I ought to be in hospital – and I thought if I arranged myself to look like an air-raid victim I should get in with no questions asked."

Marion said grimly, "It worked, marvellously. How you managed *not* to be a victim I can't imagine! Oh, Phil, you fool of a woman to get yourself into such a state! You'd better tell me all about it, for the sake of your treatment!"

But Philippa, still smiling, wearily shook her head. "An air-raid like that's enough excuse for a miscarriage, isn't it?"

Then Dr. Munro appeared and shooed Marion away. "She's better, but her temperature's still up. I'm hoping to have her well enough to-morrow to evacuate into the country, away from all this. They'll tell you if you ring up where she is."

But when Marion rang up in the evening, she was not so well, and anxiety, which she successfully hid from Paul, clouded the enjoyment of their entertainment – another show, another good supper, another dance. Marion did not try to speak of it until she and Paul were in bed, and then she did. Paul's reply was to take her in his arms, more roughly than he had been used to do, more urgently, and to say in her ear, "Don't worry. She's in good hands, and you

238

can't do a thing!" And she forgot Philippa and bombed London and all else but Paul.

In the morning there was no change, and in the evening Philippa died. Marion, who had watched over her all the afternoon, had refused to believe the sister's assertion that she would not recover; but, as experienced ward sisters usually are, she was right. She grew restless, then very quiet. Her veins were so collapsed that another transfusion was impossible. Her resistance gradually ebbed and her life with it. When Marion had not turned up to meet Paul for tea, he had rung up, and when at last she stumbled out of the hospital, he rose from a seat in the hall, where he had been patiently waiting, and went with her.

She said nothing for a while. She was too much overwhelmed by the tragedy of it; an unnecessary loss of life even when life was cheap. Her own responsibility lay heavy on her mind. She said presently, "I think it's more awful to have done what you are sure is right – and then have a frightful result – than to do something wrong that you can be ashamed of."

Paul said, "You could have done nothing else. If it happened again, you'd do it again. You mustn't blame yourself for her mistake – poor Phil."

"No one's going to know it wasn't – just the air-raid – an ordinary injury."

"There's no earthly reason," Paul said, "why they should."

She roused herself at length to say, "We'd better go home to-morrow, hadn't we?" But instead of agreeing, Paul said, "Can't we have another day or two?"

Marion glanced up in surprise and saw him smiling down

at her.

Conversationally, for they were in a Lyon's, he remarked, "It's so marvellous having you all to myself – no work, no children, nothing to get in between us. We haven't had such a time since Switzerland, have we? And – " his voice deepened, though the look of easy politeness on his face did not change – "I do love it so!"

Marion suddenly could think of nothing to say. It was so long since they had talked to each other like that. Ten years of marriage – work – disagreements – children – the war – had jostled such sentiments under. She had hated Paul's jealousy of her work and of her preoccupation with baby Martin – and yet, would not many a woman envy her a husband who could still be jealous? She could not keep her expression quite as lightly social as his as she answered him. "Snatch another two days, shall we? I may – I may have one or two things to do – Phil has got a brother, though I've never met him – I suppose he'll have to know – she's dead."

Paul said quietly, "That's a good enough excuse, anyway." And they finished their snack and went out, his arm in Marion's and her elbow pressed tightly to his side.

Marion remembered the two days, afterwards, as a queerly precious cameo, set in the crowding pressure of outside events. She alternated between ecstatic happiness at the rightness of her relationship with Paul and sadness which cut like a jagged knife when she thought of Philippa and what might have been avoided if only the child's father had not been killed, if she herself had been more understanding, more persuasive, had somehow kept

Philippa under her own eye. The intensity of both emotions illuminated every little happening, so that the short interlude formed an integrated, brilliant whole, a high-spot of feeling, every time her mind reverted to any part of it.

There were the sombre duties connected with Philippa's death, the meeting with her brother, and reminders of her, breath-taking, in his looks and mannerisms. In contrast, there was dancing, shopping, walking, and talking with Paul, the joy of which blotted out, quite effortlessly, all the shadows. Marion would have forced herself to be cheerful, for his sake. But she did not need to force herself, so all-pervading was the joy of this snatched honeymoon.

There was an air-raid warning on their last night, and they spent it, at first flippantly and then with resignation, sitting in some discomfort in the hotel's air-raid shelter. They were never in fear, because they were, for these days, dancing through life with the gods on their side. They could not imagine that there could be anything for them to be afraid of, and they were touched when, after the "All-clear" had sounded, an elderly couple came and thanked them for their gay courage which, they insisted, had kept the whole roomful steady.

"It wasn't courage, at all, of course," they agreed when they were in their own room again. "It just didn't occur to us to be afraid!"

"Lack of imagination?" queried Marion.

"I don't think so," Paul said. "I've been afraid, good and plenty, in raids on the air-fields. An awful feeling, that the men up there are bent on blowing you, personally, into little bits just because you're R.A.F. and on that spot!"

"It must have been," Marion said, "that we felt we were so utterly harmonious, such a complete unit, that we couldn't possibly be disrupted."

"Like the atom!" Paul capped it lightheartedly.

Marion, with a sudden chill at her heart, warned him, "We mustn't be too sure – it's silly, to be too sure – I wish you hadn't said that about the atom – the scientists say they can disrupt it, with a fearful bang and all sorts of troubles."

Paul said, "There'd be all sorts of troubles for anyone who tried to disrupt us, anyway — " And they laughed and forgot it in their certain present happiness, which they carried back with them to the farm and the children, so that even Martin's suspicious little soul was warmed and befriended.

Then Paul went back, and Marion felt like an empty shell, capable of nothing but echoing, hollowly, frighteningly, the noises from outside.

PART FOUR

*

Bob

1

THE noises outside became almost at once so loud and persistent that they would in any case have drowned all personal music.

Martin, due for his first term at school, started off in excited expectation, but came back at the end of the day very gloomy.

Marion, at the sight of his white face, refrained from asking questions, gave him his tea, and would have sent him out at once with Waggers. But his grandfather, coming in just then, inquired heartily, "Well, how d'you like school?"

Martin scowled. "I don't like it."

"You don't like school? Why?"

"There are such a lot of children. And they make such a *noise!* And there's a person who calls me 'dear'."

"Good gracious! Don't you like to be called 'dear'!"

"She only calls people 'dear' " – Martin was putting two and two together with some difficulty – "when she wants them to do something they don't want to do."

"What didn't you want to do?"

Martin hunched a shoulder. "I didn't want to do any of the things. They were all silly. I'm not going to school to-morrow!"

Marion said, "Well, get along out now, anyway," and, when he had gone, pulled a face. "What a bother! I did so hope he would take to it!"

"He'll shake down," Mrs. Shepherd comforted.

"I don't know that he will. He's an awful dodger!"

The next morning, Martin appeared very early, in his corduroy dungarees. "I dressed myself *all* myself!" he announced proudly, with his most engaging smile.

"So I see. But you can't," Marion told him, "go to school like that. You have to wear grey shorts, for school."

Martin's eyes became dreamy. "Oh – school. I'd forgotten about school." Then, bringing his glance back sharply to his mother's face. "I'm going to watch the calves in the field, to-day, to see that dogs don't come and chase them. I can't possibly go to school to-day."

"Sorry, old man, but that's just where you are going. So we'd better change those pants right away."

"Do I have to?" he asked forlornly.

"Of course. All boys go to school when they're old enough, to learn all the things they have to know."

He said no more, and allowed his clothes to be changed, and ate his breakfast and trotted with Joan at Marion's side across the field path and through the village. Marion let out a breath of relief when she left them at the school-gate to join the straggle of other children across the playground, and turned for the stroll homeward, calling at a shop on the way.

It was when she stopped to look in at a window that she noticed a passer-by glance at her with what seemed to be amusement, and away along the road, and then back at her, and nearly speak and then think better of it.

"Smut on my nose?" she wondered, and tried to see herself in the window glass without success.

It happened again as she went along, in that same

246

sequence; someone coming towards her glanced up curiously, with a half-smile, then along the road behind her, then back at her again; and again, this time from a young workman, a really tickled snigger. She turned quickly to follow his look along the road, but saw nothing except a commotion among some bushes in a garden, as though there were a dog among them.

She could make no sense of it until, having pushed open the door of a shop and seen at once that what she wanted was not there, she came straight out again and was almost brushed by a little figure, bent double, which scuttled past her round the corner of the next building into the lane which led home.

She shouted, "Martin! Come here, you little wretch!" and broke into undignified chase.

Martin could run, but so could Marion. She caught him up as he scrambled over the first stile, and seized him by the arm. He looked up at her, white, not quite tearful, his mouth set.

"Martin, how dare you run away from school! Whatever will they think of you?"

He gave a little whimper, like a hurt dog. "I won't go back! I won't go back!"

The impact of the whimper had given Marion a pain behind her ribs. She steeled herself, and said sternly, "Nonsense, of course you must go back. Come on, if we run you won't be late after all!" And she lifted him back over the stile, a little, light, protesting body, and set him down beside her.

He broke into real tears then. "I don't wanner – I don't

247

wanner – go there!"

She marched him along. He mustn't be given in to, of course. In the village, the passers-by were amused quite frankly now, or even shocked. Marion hissed at him, "Martin, stop it! I'm ashamed of you!" and his howls turned into snivels and finally stopped as he realized he was beaten. She took him right into the school then, and delivered him up to the teacher.

"He's still a bit shy," she explained, and the teacher took charge of him.

"Poor little man! Come along, dear!"

"Good-bye, Martin. Be good, now!" Marion said. But Martin, slouching with bent head, would not look at her.

He came home at teatime looking wretched, refused food, and presently brought up all his school dinner, and went to bed. Many times during the night Marion was up with him as he woke up retching and crying, and in the morning he was so evidently ill and feverish that she balked at the responsibility of him and rang up Dr. Hawkes.

He mocked her. "You don't really think this old man knows more about ill children than you do!"

"I wouldn't like to say you didn't! I'm just worried, anyway. One goes into a flat spin when it's one's own child. And he looks so awful, I keep wondering what I've missed."

"I'll make you my first visit," he promised her.

He was sweet with Martin, treating him in just the way Martin liked, as a responsible person, so that the child allowed himself to be prodded and pressed in a way he would never have tolerated from his mother.

"I can't go to school, can I?" he asked, as soon as the

248

examination was over.

"Not to-day, I'm afraid. Still, one day won't make a dunce of you."

"What's dunce?"

"A person who doesn't know the things everyone else of his age knows, and can't do the things they do."

"What things?"

"Reading and writing and drawing and painting and doing sums and making baskets."

"Joan can do all those," Martin said.

"Where did she learn to do them?"

Martin pulled the sheet up round his face.

To Marion, in the other room, Dr. Hawkes said, "You haven't missed anything, of course. It's schoolitis and nothing more. Wind up, in a sensitive child."

"But isn't he heading straight for a neurosis, if he finds out at this age that being ill can keep him from having to do things he doesn't like? What do I do? Hound him back?"

Dr. Hawkes looked down at her very kindly. "He'll have to go back, of course, in a day or two, when he's better. Mind you, he really is ill. He's worried himself into being ill, he isn't pretending. In the meantime – see to it that being ill stops him doing things he does like as well as things he doesn't. Keep him in, give him the plainest food when he can eat again. And talk to him – tell him how brave it is to do things he doesn't like – how you and his father – anyone he cares about – have to do them. Tell him the benefits he'll get from doing them – anything that's true and positive. It's no good saying don't's – do's are the only real help. 'You *will* be a brave boy', not 'you *mustn't* be a cowardy'. And soft soap about school being a nice place won't work with a sharp child like that who has hated it on sight. Give him some Dutch courage by pouring glucose into him, and give him a quarter grain of luminal to-night to quiet him down. And tip the wink to Miss Eagles at the school – I'll do that, she's a friend of mine, and I'm not the boy's fond parent – to make things pleasant for him the next time he goes, so that he does enjoy it."

Marion murmured, "You're very wise," and he twinkled at her.

"I've seen a lot of youngsters grow up. And never having had any of my own" – his face went bleak for an instant – "has permitted me to see the wood in spite of the trees."

"It's awfully difficult to," Marion said, "when they're your own trees."

The attack really was a worse one than usual. Marion used the few days during which it lasted for the following of "Old Salt-and-Water's" advice – refused all entreaties for dainty food, serving up glucose-water and then weak Bovril and toast and nothing else – and provided dull books to be looked at indoors in spite of suggestions that a drive with Gran'fa or a walk round the farm would be beneficial. She extolled the advantages of being able to read and write and let him try to, and of doing sums and making little mats and cardboard models; and spoke of the prizes clever boys could win.

"Am I a clever boy?" Martin wanted to know.

"I think you will be. Daddy's very clever, and I'm not dull, and boys and girls tend to be like their mummies and daddies. But even the cleverest boys can't do those things without being taught."

When the day came for going back to school, they set off very solemnly but quite without rebellion. As they reached the point where the field path joined the main road, a car drew up beside them, and there was Dr. Hawkes beaming through the window.

"Hullo! Like a lift?"

"We've got Waggers," Marion demurred.

"He can come too. In you get."

Martin was peering into the car. "Who's that in there?" he demanded, and they saw in the back seat another boy, a little bigger than Martin, and wearing the same school cap.

"John Mallory. My assistant's son. I take him along when I'm going that way."

The two stared at each other. Then Waggers made a leap into the car, and fell on the other boy, licking and wriggling, and John crowed with laughter and fondled him in the way dog-lovers do. That was enough for Martin. He scrambled in with them. "He's a nice dog, isn't he? He's mine."

The other boy looked up. "He's a very nice dog – ow! He licked me right on the nose that time – I haven't got one – I wish I had!"

Joan pushed her way in with boys and dog, and Marion sat in the front with Dr. Hawkes, and so they arrived in no time at the school.

"You'd better put Waggers on the lead," Martin instructed his mother. "If you don't, he'll follow me in."

Meekly, Marion did so, and watched the two small boys

go off together, Martin faithfully shooting his cap to the back of his head and his hands into his pockets in imitation of John. Joan turned and waved, but Martin did not even look round before they disappeared through the school door.

Marion laughed helplessly as she met the village doctor's eye. "That was most terribly nice of you. Do you – pursue your line of treatment so far with all your patients?"

"Only my pet ones," he said gravely. "It's nice to, when one can. Look, I'll pick him up there for the next few mornings, shall I? And then tell John to walk that way and meet him for a few more – and by that time it'll be a habit for them to go together."

"That would be marvellous," Marion told him. And he drove on along the village street and left her and Waggers to walk home together; or not together, as it turned out, for Waggers, as soon as he was freed, went streaking through a hedge and into the woods, and miraculously rejoined her as she passed through the farm's garden gate.

All went well after that. In little more than a week Martin seemed to have changed from a flitting elf into a sturdy, stumping schoolboy. No one asked him if he liked school, and he hardly referred to it, so anxious was he to get out on the farm as soon as he had finished his tea. John Mallory appeared at that time very often, and they marched away together, with Waggers doing high jumps around them.

One day he vouchsafed an anecdote. "Miss Eagles – she called me out to-day in front of the whole class – and she said, I want you all to look at Martin Shep'd. Martin

252

Shep'd's such a *clever* little boy!" And he put two fingers into his mouth and let out an ear-splitting whistle as he banged the door behind him.

Marion and her parents-in-law stared at each other. "D'you think she really did?" Marion asked them doubtfully.

Mr. Shepherd fussed. "Idiot of a woman if she did! Make the other boys want to kick 'im in the pants!"

"I should think," Mrs. Shepherd said, "it was just his way of telling us he's getting on pretty well now after all."

2

There had been a lull in the bombing attacks after the Battle of Britain. But now they were beginning again, tip-and-run raids by day along the coast, and occasional bigger raids on selected towns which set the sirens wailing at night.

It was one morning, when breakfast was just finished but before the children had started for school, that they heard a lone 'plane approaching. Marion had just said suspiciously, "That doesn't sound like one of ours, somehow," when a series of loud cracks brought them all to their feet.

Mr. Shepherd called, "Incendiaries!" and made a dash for his farm-buildings. Mrs. Shepherd hustled the children under the stairs. And hardly had they got moving before there was a "whee-ee-ee-ee" and a crump some distance away. The windows rattled and a tinkle of glass sounded as one of them collapsed under the strain of the blast. Marion said, "That was a real bomb!" and snatched her tin hat. The children were wailing to her not to leave them, but she shouted, "It's all right, the 'plane's gone now, there won't be any more – from that one anyway!", and, regardless of them, for she had to be, she raced for her car and shot off in the direction of the sound.

She picked up several of her First Aid people on her way through the village. The damage seemed to be at the very far end of it, where a big house stood by itself in its own grounds.

"Just too bad, if it's got the house, with all that space round it," somebody commented as the car, now loaded, rattled up the drive.

But it had hit the house. One face of it had been sheared off and lay in heaps of bricks and rubble. Rags of bright curtains fluttered like pennons from a tree. A bath stood balanced on the very edge of what had been the bathroom floor. Pictures hung askew on the remains of walls. Water was streaming from a broken pipe. As they watched, a man, covered with grey dust, climbed out through a ground floor window with the absorbed air of one who has just completed an arduous journey. Marion's car had shed its load of helpers, and he staggered to them as they ran towards the house.

Marion heard him say, "The Mistress – she's in there!" in a croaky voice.

"Are you hurt, yourself?" Marion asked him.

He shook his head, in wonderment. "I don't think I be. Not to say 'urt. Shook up. But the Mistress, she's in there.

254

And Em'ly – that's my wife – she'd just gone up to 'elp 'er dress. That" – he jerked his head to the stream of water pouring down – "that there would've bin 'er bath!"

Someone guided him to a heap of masonry, and he sat down, but quickly jumped up – "Cor, that's 'ot! Why" – he passed a hand over it, cautiously – "that be a bit of the chimney – see?"

Marion left him and joined the rest of the party as they picked their way carefully nearer the house. A beam, which had been tilted above the wreckage, collapsed slowly, with odd bricks tumbling round it, and rubble sliding into little heaps.

"There's another car here, see?" someone said. "It must've come up before we did, it's made tracks in the dust, it wasn't just standing here at the time."

Marion looked at it. "It's Dr. Hawkes's car. I wonder" – the party looked at one another in alarm – "I wonder where he is!"

One of them said, "Where on earth's the stopcock, to turn off that water? Can't hear oneself think!" He went prowling off to look for it, and in a minute the stream trickled to a stop. In the silence, a woman's voice could be heard from the ruins, calling monotonously, "Help! Help!"

The man who had come out heaved himself to his feet as they all surged towards the sound, only to check as another subsidence took place before their eyes.

"That were Em'ly!" the man croaked. "That were Em'ly – my wife!"

Someone said, "It's madness to go in there! Bits and pieces falling all round you! We want a rescue squad, with props and picks and things!"

A boy detached himself. "I'm a messenger. I'll go and get them."

As they hesitated, a sound of breaking glass came from round a corner of the building, and a man's voice called, "Hullo, there! Hullo!"

Emily's husband seemed to freeze where he stood. "Now who might that be? Who is it? There weren't no other man in there!"

They crowded round to see. And there, hardly recognizable for the dirt which covered him, was Dr. Hawkes at an upper window which he had broken, evidently, because it would not open.

"How on earth did you get up there?" Marion called.

"Stairs," he told them. "They were fairly safe. They're blocked now, by that beam that shifted a few minutes ago. Look, the old lady is all right for the present – a great wad of ceiling's being held off her by a wardrobe and a door which have made a sort of tent – quite providential. But one doesn't know how long it'll stay put — "

They chorused, "Someone's gone for a rescue squad."

He nodded. "It's the maid I'm worrying about. Emily. I've only just found her. She's under a bit of wall. She's in pain."

The man outside caught his breath and pressed to the front, and the doctor saw him. "Oh, you're there, Foster. That's good, I was wondering about you. Well, I'm just going along to give her a shot of morphia to make her comfortable." And he withdrew his head.

They shouted as one man, "Be careful!" and stood listening. But there was no sound now but the little creaks

256

and plops of small fragments moving. They felt helpless, standing out there.

"Nothing we can do till the rescue people come. Ladders, we want. Get the stretchers ready and stand by — " they gave their opinions.

Someone said, "Dam' plucky of old Doc, dashing in there – he's not a young man — "

Another expressed the anxiety they felt for him – "Dam' foolhardy!"

Someone else explained it all. "Old Lady Mary's a patient of his, and of his father before him – he'd feel he'd got to do something if he could."

And at last – "Here's the rescue squad!"

They came on a converted lorry, a dozen strong labourers directed by a young farmer. They hullooed, and in a minute the doctor came to the window again.

His eyes sought Emily's husband first. "She's all right. Leg broken, I think, but no worse. She's had her morphia." Then he turned his attention to the rescue party. "You can get to all three of us from here, reasonably safely, I think. I don't know about getting them out this way – you'll see."

Watching the men handle the ladders and move lumps of stonework to make room for them, Marion was impressed by their strength. One of them went up the ladder and forced the window-frame out with an iron bar and climbed in, and another followed him. One came back and called for some implement, and a third man took it up. Some others explored the possibility of moving the beam from across the stairs, and reported that it was no good, because a whole lot of roof had come down on top of it.

Then one of them called, "Splints, please! Long ones!" Marion grabbed them, and wool and bandages, and said, "I'll go!"

She looked up at the window, and the man there shouted to someone inside, and then nodded. "Doctor says O.K., you can come!" She clambered up. She did not mind heights, and the ladder was wonderfully steady. Getting off it through the window looked difficult, but if the others had done it, she could. She handed in the splints, swung one leg over the sill, and found herself firmly supported from inside.

"Right – keep close the wall, the floor doesn't look too good – through here."

The room they came into was open to the sky. The floor of the attic above had come loose at one end and sagged in a dismal curve of slats and canvas. Curtains and carpets were in shreds, and the front of a heavy wardrobe looked as though it had been splintered with an axe. It was the side of this same wardrobe which had fallen across Emily and broken her thigh just above the knee. It had been moved away now, and she lay there on the floor, in an old-fashioned print dress and apron, a little elderly woman, beady eyed, tight-lipped, reminding Marion of old Ethel. Dr. Hawkes, kneeling beside her, smiled at the newcomers through his grime.

"She's more comfortable now. The morphia's doing its job. Splints? Good. Get it tied up – it's compound – then we can move her."

He took the splints from Marion, and she bent beside him, and they worked together, harmoniously, as they had

258

worked on Marion's punctured tyre and on the leg of the boy in the ditch at their first meeting. Some others of the First Aid party came up with the hand-stretcher, and Emily, uncomplaining, was rolled in it. She thrust out a hand suddenly to Dr. Hawkes, and he pressed it and firmly tucked it in again, and they got her down, inch by inch, and went back for her mistress.

Marion turned to go with them, but Dr. Hawkes prevented her. "There's no need. She's quite unhurt, and there isn't much room."

It was not long before the old lady, still in her frilly nightcap and bedjacket, and the maid, were together in the ambulance. Marion liked the quick look, as between friends, that they gave each other. "You'd better go too," Emily's husband was told, and he went up beside the driver.

Someone called to him, "No one else likely to be in there?" He shook his head. "No one else. Only the cat — "

The messenger boy shouted, "I've got her! I found her down the drive, covered with dust. I'll take her home."

The rescue party were mopping their brows.

"Cor, she had an escape, the old girl!" One of them exploded. "Half a ton of ceiling two feet above 'er head, balanced on a broken door and a bit of furniture! And half the floor of 'er room in the garden! I don't know how the doctor managed to get to 'er without a ladder, that I don't!" "Only got to tread on something rickety, and down 'e'd 've gone with the whole lot boilin' on top of 'im!"

"Doctors don't have to think about their own safety," someone said rather unctuously. "Wouldn't be able to do

259

their jobs if they did. Would they, Dr. Shepherd?"

Marion said, "No one thinks of much beside their job – when they're doing the job, do they?" But she herself thought suddenly of Paul's maxim – a live airman's an asset, a damaged one's a liability – silly, it wasn't Paul's but someone's higher up, preaching to the men. Paul was as brave as Dr. Hawkes was, any day.

But Dr. Hawkes *was* brave, there wasn't any getting away from that. He was smiling down at her, sheepishly, and running his fingers through his gritty hair.

They lingered, looking back at the ruins. "A pity – such a nice old house, it was," he said, "full of lovely things."

"Doesn't it make you *angry!*" The queerest mixture of rage, sorrow, and excitement made Marion feel as though she might burst into tears. She took some trouble to control herself.

3

It was three days later, at breakfast, that a small boy arrived at the farm with a message. Would Dr. Shepherd go and see Dr. Hawkes, please, as early as she could? He didn't know why, he only knew that the Doctor's old cook had given him sixpence and told him to come.

The same old cook met her at the door.

"The doctor's very queer," she said. "No, he doesn't know I've sent for you, Ma'am. I don't think he would have let me. That was why I sent the little boy, not wanting him to hear the 'phone." And she pushed open the door of the little morning-room.

Dr. Hawkes, in a dressing-gown, his hair on end, was sitting by a newly-lit fire. He had one sleeve rolled up almost to his shoulder, and he was gloomily contemplating his forearm, which was immersed in a bath.

He half-rose when he saw Marion. "What the blazes – I suppose that old witch-woman asked you to come!" Then, following her eyes to the steaming bath, he grinned. "Yes, salt and water!" he said. "I got a few scratches the other day – unavoidable, climbing about in all that mess – and something must've had a streptococcus in it. Anyway, the thing's all swelled up, and I alternately shiver and burn – and there you are! What finished it was that I found this morning I could hardly stand – head swimming – legs wouldn't work – I've never been ill in my life!"

"And what are you doing about it?" Marion asked.

"What you see!"

"Hadn't you better," she suggested, "do a bit more? You ought to be in hospital."

He snorted. "Hospital! We don't send people to hospital in the country unless they'll die if they stay at home. Don't you townees ever tackle any treatment?"

"Now and then!" Marion countered. "But it's your right arm. You wouldn't be much use without it."

"You won't get me into hospital," he asserted. "To be bossed about by Irish chits and boys who still smell of the dissecting-room!"

"You ought at least to be in bed and swallowing these new M. and B. things, that kill the streps while they're still swimming about in your blood stream."

He gave her a funny look, a blend of the countryman's suspicion of everything new-fangled and the hope of a sick man in the magician whose help he will trust.

"I don't mind *you* bossing me," he acknowledged. "I'll get the gardener to put up a bed in here and lie in it, if that will satisfy you. Save Mrs. Bean a lot of stair work . . . D'you know anything about the M. and B.s?"

"Quite a bit. I was visiting a friend of mine who had – peritonitis – in hospital, and I found out about the dosage and so on then."

"Good girl. You'll never get them from that one-eyed chap in the village though. Have to send to Brighton."

Marion looked down at him. "No good sending and waiting for days. You need them now. Couldn't Mrs. Hawkes drive in for them?"

"She doesn't drive," he said at once. "And anyway – " He lifted his arm out of the bath and studied it minutely. "Fact is, she went off to stay with her sister at Ambleside the day the bomb dropped. Can't blame her. Why should anyone stay about here who doesn't have to? I do have to, though she wouldn't see that. Are you staying yourself?"

"I? Of course. My in-laws wouldn't leave the farm, and I don't want to leave them. The children don't seem unduly upset . . . Well, I'll go into Brighton myself, if you'll tell me a likely chemist."

He blinked up at her with comical surprise. "Practical, aren't you?"

"Women are," she said.

"And astonishingly kind. But I wouldn't let you do that.

262

Might get another bomb, at Brighton. The nearer the coast, the more likely. No, if you ring up Curtis, the chemist near the bus stop, he'll put it on the bus, and someone can pop out and meet it here. I often do that, with things I want urgently."

Marion said, "You're pretty practical yourself. I'll go and 'phone now."

When she came back, she asked him, "Would you like me to see any patients for you?"

The gloom which had settled on his face cleared. "I was hoping you would. I'll just get my book."

"You'll do no such thing."

"Tyrant! How women do like power!"

Unmoved, she said, "Not woman. Medical adviser. Sit still and tell me where it is."

"In the surgery, on the desk . . . I left it all in a bit of a mess last night . . . felt awful!"

Marion collected the visiting-book and a tin of kaolin plaster. She set it to heat, and when the matter of visits and surgeries had been settled, fetched it in, and encased his arm in it in spite of argument and protest; brought Mrs. Bean into the room and gave her directions about what he might do and eat, in front of him; telephoned to the farm; and went back to the surgery.

She sat for some minutes at the desk, composing herself into the mood – how long ago it seemed since that mood had been her usual one – of planning a day against time.

And time was her greatest enemy, from then on. She would be up at half-past six, tidying rooms, getting the children dressed and fed and off to school. A morning surgery, visits, some of them far away, an evening surgery; and, twice a day, a professional attendance on Dr. Hawkes. He was quite ill, and looked even more ill than he was, unshaven, his face frowning, or gloomy in repose, his bed hopelessly untidy five minutes after it was made. Fever and the M. and B.s between them removed his inhibitions, and he liked to talk as long as Marion would listen.

He talked much about his wife, whom he seemed to think might be blamed for her desertion.

"A rotten life for a woman, married to a G.P.," was his opinion. "Has to play second fiddle to his practice all the time. Sheila had never been used to playing second fiddle. She just couldn't understand it. She was always wanting me to take her away for week-ends – she would make arrangements without consulting me, spring them on me as a lovely surprise – and then I wouldn't be able to go, because someone was very ill, or a confinement was due. She couldn't bear it that her wishes didn't come before those things. Thought it was the money they paid me which held me to them. I suppose no one who isn't a doctor can understand that one hardly thinks of the money side of it – but the human need gets under all one's defences – the duty one has to people when once one has assumed responsibility for them. *You'd* understand, of course . . . It wasn't long before she hated the practice, and soon she hated the patients as well. I remember the first time I realized that . . . She was in the front garden, and a big fat blowsy woman came and leaned over the hedge – thirteen kids she had and a heart of gold, but no polish at all – and she called to Sheila, 'Will you tell the doctor to

264

pop in and see my Willy, 'e's got the ear-ache!' Sheila stood up straight and looked at her as though she was something the cat had brought in, and rapped out, 'D'you mean your son needs a visit? My husband doesn't pop!' "

Marion could not help a smile, and he paused and looked glumly at her. "It sounds funny to you, but it didn't to that woman. She wasn't used to being taken up like that. She'd thought of us as friends, who understood her. She stammered, 'Beg pardon, Ma'am, I'm sure!' and scooted round to the surgery door." He paused again. "Sheila was a lovely thing when I married her. Slim and straight, like a young tree. Willowy. And gay. She'd say the wittiest things, and she was always laughing, the prettiest, tinkling laugh. And now – the tree's stiff and brittle – and the wit is prickly, barbed – and the laughter crackles like dry leaves – and there's no kindness in her. But it's my fault she's as she is – I didn't give her the life she expected. My fault." A tear trickled down his stubbly cheek.

Marion spoke breezily. "Paul – my husband – didn't like the practice much, either, or the patients. I thought he was unique in that, but I see he wasn't. I agree, being married to a doctor can't be any joke at all. Even the children hardly get any medicines except samples – like the shoemaker's children never getting any new shoes!"

She was unlucky, for she only set him off again, "Children! If only we could have had some. They would have kept her younger, softer. But we never did – we never did!"

"They're not an unmixed blessing," Marion said lightly. "Little devils!"

He murmured something about clouds of glory, rather maudlin, and she firmly shut him up. "You're talking far too much for a sick man. Go to sleep now – and don't forget to drink that orange juice before you settle down."

She waved a hand, and left him slumped there in the shabby, dun-coloured little room whose windows looked into a clump of unkempt bushes. Next time she came, she brought some chrysanthemums from the farm greenhouse and set them on a table where he could see them.

He received them peevishly. "Sheila always wants to clutter up my rooms with knick-knacks. I won't have 'em."

"Flowers aren't knick-knacks. Cheer you up! May I take your temperature now!"

It was four days before the temperature stopped spiking up in the evenings, and drenching him with sweat as it fell during the nights. The M. and B.s made him feel sick and wretched, and Marion had the greatest difficulty in persuading him to go on taking them. When they had done their work, however, and the arm faded from fiery red to plum colour and then to pink, and the throbbing pain went out of it, he gave the hated tablets, and Marion's use of them, grudging praise.

"I don't mind telling you I was making plans for multiple incisions and even for amputating my arm," he said, when those dangers were obviously over. "I'm extremely grateful. I hold you in the highest regard." He twinkled at her. He had shaved now, and looked more like himself, if somewhat wan. "Was I a good patient?"

She said, "Simply frightful!"

He laughed and teased her, "Doctors always are!"

4

The unexpected return to the practice of medicine showed Marion that she had not lost her interest in people, as people, as distinct from cases. The sharp impression which the general practitioner receives, of personalities dealing with stress according to their different lights, the swift intimacy of troubles shared, excited in her, as it had always done, a wish to know more of their circumstances and their past history. She found that it was easier to get to know them, here. Perhaps they were simpler than the townspeople, perhaps it was just that there was more time. Or perhaps Dr. Hawkes's jibe about not sending them to hospital was a clue – one saw them here through an illness from start to finish, whatever the finish might be.

At first she could not get away from the impulse to get a second opinion – so easy in a town, so difficult and expensive in country districts – about anyone who worried her. The labourers with rheumatism, or splinters in their hands, or hacking coughs, the common ailments of the essentially healthy children, the few aches and pains which the women had time to acknowledge, these she could deal with. But there were more complicated illnesses which brought her up short – temperatures which might be this, that, or the other and must be differentiated, without the aid of the laboratory, before they could be treated; hopeless cases who died at home instead of in hospital wards, and whose last days must be eased as best she might.

Mrs. Field, for instance, a woman in her early sixties, dying of cancer; she had been beautiful, had traces of beauty still, and, clinging to the memory of it, still wore pretty bedjackets, and pearls round her mud-coloured, wrinkled neck, and made her daughter curl her faded, lifeless hair. She resented her illness fiercely. "As soon as you doctors let me get up," she told Marion, "I'm going to the best hotel I can find in some fashionable town – Bath, or Cheltenham, they're still inhabitable, I believe – I'd have liked Bournemouth, but the coast is not too healthy now, is it? – and I shall buy myself the most expensive outfit I can get, and enjoy myself again – enjoy myself. And find something really profitable to put my money into – there must be something that'll bring me in more than a miserable three per cent, though my daughter says there isn't, any more!"

Marion thought it was grim that, with only a few weeks to live, she should be thinking of nothing but these things and of such little comfort as she could get.

"Doesn't she know she's going to die?" she asked the daughter brusquely one day. The younger woman shook her head and set her lips.

"No. And I can't have her told. It's I who have to bear the brunt of her moods. Some days she cries and complains without a break, even as it is. It's awful, to have to watch it."

Marion said, "Don't you think part of her unhappiness is that she lies there bewildered because nothing seems to be done to make her any better? Wouldn't she prefer to know the truth, wouldn't it calm her down to realize there was no point in all this frenzied planning?"

"She'd never face it. She's always been a self-kidder,

simply won't see a thing if she doesn't like it. She'd just be hurt and angry and tell me I was glad I was going to be rid of her. She mustn't be told – please!"

Marion worried about her and, meeting the Vicar one day in the street, stopped impulsively and asked him to visit Mrs. Field.

The Reverend Brian Bennet was a man in his forties, thin, with deep-set, eager eyes which gave him the look of a saint. He said doubtfully, "Does she want me to come?"

"She hasn't said so. But she's so grousy and miserable, and I can't help her much. I thought you could, perhaps."

"I could go and try. There's nothing against a Vicar calling on his parishioners, she needn't think it means anything more than that if she doesn't want to. Miss Field's been to my church a few times."

"Wouldn't you go, if she hadn't?" Marion asked curiously. He temporized. "Well, they might be Nonconformists – or Romans – or atheists – and resent intrusion."

"Gentile!" Marion shot out, and then flushed and said, "I'm sorry. That wasn't very polite. I meant – if she's dying, it can't matter much what her denomination is, can it? Isn't that the meaning of 'In my Father's house are many mansions'?"

He smiled, and looked at her with some interest. "It may be. I was only thinking that, if she were a member of some other church, someone of her own sort might help her more than I could. However, we have no evidence that she is. I'll go. Thank you for suggesting it. I'll certainly go."

5

Marion formed the impression very soon that Dr. Hawkes was somewhat slapdash in his methods. A man came complaining that he was deaf and had noises in his head. "Ears feel all stopped up, to me, but the Doctor, 'e never suggested syringin' them." He looked expectantly at this new medical adviser.

Marion said, "I'll look and see if they need it," and did so. "Good gracious!" she grumbled to herself a minute later. "Doesn't the man ever look into ears?" To the man, she said, "You have got some wax. We'll clear it out — "

He said, "Ar?" and watched her moodily as she collected her tools. But his face cleared when she showed him, later on, a repulsive dish of soupy fluid and lumps of wax. "Ar! That do be wonnerfully better! Shall be 'earin' more'n they want me to 'ear, now, I reckon!" And he went off beaming.

She was summoned by a stout lady who complained of dizziness. "Dr. Hawkes says I've got a blood-pressure," she informed Marion. "He gives me a diet and some little tablets, and forbids any exertion. No housework, no gardening."

Marion scooped her sphygmomanometer out of her bag. "If you wouldn't mind taking off your coat and rolling up your sleeve — "

The lady pulled her chin down into her neck and frowned. "Dr. Hawkes didn't do anything like that. He could tell, from my pulse, immediately."

"I like this way better, myself," Marion said cheerfully.

"Can I help you off with it ? Thank you — "

"Dr. Hawkes knows me so well. Of course, he's had more experience. Well, if you must — "

The blood-pressure was perfectly normal, the arteries so soft and healthy as to be barely felt. Marion was quite sure there had never been any abnormality. She said, "It's very much better now. You could do some oddments in the house and garden now without the slightest danger."

The stout lady did not seem best pleased. "I shall wait until I see the Doctor again," she stated. "One can't be too careful, with a complaint like this. And I can go on with the tablets and the diet?"

"Why, yes, if you wish," Marion said. And added mentally, "I wonder why the dickens you sent for me?" And then remembered that she hadn't, she had sent for Dr. Hawkes, which, it appeared, was something very different. She commented on it, when she saw him next, by which time he was beginning to get better and liked her to tell him what she had been doing.

"I've been to see the lady in the end house on the right. She thought she had a high blood-pressure."

He grunted, "M'm?"

"She hasn't a high blood-pressure at all."

"Oh, well," he said amiably, "she might have had. And it gives me an excuse to diet her without telling her she's far too fat, and gives her one to get out of jobs she hates doing."

"And the tablets?" she asked suspiciously.

"Are sugar of milk."

"Oh, Bob!" she protested. "You charlatan!"

His eye gleamed at her first – and involuntary – use of his name. "Not at all," he said. "Her very good friend!"

The Vicar took the trouble to come to see Marion about Mrs. Field a few days later. He arrived as she was about to leave Dr. Hawkes' house after a surgery.

"I've been to see your sick lady," he said. "But you know, you've given me a task quite beyond my powers!"

Marion said, "I can't believe that."

He sat on the edge of the couch, his long legs swinging. "First, I had to promise her daughter it would be simply a social call. The next world was not to come into it at all. I kept that promise quite literally. But it involved listening to a long recital of Mrs. Field's wrongs. She'd had a bad father and mother, a bad husband, bad children. Even the daughter who spends her life looking after her is selfish and inconsiderate, so she says. All her doctors have been fools or knaves, or she would never have been stricken with this disease. She herself seems to be some sort of shining saint."

Marion interjected, "I've never come across a more querulous, self-centred old woman. She can't even say thank you to the people who do things for her. She hasn't any friends. Even the District Nurse, who's used to sick people's whims, won't go into the house except for absolute necessities."

He nodded. "I'm afraid her whole spiritual edifice needs pulling down and rebuilding from the bottom. A tall order, at her age and with little time to live." He surveyed Marion over his glasses. "I tried to get her to pray with me. But she would do nothing but interrupt and tell me I was praying for the wrong things. It was no good suggesting that she

272

accept God's will. The Almighty was to be coerced to fall in with hers. He was to make her well, in double quick time, so that she might return to her life of pleasure. An imperious woman, full of pride. I don't know that I've ever met one like her."

"I suppose," Marion said, "you don't meet really wicked people, do you? I mean, they must have some urge to be good – and therefore have lost much of their wickedness – before they seek you out."

"You mean," he said, "one ought to go into the highways and hedges, not wait for them to come to one. You're right, a minister of the church does not meet the utterly unregenerate, except by chance."

Marion spread out her hands. "I wouldn't presume to teach you your business. Your job's to save souls, mine to save bodies. And although the Almighty did make bodies too, one can't deny that your job is the more important."

He seemed surprised. "I thought most medical people had no use for the supernatural. St. Paul's vision was an epileptic fit, the blind man wasn't really blind, and so on."

"You're out of date!" she flung back at him, smiling to disarm her words of any sting. "Right back to Darwin and the old war between religion and science. We see no war, now. The only thing we know about the missing link is – that it's missing – will always be missing, because it never could have been! I was only thinking that if preventive religion could be as active as preventive medicine, we should be quite different people, most of us."

"Highways and hedges again," he said very seriously. "I can't help seeing that you've touched a spot. But it's very

273

difficult. They all begin with one accord to make excuses. Perhaps it's the dog collar. Perhaps a certain unctuous assumption of superiority in the clerical manner. An assumption that often isn't intentional. One knows so well that the only way to influence people is by trying to be good oneself and hoping they may notice – but that's limited – and slow. Too slow, I'm afraid, for the lady in question, even if she did notice. But I'll go and see her again."

"You don't think," Marion asked, on impulse, "it's any good – praying for her to get well – if that's what she wants so badly?"

The Vicar searched her face, as though to find out whether she might be mocking him; and then, as though uncertain, avoided her eyes. "In this particular case," he said deliberately, "I'm sure it could be of no use at all." And he sprang down from the couch and scurried away. Marion looked after him. One strained every nerve to keep people alive, and in the last resort did one's best to make their passing peaceful, often, as now, to keep the certainty of its coming from them altogether – but what then? And what about this question of praying, anyway? Was there any sense in praying for one's people in the Forces? Or for the sick, as one heard them every time one went to church? She wondered if the Vicar could be made to talk of it – or if he would just hedge, as he had done to-day.

By the time Dr. Hawkes was well, the routine of practice had so got under Marion's skin again that she hated the thought of giving it up. And as the village doctor had been much put out by the prospect of a return to work uninterrupted by even a half-day a week, they came to an amicable arrangement whereby she was to act as part-time assistant to him, doing surgeries or visits as he found most convenient.

To her pleased surprise, the Vicar dropped in to see her on another day quite soon, and promptly asked her views on spiritual healing. "I don't mean Christian Science. That's bogus. I mean healing by prayer."

Marion looked doubtful. "I haven't formulated an opinion. It hasn't come my way."

"D'you believe the miraculous healings of the Bible?" he asked her.

She said, "Yes. I don't see any reason to doubt them. But – we haven't Christ here now, in human form, to do them."

"It wasn't only Christ, or only while He was here. St. Paul healed, and others of the apostles, after the Ascension."

Giving serious thought to it, Marion said, "I don't see why it shouldn't be possible now, as then, given the same conditions."

"Which are?" he pounced on her.

"A healer who is a very good man – or woman, and who believes absolutely that by prayer he can transmit a healing power. And a patient all keyed up to receive it – wanting with all his heart to be healed and believing that he can be – I think he would have to be a good person, too – or a child – or he would be afraid, or sceptical. And there are heaps of people who don't really want to get better, of course, for one reason and another. Those who honestly do want to, get better much the quickest."

"But not," he said, "of things like cancer."

She said thoughtfully, "No. But it doesn't seem to me impossible, all the same, that a frame of mind, induced by hope and belief, might so influence the circulation – or the body chemistry – or both – that a cure might result. The body does put up some defences, even against cancer, only they're generally not strong enough. And if you think it's impossible that a state of mind should influence the body – well, the purely emotional state of sorrow leads to the purely physical production of tears."

He was following her intently. "You mean – a miracle may not consist in the abrogation of what we call natural laws – but, on the contrary, in speeding them up? In such a case, by enabling the body to do perfectly what it already attempts to do imperfectly?"

She nodded. "There's a parallel with the wireless, which our forefathers would have considered to be a miracle. It doesn't make new natural laws, it only uncovers and uses those which are already there."

"That's a helpful way of putting it," he said. Then, as though explaining himself, "I just thought I would like to know what you thought. We've had some of the healers from Millingdon Abbey here from time to time, and there have been – results. None I can actually show you at this moment ... "

"I'd be interested," Marion said. And added, "Why did you say it wouldn't be any good for Mrs. Field?"

The Vicar answered at once, "Because she would never co-operate. She would interpose her own will, her own wishes, and I don't think she's capable of trust. She must always know more than the other man. More than God himself, it seems sometimes. And I'm convinced that one must have co-operation, in this as in any other relationship between God and man. The Holy Ghost has to be invited, he doesn't just blunder in."

6

Many letters came from Paul, graphic letters in which personalities, places, and episodes sprang to life in a few apt words. The sum of them was that he was pretty safe because nothing much was happening, so far anyway; he liked his job enormously, education was important because there was little else to occupy the men; but that there seemed little hope of an early return home. He seemed very far away, the more so because, in some ways, Marion herself had gone back to the sort of life she had lived before she had ever known him.

In her work, little peaks arose now and then from the level to make their lasting impressions on her. The deaf labourer whose ears she had syringed lumbered in one day for a cough mixture. When she spoke to him in her usual voice, he automatically put his hand behind his ear. "Ar?" She repeated her question, more loudly, and louder again, and finally he answered it. Then she shouted, "I thought you were hearing better, after your last visit?" The man grinned. "Ar – them ears. They did *feel* better. But they didn't *work* any better. I reckon that's Anno Domini, that is!" He went off, chuckling, and Marion again revised her

277

opinion of Dr. Hawkes's slack methods. What was the good of wasting your time syringing ears which were already hopelessly deaf? Dr. Hawkes had, she found again and again, a certain broad wisdom which she herself had not so far acquired.

There was Miss Tilly, an eccentric old spinster who lived alone. She called Marion in one day for some trivial ailment, and said, in the course of conversation, "I wouldn't have bothered you, except that I was afraid I might be infectious. I'm not long for this world, anyway."

Cautiously, Marion asked, "I wonder why you say that so positively?"

"I've got a growth," the old lady told her frankly. "I've had it for some years. It'll carry me off pretty soon, now."

Something in the healthy look of her set Marion doubting. "Does Dr. Hawkes know about it? Has he examined you?"

"I've told him about it. No, he hasn't examined me, I wouldn't think of allowing him to do so. But he tells me there's nothing that can be done."

Marion said with some indignation, "I wouldn't be sure of that, nowadays. Something to ease matters might be possible, if nothing more. Won't you let me see?"

The old lady's clear gaze rested on her for a minute. "I'm not at all afraid of being carried off. Of death, I mean. A natural affair, at my age. And" – she smiled – "my money'll just about last me out and no more."

"And you don't get any pain?" Marion persisted.

She blinked for a minute. "I do, a little. If you could ease that for me – I don't deny it would be a comfort."

So Marion examined her, and the growth turned out to be nothing more than a couple of piles.

"Not cancer? Are you quite sure?" the old lady reiterated, when she was told the news. "And I'm not going to die?"

"Not from that, anyway," Marion smiled at her. "And I should think, by the look of you, not for years."

She seemed bewildered. She had, after all, lived for a long time with her "growth", faced it bravely, made terms with it – and now it had vanished and left her almost lonely. She collected herself. "Well, that's very kind of you, Doctor, very kind indeed. And you think the ointment and the emulsion will take away the pain?"

"I'm sure they will," Marion told her; and went away, pleased and amused. The funny, plucky old thing!

But a few weeks later Dr. Hawkes said to her, "Didn't you go to Miss Tilly some time ago? I've just had to send her into the loony-bin on an urgency order. Quite off her nut all of a sudden. Smashed two of her neighbour's windows and then went for her with a hockey-stick."

"Oh, poor Miss Tilly!" Marion exclaimed with feeling. "I can't imagine her in any sort of institution! She was all right when I saw her – or was she? She had a very fixed idea that she had a growth which was going to kill her off quite quickly, and she did seem a bit upset, in a funny sort of way, when I assured her that it was only piles and she'd got quite a while to live."

Dr. Hawkes's mouth dropped open. "You de-bunked her growth?"

"Of course I did! She hasn't got a growth! And you knew she hadn't!"

"I suspected she hadn't, of course. She's far too well. She wouldn't let me look at her, or get herself X-rayed or anything – and she'd lived for years in the belief that she had a growth and was being very heroic about it – and it wasn't doing her a ha'porth of harm, so – well, it had just become one of her eccentricities."

"She's been living on her capital, in that belief," Marion said. "And one supposes that if she'd known the truth, she wouldn't have done so."

Dr. Hawkes chewed his lip. "Has she, though! That's something I hadn't thought of. Still, it seems that her growth kept her reasonably sane, and now she's lost it she's lost her sanity too – so where are we?"

Marion shook her head. "You may argue — "

"And you may call me a charlatan. You don't know the obstinacy of these untaught country people. One has to treat them as one best can, for what one judges is their own good."

In spite of this, Marion was still sure that she had something to offer which Dr. Hawkes had not: careful precision in examination so that she did not work by guess but by certainty, a method so drummed into her by her teaching hospital that she could never abandon it; and more recent contact with first-class brains and modern forms of treatment. They had the material, between them, for a good team.

She said so, one day. Dr. Hawkes agreed immediately. "Better than I'd ever dreamed of. I'm most grateful."

"But so am I," she protested. "I'm glad to have been dragged back to work. And you're teaching me a lot."

He looked at her with wistful, spaniel's eyes, and a flush of pleasure crept up under his weatherbeaten skin. He said, "That's nice of you," and seemed about to say more, but thought better of it.

They were talking in his front garden as Marion was leaving the house. As they looked out over the gate, a man limped by, walking very slowly and with the most painful difficulty. He smiled and raised a hand to them as he passed.

Dr. Hawkes looked after him. He said, "That's the worst of staying in one place for a very long time. One is haunted by one's mistakes."

"What's the matter with him?" Marion asked. "And how is he a mistake?"

"The mistake was about a week after I came here, immediately after qualifying. My father wanted me, and neither of us realized the value of house jobs in giving one experience. He'd never done any, and nor did I. Anyway, this fellow came a cropper – he wasn't a young man, even then, he must be getting on for eighty now – just fell over a mat in his own house. I thought he was a bit tight. Got up again, with his wife's help, hobbled to a chair, and sent for me. I didn't think much of it – he'd walked – he didn't look ill – he was fully dressed and it would have been a job to examine him properly – he was making a bit of a fuss, but I put that down to the one over the eight I was sure he'd had. I ordered a liniment and came away. He refused to leave his bed the next day, and after a week he wasn't any better, so they sent for me again. It was easier to look at him, in bed – and there wasn't any doubt that he'd

281

fractured his thigh, and, although I gave him some gas and fixed it up in good position right away, it never united – and he's never done a day's work since."

Marion said, "He doesn't seem to resent it – the mistake, I mean."

"That's almost the worst of it. He goes about telling everyone how kind I've been. Perhaps I have. It's the least I could do. The thing would have healed if I'd spotted it and got it splinted when it was first done."

"It might not have. They don't always, even with the best possible treatment, do they, those fractures?"

He grunted gloomily. Marion liked his honesty.

7

And so the months jogged by. Miss Tilly died after a few weeks in the County Mental Hospital, of bewilderment, Marion was sure, at her new surroundings. Mrs. Field became gradually weaker and surprisingly, to her daughter, sweeter in temper. She said to Marion one day, "Is there anything about my illness, Doctor, that you think I ought to know?"

Marion looked her honestly in the face and replied, "Nothing, I think, that you don't know for yourself already." Their eyes held for a long minute. Then she said, "Thank you, Doctor." And after that, there was no more planning, no more rebellion, and she died peacefully a few days later.

Babies were born in spite of the war's disintegration of family life. In one house, twins and a litter of mongrel pups arrived almost simultaneously. "I shall have to be careful," the embarrassed grandfather was heard to proclaim, "that I don't drown one baby and find a home for the other!"

There were illnesses, accidents, and recoveries; bereavements, emotional upheavals, marriages. The months lengthened into years. Pearl Harbour brought America into the War, the Japs menaced Burma and India. There seemed little likelihood of Paul's return for a long time. Although his letters came often, Marion was shocked to find how seldom she thought of him. Now and then she missed him fiercely. But for the most part, her life-long habit of living in the present blurred the past for her, and her husband along with it, and debarred her from thinking about the future.

The children were growing up. Joan was a leggy, pigtailed girl, a little solemn, with steady eyes, the sort of dependable all-rounder who would be a prefect at school and later a mainstay at home until she married. Martin had his incalculable moods and rebellions, a quick temper and great charm. He had settled down at school, where he was considered brilliant, and he had made a real friend of John Mallory. The farm was a great outlet for all his phases. He could hide for hours together if he wanted solitude, and he could, from his very familiarity with the place and its inhabitants, be a leader to John and the shifting crowd of other boys and of Joan's girl friends who were so often in and out. Marion was enormously interested in them. Their many crazes, their slang, their questions, the difference

283

between their outlook and that of her own childhood, stimulated her. The mellow, happy wisdom of her parents-in-law was a steadying influence, hopeful in a different way from the children's thoughtless eagerness. She found great pleasure, too, in her friendship with the two men whom chance had brought in contact with her – Bob Hawkes and the Vicar. She talked much with them, worked enjoyably with the one, and took to going regularly to church to hear the other preach and watch the intent devotion on his face as he conducted the service. She was soberly happy at this time. Life made demands on her, but she was able to satisfy them. There were no conflicting claims, one pulling this way and another that, but an integrated whole which used all her talents to the full.

There was a period of weeks when no letters came from Paul, and Marion was conscious of a gap in her life's pattern. But whenever she turned to think seriously about this, some interruption would divert her – a ploy of the children's, a call from Dr. Hawkes – and she would withdraw her mind from the unease until, she told herself, some convenient time. When at last the anxiety of Paul's parents, and the length of the silence, forced her to realize that something was most probably wrong, ten letters arrived all at once, tied together with string, and no one ever knew the cause of the delay.

Later that year, there was another silence. It followed two scrappy little notes, lasted a month, and there was only one letter at the end of it, a short one saying that there had been a great rush of work and that Paul had been none too fit but was all right now. Marion worried more about that letter than she had done about the silence. She was sure, that time, that there had been something really wrong. But after it, letters came regularly again, and were as colourful and informative as they had ever been.

Marion herself had written regularly all the time – about the children, the farm, village gossip, about herself sometimes, but little about her medical work. Paul had never much liked to hear about her work.

The village had no more bombs. Lady Mary, that stout-hearted old aristocrat, came back to live with her sister some ten miles away and brought the faithful Fosters with her. But Mrs. Hawkes, and the few others like her who had fled to areas supposedly safer, did not come back. They wrote, instead, of all the important war-work they were able to do where they were.

Marion, hearing of this from Bob Hawkes, and remembering the First Aid exam, asked naughtily, "What does she do, exactly?"

"She's a Welfare worker in a factory. Bosses them all around, I haven't any doubt. She'd be happy enough, as long as she could be the centre of the picture." He smiled as he said it. He did not sound bitter, just not very interested. Marion felt that he thought his wife was better where she was.

285

8

During the summer of 1944, they heard the sound of the flying-bombs, not very near them, on their way to London, and saw from the downs the barrage balloons set up to intercept them. But none dropped anywhere near, and the alarm they had first felt at the eerie noise was gradually forgotten. Even Martin, who had shown a particular repugnance to their whining, took no notice of it as time went on.

He was, however, more than usually nervous that summer; perhaps because of the flying-bombs, perhaps, they thought, because John Mallory was leaving the village school and going to a preparatory school as a boarder. He was very full of talk about it, and Martin with one side of him wanted to go too, and with another was afraid to, and in any case was at variance with his friend instead of in step with him, and that was worrying. He hated the idea of the village school without him.

In early September, when John had just gone and Martin himself had been back at school a couple of days, he went down with one of his attacks of sickness, which had lately been much less frequent than when he was younger. As usual, Marion asked Bob Hawkes to come in and look at him, and as usual the boy brightened up at the doctor's cheery talk.

"Want to see my tum?"

Bob, hands in pockets, looked down on him and laughed. "Not particularly. Why?"

Martin smiled his funny puckered smile, raised his

eyebrows, rolled his eyes. "Don't know. You did one time you came to see me."

"I know what it looks like, now!"

They both chuckled.

"See you to-morrow?" Martin asked expectantly, and Bob said, "You'll be better by then, you won't want me any more."

To Marion, at the front door, he said, "You don't need telling what to do. Glucose and lots of drinks and keep him quiet – I expect it's his usual nervous reaction – missing John and all that."

He was sick twice during the night, and Marion had to get up to him, but that was usual in these attacks. In the morning he was restless and whiny, and Marion left him in bed. She had a busy morning seeing patients and came home late for lunch. She met Mrs. Shepherd coming downstairs with Martin's tray – weak Bovril and toast was what he usually started on and ravenously consumed once the attack was over.

"Wouldn't touch it," Mrs. Shepherd said. "He doesn't seem at all well."

"A long one," Marion commented. "He's generally better by this time."

She went up to him, and came down again rubbing her chin and trying to ignore the fact that her heart was thumping uncomfortably against her ribs. Instead of eating her own lunch, she went to the telephone, which Bob Hawkes answered himself.

"Bob – I may be doing a fussy parent act – but I don't like the look of Martin." An interrogative grunt came from the other end, and she went on. "He says he's got tummy-ache, and he's never really stopped being sick, and he's got a nasty anxious look."

Silence a minute. Then, "He didn't say anything about tummy-ache before, did he?"

"No, he didn't. But we didn't ask him, and he's a funny silent chap, he never does volunteer anything."

"And he did suggest I looked at his tummy." Marion blessed his honesty again, she had not intended to remind him of that. "Did he volunteer it just now?"

"No. I tried to pull him up in bed and he yowled. I *may* be just fussing — "

"I hope to God you are," he said. "I'll be with you in a few minutes."

It was an uncertain little smile that Martin gave him when he said, "I think I will look at your tum to-day, old man." And when he added, "Does it hurt?" Martin gulped, and acknowledged grudgingly, "Yes, it does."

The tummy was blown up and tender, the boy's pulse racing, his temperature subnormal. Dr. Hawkes covered him up again gently, remarked, "We'll soon put that right," and went into the passage with Marion.

There, he remarked forcibly, "Blast! Perforated appendix, of course, with general peritonitis. Why didn't I think of it? Why?"

Bleakly, Marion tried to comfort him. "It seemed so exactly like his usual do. There was even the right sort of reason for it. I'm to blame, if either of us is. I didn't give you a lead. If — "

"If only I'd felt his blinking little tum!" Bob Hawkes said.

288

"Just to satisfy him! Instead of turning obstinate. It's how one always misses things – not looking for them. How I missed old George's fracture, all those years ago. Somehow, one never learns. And now – Martin, of all the little boys I'm always seeing!"

He stood for a minute, looking so old and desolate that Marion, impulsively, hooked a hand in his elbow, and he glanced at her and squared his shoulders. "May I use your 'phone? I'll get hold of J. B. Jackson and get him to fix something in Brighton. There's nowhere here I'd trust with the nursing of him."

9

Martin's eyes, questioning, not exactly alarmed, following her round as she opened drawers and packed a suitcase for him; Martin biting his lip and gripping her hand when the ambulance men rolled the stretcher in under him and folded him in blankets and carried him down; his urgent, "Come with me, Mummy!" when they slid him into the ambulance; the tackety-tack of heels on tiled corridors, the hospital smell, the swish of nurses' skirts; smooth green walls of a side-ward on the children's floor, and a little round face peeping over the side of one cot while Martin was tucked into another; holding his hand again – his eyes really were alarmed, now – while Bob Hawkes and a younger man with a keen, pleasant face felt him cautiously over again, and then while a nurse injected atropine into his arm – he didn't cry, only gave a surprised, "Oh!" and frowned at her; coaxing him to swallow a small yellow capsule and thinking that it wouldn't do him much good because he would certainly be sick; only he wasn't, and presently she went with him up to the theatre floor and a white-coated anæsthetist put a mask over his wonderfully unprotesting nose – these were the impressions which chased themselves through Marion's brain as she waited downstairs, having refused an invitation to watch the operation.

People passed and re-passed, but she hardly saw them. She thought wryly of her opinion, often stated while she was a house-surgeon, that she would rather deal with twenty patients than one relative. It would be the ward-sister's opinion, too, it always was. What a time they were. It must be a terribly bad appendix. The clock must have stopped. Then Bob Hawkes and the surgeon were with her, and the surgeon was saying, "He's all right so far. It was as we thought – a bust appendix with commencing peritonitis. Mercifully it was easy to reach. I put in a tube, just for safety, and scattered sulphathiazole powder all about. He'll have a few stormy days – but he should do."

Marion said, "Thank you. It was good of you to mobilize everything so quickly."

Bob Hawkes said, "One peep at him – and then you must come and have some dinner."

Martin did have a few stormy days. Marion was with him a great deal, and sometimes he knew her and sometimes he didn't. He was propped up in bed, and his eyes were round and wide in his flushed face, and his expression was

290

anxious and his breathing rapid. He talked, in tones which sounded reasonable, but what he said was mostly rubbish, and he never smiled.

The surgeon, J. B. Jackson, brought a colleague, then a physician. Martin had more injections, some of them the recently introduced penicillin. And it became evident that, in spite of all of them, he was not going to do.

They held a conclave, Marion, Bob Hawkes, and the three men from the hospital staff, and the ward sister, and their faces told Marion what they thought. They faded away, one by one, murmuring that everything possible was being done, and left Marion and Bob Hawkes together.

He walked, with his hands in his pockets, from the window to the door, and back again. Then he said, "Would you mind if I asked Brian Bennet to come and see him?"

Marion's heart missed a beat. "The Vicar? D'you think he's as bad as all that? And can it do any good? Mightn't it frighten him? He hasn't been confirmed, he's too young for" – she gulped at the word – "a last Sacrament."

Bob Hawkes stopped his walking and straddled a chair, facing her. He said, "I don't mean that. I mean – what about his Faith Healing? Here's a case for it, if ever there was one!"

There was silence for so long that it became oppressive. He got up again. "It's the only thing I can think of – to help us – now."

Marion shook herself. What did it matter what the hospital people thought? It was Martin's life that mattered. She said, "Go and get him, Bob, as quick as ever you can!"

10

It was early evening when they came back, Bob striding in, the Vicar lagging a little.

"He wanted to send for someone from Millingdon Abbey," Bob explained. "But it would be to-morrow before they could get here. I said he'd better come himself."

"I thought they would do better for you," Brian Bennet said simply. "I still think so. I've no experience."

Marion caught his hand. "We're always having to do things of which we have no experience, in my job. If we can, you can. And time matters so much, now."

"Does it?" he said. "If you're asking for a miracle?"

"But of course!" Marion spoke fast and eagerly. "If a miracle is what we said the other day – not holding up natural laws or reversing them, but giving them free play! After all, Nature always heals us if she can! He might – be dead – by tomorrow – and I think that would tax even your belief!"

He said gravely, "I'm ashamed to say it would. And so – as you will, my dear."

Martin did not seem frightened as they went in. He was past being frightened, past taking things in. He did not resist Brian Bennet's hand on his, and presently his own fingers tightened round it, as though he liked the feel of it.

Marion thought, "He said one must have co-operation. That's about all he'll get of it, from Martin. P'raps it's enough. He's got mine" – she looked at Bob Hawkes, whose eyes were fixed on Martin – "and Bob's." The two of them moved, with one accord, to the window, instead of leaving the Vicar alone with Martin. They felt they must not watch him, but they wanted to be there, to give what silent help they could.

And so they waited, for fully half an hour, looking out, unseeing, to the little steep road, their ears alert for any sound. At last they heard the Vicar sigh, and move, and turned to see him getting to his feet.

Martin's face, deathly pale, had fallen sideways on the pillow, and he was not gasping any more. Desolate in her disappointment, Marion gripped Bob Hawkes' arm. "Bob – he's dead! He's dead – we've killed him!"

But the village doctor, bending closer, moved his arm suddenly until it was round her shoulders, pulling her gently down beside him.

"Listen!" he said. "Quiet – listen!"

And in the silence, she heard Martin breathing, quietly, regularly. The hand that had been plucking at the blankets was curled, relaxed.

She looked dumbly at Bob Hawkes, who was smiling; at Brian Bennet, who was gripping the bed-rail and passing a handkerchief across his brow. The three of them tiptoed out.

11

When Marion came back later the ward sister was there. She said, "Temperature and pulse are normal, and he's taken some glucose water without being sick, and he's passed some wind."

They stared at each other. Marion said, "It's wonderful!" And then, with a chuckle, "Such funny things to be so glad about! But I *am* glad – aren't you?"

"Of course. You know," the sister said, "he's just like a pneumonia after the crisis, in the days when pneumonia used to have a crisis, before we had the sulphonamides. Mr. Jackson says it's the penicillin that's done it."

Marion said, "*I* think it was the Vicar!" and the ward-sister said, "It's very difficult to tell!"

Marion stayed for a time, and then, since Martin was sleeping so peacefully and so obviously on the mend, she went back to the village.

She drove straight to Dr. Hawkes' house, and found him sitting there with the Vicar. She advanced on them with hands outstretched. "How can I thank you – both of you – enough?"

"He's still better?" they asked, both at once.

Marion sat down. She was simply too overwrought to stand. She told them what the ward sister had said, penicillin and all.

The Vicar asked, "And what do you think yourself?"

"I think it was due to you. I said so. I expect the penicillin and all the other things played their part – but before you came Martin's body was not in the right state to make use of them, and afterwards, it was. D'you see?"

They nodded, gravely.

"And there's just no way of thanking you."

The Vicar said, "Don't thank me, thank God."

"You, too," she insisted. "Both of you."

Bob Hawkes stirred. "We have to thank you, too, you

294

know," he commented.

"Me!" Marion cried out. "What have I done? What could I do?"

"You've put us on our toes," the Vicar joined in. "We were saying this to each other before you came in, now we'll say it to you. A certain 'never-say-die' attitude, shall we call it? Not about this only, but ever since you've been here. Who else would have thought of doing anything – anything at all – for Mrs. Field? 'Give me my bow of burning gold' that's how I've often thought of you!"

Bob Hawkes crowed applause. "That's right! That's just, exactly right! 'My bow of burning gold'!"

She looked from one to the other of them, her face aflame.

"Setting a high standard without even thinking about it," he was going on, "and taking for granted that we can reach it. That's what you're doing for us."

"It's terribly nice of you – saying all this," she mumbled. "I've never thought any such thing, of course – I mean, that you needed putting on your toes. You didn't — "

Bob Hawkes chuckled. "That's what you think! You've no idea how comfortably slack one can get, with no competition and no one to criticize."

They sat beaming at her, and presently the Vicar stood up, and went off home, and Marion and Bob Hawkes sat talking, intimate, contented talk, about secret thoughts that they normally kept to themselves: until at last Marion too, feeling curiously light-headed, went back to the farm with her good news.

12

Martin just steadily recovered, after that day. He was not miraculously quite well all at once, he improved from day to day as if, as sister had said, his illness had reached a crisis and then been flung back and defervesced.

He was pushed out on the balcony to enjoy the autumn sun, and Marion and Bob Hawkes or the Vicar would visit him almost every day, and some days people from the village would come, shyly, with fruit or flowers from their gardens.

It was after one of these visits that Marion and Bob came home together and lingered in the doctor's garden because there wasn't really time for Marion to go to the farm before the evening surgery which she was going to do, and to watch the sun setting over the downs in a glitter of scarlet and gold.

They sat at the two ends of a little slatted wooden seat, with the red wall of the garden behind them, cut off from the house by a yew-hedge, and with the fragrance of tobacco-plants and heliotrope rising all around.

Marion said, "Isn't it marvellous, to think we'll have him home in a few days now! It feels like a lifetime since that day we took him off in the ambulance."

"We've packed more experience into these few weeks than most people get in a lifetime. The ordinary hum-drum jogging along – and then dreadful remorse, tearing anxiety – a fight and a victory. The wonderful comradeship of the three of us . . . Bennet and you and me working together for the good of someone else, not thinking of ourselves –

296

and, running through it all, this other wonder – of coming closer and closer – to you."

Marion had been only half-listening, her thoughts on the colours and scents of the evening, on Martin and what she would do with him when he came back to the farm. She turned a startled face to her companion – and found him leaning forwards towards her, his head up, lips parted, his spaniel's eyes sad no longer, but ablaze, demanding, young. He said, "I think you must know how much I love you." He took both her hands between his own, and held them, tenderly, but very tightly.

She said, "Why, Bob – why, Bob – of course I didn't know – I never thought — " and then, in a despairing wail: "Oh Bob, dear, we've been such good friends!"

It was at the word "dear" that he let out his funny crow of joy. The rest was smothered as he pulled her close to him. And Marion found herself resting there, infinitely contented, utterly at peace, listening as he told her just what he found so delightful in her: her kindness, her steadfastness, and many other qualities which she did not know she had and which she had not heard spoken of for a very long time; her beauty, her gaiety, the music of her voice. When he kissed her, she could not resist him, could only return his kisses in an amazed happiness. It seemed to her that she had never felt so grateful to anyone, had never been in such harmony. She stayed in his arms, her head on his shoulder, his lips murmuring into her dark hair, until the sun sank and the cold of the misty autumn evening sent a shiver through her and brought her back to reality.

She sat up, and brushed her tousled hair from her

297

forehead with a gesture that was groping, puzzled. "Bob, I don't know what came over us!"

He looked at her with delight. "You don't? I do! I've never been so happy in my life! A little longer life than yours, my darling, my lovely, vital dear, but not so long that I can't love!"

Marion tried laughing at them both. "Oh Bob, we're idiotic! It's the sunset, and the moon, and the tobacco-plants, and being so glad about Martin!"

"It's nothing of the sort!" he said indignantly. "It's been growing ever since we first met . . . all the feelings one ought to have for one's beloved . . . first, just a terrific interest – any excuse to see you – the whole day wasted if I didn't see you – a sort of awe when I realized you liked me . . . that we fitted together so well . . . and now . . . Marion, I think you love me too!"

She could not, somehow, say that she did not. "In a sort of way, I do," she said slowly.

"Any way's good enough for me," he declared. Then, urgently, eagerly, "What are we going to do about it, Marion? What shall we do?"

She looked at him again then, wondering at the light she had kindled.

"We can't do anything," she said, very softly because she felt rather sad about it. "It's just – one of those joys – one must kiss as it flies."

She thought, perhaps, he would see sense then, and the light in his eyes would fade. But it did not, it blazed the more brightly. He took her hands again.

"Marion," he said, as though he loved the very saying of

her name. "Marion, dear, I've thought it all out. You're happy, with me, aren't you, and I with you. Why should we shut ourselves off from such happiness? Our work has been our life, for both of us. Perhaps, in both of us, as a compensation because we haven't been quite happy apart from it. My wife hates it, your husband hates it. If we had married, you and I, we would have worked together, as we do now, loving our work and loving each other too . . ."

Marion said flatly, "But we didn't, Bob." Then, for honesty's sake, she added, "And you know, I haven't been unhappy. Certainly not since I gave up my own practice. I was a bit bothered while I was trying to do two things at once."

He waved her protest aside. "A shame, that you should have to give it up. You, who are so good at it! I don't believe you *could* be happy without it, wasting half yourself. Let's go away together, to Scotland, to Wales – to South Africa, p'raps, when the War's over – it's nearly over, now – and run a practice together as we're running this one, and a home too. Everyone's snatching at happiness, now, when they see it crumbling round them. Ours wouldn't crumble. It would last . . . till death parted us – and after."

He was panting a little in his eagerness; so different, so very different from the gentle, elderly man she had known – as if a dam had burst in him, setting free some ardent spirit long imprisoned.

Marion said, almost under her breath, "Bob, we can't. You must understand, we can't do a thing, a single thing. There are the children, there's Paul – and Sheila, too."

He brushed the last two names aside. Paul he had barely seen, his wife Sheila he had gladly forgotten. "We could take Martin with us. He's fond of me, you say he doesn't like his father. Joan could stay here, she's self-contained, she gets on well with him. That would be a fair arrangement – any court would let you have one of them, as long as their father agreed — " He stopped, before Marion's look of horror. "I'm sorry – I'm going too fast. I've thought so much about it – I forget that you haven't. I suppose you haven't, have you?"

She said severely, "Of course I haven't. None of it had entered my head until to-night – none of it at all!"

But Bob Hawkes, that evening, was unsquashable. He said amiably, "I believe you. But will you, please, think about it now? It's worth a little thought, I promise you!"

Before his eager assurance, Marion could not deny her thoughts free play. Sitting back again in her corner, a possible future floated before her. Work, with Bob, its interests and its anxieties shared . . . Martin, growing up with someone he loved and trusted, to whom he owed his life (and, the thought bubbled up, so nearly his death). The comfort and harmony of a home with Bob, who would back her up, always, and need backing up by her, would never pull obstinately in an opposite direction . . . living with Bob – in every possible way. Her thoughts took flight, suddenly, to London, to Paul's last leave, and she jerked back to reality. She was young, what did she want with comfort and harmony? Life was a battle, had always been a battle, and there was joy in the parry and thrust of it, a bright, hard, golden joy . . . not a vuzzy bear, vuzzy-voiced, bedside-manner, flabby, feather-bed comfort.

She saw Bob Hawkes again as she had always seen him – a little pathetic, gone to seed, a very good friend. Her vision of him this evening was, indeed, a vision of what he might have been – perhaps of what he might still be if she gave him the chance he was begging of her?

Perhaps, if that week-end in London with Paul had never been, she might have considered giving him that chance.

She said, "Bob, we've been temporarily and very enjoyably up the pole. I'm happily married – yes, I am – and I've got two children I'm very fond of, and I don't even want to break it up. You're married too, and I don't think too unhappily, really. You didn't think so till I came along. Can't we be grateful for this – rather lovely interlude – and go on being good friends?"

She never knew what Bob Hawkes might have said then. For footsteps came towards them from the house, and Mrs. Bean's voice called, "Doctor? Are you there, Doctor? The waiting-room's just packed with patients – you must have forgotten the time!"

Marion called back, "Good gracious, yes! I'm coming!" And she fled and left him sitting there.

13

Marion did not see Bob Hawkes at all during the next few days. When she was at his house for surgeries he was out. Nor did he ring her up. So that when, nearly a week later, she went to collect Martin, it was in her own car, and alone.

Martin asked at once, "Where's Bob?"

"He was busy, he couldn't come."

Martin wrinkled his nose. He did not approve of friends who were too busy to come when he wanted them. He remarked, "Who's going to carry me down, then?"

As it happened, the house-surgeon did, which was a great honour and put him into a good humour again. And when they came to the farm, Marion acknowledged to herself that, although she felt Bob ought to be there at this home-coming, it was somehow rather pleasant and family-ish to be without him. Grand-fa' Shepherd carried Martin upstairs, Grand-ma Shepherd fussed round him, Waggers rushed madly round in circles, on the furniture and off again, Joan stood with her hands in the pockets of her shorts, saying snortily, "Well, fancy going and getting ill like that and making all that bother!" but her face shining with pleasure at having him back.

Quite early in the morning, she heard a car in the drive. In spite of herself, her heart began to thump. There was, unfortunately, no doubt at all that it was possible to love two men at one time; certainly if one was with you so very often and the other so far away that he was almost nothing but a memory; except when you saw Martin's funny little smile, and a certain blue straightness in Joan's glance, and these things turned your heart over so that, for an instant, you could not draw a breath. And the fact remained that, loving one in the present, you were tied to the other by that love of the past and of the future, and so, the present love must go by the board whatever your inclinations.

There were voices below; the older Shepherds exchanging comments, giving directions, dallying, it seemed, an awful time before anyone went to the door.

Then a door opened, and Mr. Shepherd's voice rose in surprise, "Why, Doctor! I'm so sorry I kept you waiting! I thought you were a ton of manure, and I couldn't think where you'd better be put!" Bob's well-known burst of laughter, and then Bob's voice, solemnly, "I've been called many things – but never that, and never in such quantity!"

Then the two men were chuckling together as the doctor came in. Marion's pride evaporated with her doubts and fears, and she ran downstairs.

For an instant her eyes met Bob's – sad spaniel eyes which looked tenderly, humorously, into hers.

She said, "Martin's back. Did you know?"

"Of course," he said. "I came" – and he raised an eyebrow at her – "specially to see him."

They went upstairs together, Marion lighthearted, light of step. Everything was as it had been, but with an added spice of enjoyment. She took Bob's hand for an instant as they went into Martin's room.

14

The war was going well on the Continent now. The Pas de Calais had been taken, and no more flying-bombs came over, and, after the epic of Arnhem, allied troops were pushing forward through Holland. In the Far East, however, the Japs were very menacing. Paul's letters no longer told that education was important for the men because they had nothing else to do. He wrote rather of plays and concerts got up for their entertainment on leaves from more active areas than the one where he was himself. He took, it seemed, a great part in these, and was writing a good deal, plays and poetry. It did not seem that he was in any particular danger, but he did not give any hint that he might soon be coming home.

Mrs. Hawkes wrote that she was coming soon; then the news of rocket-bombs became public, and she changed her mind.

Bob Hawkes coaxed Marion into his garden again, and Marion went with him. Why not? He was her very good friend. And just supposing Paul did not come back – or, having come, proved, as so many husbands did, to be tired of her. His letters, vivid though they were, might have been written, lately, to any acquaintance, they said so little about him, asked so little about her. What was the harm of holding lightly to this second string which had been waggled so temptingly before her without her asking?

Bob Hawkes pleaded with her, eager again, alive. "Have you thought of it – the future? Is there a spot of hope? I'm so sure we could make a do of a home together – anywhere you say."

Then, without her volition, there came to Marion a vision of their house outside the University town, on a ridge looking down over fields and trees, with the wind blowing round it and all the windows wide; and of this one, tucked into the shadow of the downs, sheltered, warm and safe as Bob's inherited practice, unadventurous. She couldn't imagine Bob transplanted, making his own way.

She shook her head. "It's no good, my dear. Oh Bob, did I lead you on or something?"

He grinned ruefully. "Can't say you did. I just hoped . . . Is there any news of Paul getting leave?"

She said, "Not so far. But several of them have done – people who went out with him."

Bob pursued his own line of thought. "You know, lots of the men who come back – especially from the Far East– are very funny. Can't settle down, don't like their children, squabble with their wives. I've seen a number like that. Find life hum-drum, can't get down to it . . . if that should happen with Paul, you've only to let me know — "

Marion looked up, startled because his thoughts had run in line with her own, wondering if he knew that this was so. But he was looking at her with his touchingly humble smile, which always, now, so dangerously made her want to hug him, to make up for the youth he had lost, to turn him into the man he might have been.

She said, "You're a bit of an old darling," and they walked back across the garden rather far apart, because they could not quite trust themselves.

That note they managed to hold throughout the winter; becoming, it seemed, more and more indispensable to each other in work, in interests, in friendship, but in nothing else.

In the early spring, an orgy of polishing and cleaning began in the old house. The Lalique lady danced once more

305

on her steel table, and the rooms were filled with flowers and budding branches. Dr. Hawkes went up to London to meet his wife, and for weeks she entertained her friends and talked about her own work, as though she had taken a tremendous hand in Britain's war effort while her husband and the rest of the village people had stayed behind in safety and idleness. Marion came and went to do the surgeries, but she did not stray into the garden or the lounge, and her encounters with Bob Hawkes were no more than a few sentences in the front garden, perhaps, reporting on a patient, or a visit passed on over the telephone. One wet evening when patients were few, he came with determination into the consulting-room and sat there talking – of practice matters, of the War's progress, of Martin. After ten minutes or so, his wife's voice came, calling. "Bob! Bob? Wherever is the man?" And he heaved himself up, with veiled eyes, and said, "Good night – my darling!" and went slowly off, as though he would have turned back again if he could have thought of some word that might be said.

Another day, Mrs. Hawkes came upon them in the village street. Marion was in her car, and Bob Hawkes had left his standing, its engine still running, so hasty was his need to talk to her, and had his head through Marion's window.

His wife said, "Oh, there you are!" She turned an artificial smile on Marion. "I wonder if you're as blind when you're driving as my husband is, Dr. Shepherd. I could practically have patted the car when he slowed up for the corner along there – and he just went on without seeing me. Didn't want to see me, I always say! It isn't the first time, or the second.

306

Didn't want me to ask him for a lift!"

Bob stood back from the window and shook himself – an irritable little shake, though his voice was good-humoured. "Don't be a fool, my dear. How can one possibly notice one pedestrian in this street on a market day! One's whole attention is on the traffic."

Mrs. Hawkes pursed her lips, bobbed her head, spread out her hands. "And the whole of his thoughts on his patients!" She threw a sharp glance at Marion, and went on, in the curiously intense tone which made Marion wonder how long it would take her to work up one of the tantrums which her husband had unguardedly mentioned. "Patients! How I hate them! Tell any lies to get him to their houses. And never a thank you, much less an account paid. And he loves them! They matter far more to him than I do!"

Marion did not dare to meet Bob's eye. She said, "I was just hearing that Dr. Mallory's being demobbed very soon. He'll be much more help than I could be, and that'll make things easier."

Mrs. Hawkes said, "It won't make the slightest difference. My husband will still insist on looking after all his pets, and he'll give each of them twice as much time as he does now. That's all. They're the ones who will score."

Bob interposed, "D'you still want a lift?" and when she said "Yes. I want to go to Mrs. Smart's beyond the Green," they bade Marion good-bye and went over to the car together.

Marion sat where she was. Did Sheila suspect anything? If she did, Bob's life would be hell. Well, when Mallory did come back there need be no more connexion between Bob and herself. No Bob, no work. She did not think she could bear life without her work again; that queer, centrifugal life which forges bonds of sympathy with all types, all classes, all ages, and can make of the man or woman who practises it, in understanding though not indeed in performance, a second Shakespeare.

Her mind kept coming back to Bob's plan for their joint future.

15

Martin's illness, queerly, seemed to have given him a new poise. He was more sociable, expected people to like him, was far less shy. He had welcomed the trail of visitors who had come, all sorts and kinds of them, some out of curiosity, some out of regard for his mother or his grandparents, to show their pleasure at his recovery. He had turned on them all his charm, none of the sudden rudeness to which he had been so prone before. Marion, still thinking of the future, was glad that the children had their own interests now. She thought perhaps they valued her more as she was, a power who could descend and give them treats or punishments, than they would have done if her concern had been for them alone.

One day she had arranged to take them with her on a prearranged call to a village some miles away, where there was a teashop in an old cottage with a little zoo attached to it. They were to have tea there, and the children, with a couple of Joan's friends and one of Martin's, were to be left to explore while she paid her professional visit. Such treats were so rare now, in the absence of any petrol for pleasure use, that they were greatly prized.

"You won't let anything interfere with it, Mummy, will you?" Joan begged her more than once. "Not anything?"

"My dear, I won't if I can help it. But you know what patients are – if someone chooses to be very ill, or have a baby, it'll have to be put off till another day. We *could* go another day — "

"Oh Mummy, we couldn't! At least, it would be an awful bother. You don't know what a job it was to get Valerie to come."

"I don't know Valerie, do I?" Marion inquired.

Joan's voice sank to a tone of awe. "No. But I think she'll like you. She's wizard! She's sixteen, and she's in the First Eleven. She's – Oh well, you'll see. Barbara and I think she's enormous, and we had to simply *wheedle* her to come!"

Marion said, "Oh, it's like that, is it? Well, all we can do is to hope."

The telephone often rang for Marion several times during breakfast, and anyone who did not happen to be eating or drinking answered it. Joan answered it once on the morning of the expedition, and because she seemed to be taking an extra long time to get a message, Marion went out to see if she could help.

Joan was standing away from the 'phone, with her back to it, looking out of the window. She turned as Marion approached, and her face crinkled with rage.

"It's Mrs. Howard. She says she's going to have her baby *to-day!* I hope" – Joan fairly spat the words out – "I hope she'll have it in the 'phone box. And I hope she'll have *two monkeys!*"

She whirled away down the passage. Marion, startled, took up the 'phone. "Mrs. Howard? But you're not due for a couple of months!" She listened to a garbled message about backache and tummy-ache and a meal of bottled gooseberries which might mean anything or nothing.

"Don't go and upset your friends about putting off this afternoon yet," she told Joan. And added, "What do you know about having babies, anyway?"

Joan eyed her with some alarm. "I know about calves!" she spurted. "I saw one come. I hid in the loft. It was marvellous . . . so neat and lovely . . . all folded up . . . and the cow looked so pleased when she turned round and licked it! It wasn't the least bit frightening . . . or nasty . . . or anything. I suppose . . . babies aren't very different, are they?"

Marion said matter-of-factly, "Hardly different at all. That's all right. Only you'd better not talk to the girls at school about it. People who aren't farmers think things like that aren't quite proper."

Mrs. Howard's fears proved unfounded, and the expedition went off well.

"Did Valerie approve?" Marion asked afterwards, and was rewarded by a brilliant smile from her daughter. "Oh yes, Mummy! It was a smashing party!"

"Thank you, M'am!" Marion said, and went indoors, leaving Joan and her friend Barbara, Valerie having been dumped at her own gate, giggling happily together.

She came out again in a few minutes, to fetch something she had left in the car, and the two girls were still in the garden, leaning their elbows on the low brick wall that separated it from the garage path, jabbering so hard that they did not hear her coming.

Joan was saying, "Wasn't it a narrow squeak? You know, I do *admire* Mummy, most awfully . . . she's like a horse . . ."

Marion could not help but stand on one foot, listening.

"A nervous and courageous animal . . . she hates doing things, but she does them all the same, d'you see what I mean? But I do think really, Mummies should just *be* Mummies . . . not doctors or something as well. You can never make plans in our house. If you do something nearly always turns up to wreck them, and it's *devastating* when there are other people involved, like to-day!"

Barbara murmured something about it being rather exciting to live in such a house.

"*Exciting!* That's what *you* think!" Joan's voice was so withering that Marion passed hurriedly, silently on.

Other people involved? Other people were always involved. One couldn't get away from them.

The next morning a wire came from Paul. He was in London, he would be with them in a few hours.

16

Marion decided to meet Paul by herself, in spite of wails from the children that they ought to be allowed to go too. She knew that she was a different person from the wife he had parted from, and Bob Hawkes's hints of probable changes in Paul had further unsettled her. She must see him, and he must see her, this first time, without anything to distract their attention from each other.

She saw him the instant he left the train – taller than most of the crowd, his fair hair bleached against his bronzed skin. She watched as though she were seeing him for the first time – a man whom anyone would look at twice, quiet, graceful, good-looking, a person of character. She took her lower lip between her teeth, to control herself, as he moved slowly, inevitably, towards her.

Then he saw her, and his face lit up with his little-boy grin, and he raised a hand and took longer, quicker strides. And then again at last his hands were on her elbows and he was kissing her, quite unashamed, and she was hanging on to the lapels of his coat, and then they were side by side, swaying together among the jostling people.

It was a happy homecoming. Joan led her father round the farm and round the country, showing him the things her quick observation had picked out to love, and found that both love and observation, strangely and most satisfyingly, echoed his own. Martin, with his new sociability, scrutinized him for only a minute before beginning to talk about school, and Paul at once changed gear and became an educationalist instead of a countryman, and followed his son's mood and imperceptibly led his thoughts. And as they walked or sat and talked together, Marion would see Paul's swift sensitivity at work and pick it up in glances coming to her over the children's heads.

Paul's parents were happy, too. His mother provided marvellous food with the help of the farm's eggs and cream. His father asked questions and listened intently to the answers, and lured him away to smoke a pipe and give his opinion on the new bull calf.

It was three days before Marion had any long spell of time alone with him. And then he contrived it by suggesting that they should walk to the village together. They strolled on, after they had bought the tobacco he had come for, along the path to the windmill, and sat down on the seat behind it, looking out across the fertile valley, dotted with farmhouses and copses veiled now with young green, and intersected with little rivers, to the velvety folds of the downs. A tractor chugged across a meadow, a horse galloped and neighed beyond a hedge, a lone man leaned on his hoe, cloud shadows floated over.

Paul drew a long breath and looked back at Marion. "Remember the first time we came here? In mid-winter?" he asked.

She nodded. "Always, whenever I come. We were enchanted — "

"And the enchantment," he said, "has never quite gone. Although we've travelled a long way since then . . . I want to tell you a bit about the travelling – my part of it."

Marion felt a sudden sinking; as though these three days had been too perfect, her hopes for the future too high, and

313

now she was going to see the changed Paul whom Bob Hawkes had foretold, who would not fit in any more to life as she knew it. She was glad Paul was not looking at her, for her face felt stiff and white. She said very steadily, "Carry on —"

He told her how he had hated, at first, living in a crowd, of the discomforts of camp life in a hot climate, sketching lightly as though to give her a background; of makeshift classrooms, of the subjects they taught, of the surprise the teaching staff had felt at the men's keenness and interest; and then, warming up, of the men themselves, names and faces at first, then voices, recurring phrases, points of view, ultimately well-defined persons; and of the sense of comradeship which grew up, of helping this man, guiding that one, protecting another, many shoulders bending to one task.

Marion interpolated now and then – "You wrote about that man . . . you told me a bit about that in a letter . . ." and he would nod his head and go on.

"It made all the bad parts seem worth while – that solidarity, that sense of being part of a plan."

Several friendships emerged from his crowd, and one of them, it seemed, was the Padre. His name kept cropping up, and Marion formed a picture of him, a thin, quiet man with eager eyes, courageous and very good.

"He didn't preach to the men, he talked to them and listened to them. And it wasn't so much what he said as what he *was* that had the effect on them. Not that he set up to be an example, he didn't, he had far too much humility. But they – even the toughest of them – sensed his goodness,

314

and heard him out and tried to please him and – does it sound odd? – became better people themselves."

Marion realized then that her picture of Paul's Padre was a picture of Brian Bennet.

Paul went on, "It's funny, that effect people have on each other. Specially at close quarters, as they are in a unit of that kind."

Marion said, to herself, not aloud, "And in a village, too." A queer excitement was mounting in her. She waited for more.

"A sort of diffusion of qualities from one man to others. I felt it in myself, too. The Padre had charge of their souls, I of their minds, and what I was had more effect than what I said. I had to keep my own mind clear, sharp, logical, critical, d'you see? To help them keep theirs so. If I thought about myself, and the impression I was making, I lost touch. If I kept my mind on a subject, I kept their interest on it. It gave one the queerest sense of responsibility . . . Am I being pompous? Lecture voice?"

Marion said, "Of course not. Go on," and he sensed her eagerness and smiled.

"The Padre had his effect on me, too. I've always fought a bit shy of parsons and people who call themselves religious – I don't know why, I was brought up in it in a mild sort of way – but now – well, I know it has a message I want to hear more of . . . Your letter about Martin's recovery interested me no end. Made me think you might understand what I had come to feel. Before that, I was doubtful if you would."

"I do," Marion said. "I do . . . I'm already seeing your

Padre and my Vicar as Heavenly Twins."

Paul smiled at her very warmly, and then was silent for some minutes. Marion said nothing. She felt there was more to come and that speech, even agreement, might interrupt it.

"There was another thing, too," Paul continued, slowly, and, Marion thought, with some effort. Was it coming now, the change she had dreaded?

"I've told you about the Padre and the various chaps and the way we lived, but I left this out, even from my letters, not because I wanted to keep it from you, but because I was afraid you might take it the wrong way. Because, too, I wasn't quite sure myself, sometimes, what way it was going to take. It was another friendship. With a woman. A W.A.A.F. You'd have liked her, I think. She worked with me, we were in daily contact, and . . . we came to love each other."

Marion thought, "This is it." Her voice seemed to come from a long way away as she said, "Yes, Paul? Go on, please."

He shifted in his seat, his eyes on the line of the downs, or on nothing. Then he turned to her.

"It was very – lovely, while it lasted," he said. "Good and wholesome. Somehow lit everything up. She worked for me – did what I told her, and gave in to me, and looked after me . . . and thought I was wonderful . . . she wasn't a soft sort of person, either, some of them were terrified of her. I revelled in it . . . And then, somehow, I would think of you and me and how we used to fight – and laugh, didn't we? . . . And how I revelled in that, too. And I knew, when

316

I thought about it, that our relationship was the better. Yours and mine. It seemed as though it was possible to love . . . both you and her at the same time . . . with that distance between us. Yet there came a time when one had to choose. One couldn't take both loves . . . one of them had to go. Marion" – he stretched a hand to her, and his voice had a curious appeal in it – "can you understand that? Can you?"

She took his hand, and the colour came flooding back to her face. "I can, Paul – Oh, I can. Only – you must tell me quite clearly, please, which love you did choose."

"Why, my dear," he said, "My dear, do I have to tell you?"

"Why, yes," she said. "You do!"

After a while she asked him, "Have you finished? Can you listen to my tale now?"

He was sitting with an arm about her, and he rubbed his chin on her head and looked down, as though he were amused. "Of course. Selfish animal, aren't I? But one of us had to begin."

"What struck me, all along, as you were talking," Marion said, "was how curiously parallel our growth has been. Perhaps not curious, in man and wife – but somehow rather wonderful. My Vicar and your Padre. That sense of personal responsibility, you to your men, mine to the children and the patients. The understanding of how it matters what one is, more than what one does, in such relationships. I've found that out, too. And the sense of solidarity there is in people working together to one end, I know that. And — " She swallowed, hesitated, wondered how to say it. "I had a choice to make, too."

317

Paul, staring at her, half-rose. "The devil you did!"

"The same sort of choice. And . . . I chose the same as you did."

It seemed to take him some time to digest what she had said.

He rubbed his nose, took out his pipe and put it away again. He said presently, in a carefully nonchalant tone, "I hadn't thought of that one. I hadn't thought of that, at all."

Marion, moving closer to him, looked up and saw that his face was haggard. She said, "My darling, it's all right. You don't have to worry about it."

A little smile played stiffly round his lips. "I suppose – I don't. If it was all right for me, it was for you too."

She smiled up at him confidently and said, "Why not?"

He took her face between his two hands, and his eyes bored into hers as though he would read her very memories whether she would or no. She flung her arms up round his neck and met his scrutiny until he, too, broke into a smile.

"I wondered whether to tell you," he said inconsequently. "I did, because I hate secrets, they only ooze out and make trouble."

"I was going to tell you too," she said, "though I was a bit afraid to!"

Ferociously, he said, "Who was the blighter, anyway?"

"Must I tell you?" she fenced.

He studied her for a minute, and then said positively, "It was old Salt-and-Water!" and she flushed and dropped her eyes.

He said wonderingly, "But you couldn't love that old

318

feather-bed, Marion! Not you!"

She moved in his arms. "I suppose not, really. He's been so kind. So appreciative of all I did. So much more alive than you'd think he could possibly be, just to talk to him. And, as well as being grateful, I was so sorry for him."

"A very fatal combination!" Paul said solemnly, and their eyes met and they began to laugh again. Marion, snuggling into her husband's side, said, "So that's that!"

Looking out over the valley again, she said presently, "I've grown so fond of this place. I shall be sorry to leave it. But it'll be lovely to get back to a home of our own." She turned to Paul. "Shall we be able to get the house back? One hears these awful tales of sitting tenants who can't be displaced."

Paul sat silent for so long that she poked him and said, "Wake up! What's biting you? Don't you want to make a home with me after all?"

He pinched her and laughed again, and then spoke seriously. "I've been wondering about this work of yours, that I always quarrelled with. You've been so happy, haven't you, doing it again?"

Marion sensed some conflict going on, and realized that she must tread carefully. "I have. I've enjoyed it no end. But I've had a good whack at it. I've quite decided to give it up now and be a good wife and mother for the rest of my life. Have another family, if you like. I've always thought four's a good number."

She glanced up. Paul's face was full of horrified amazement, there was no sign on it of the eager gratitude she had expected. She said, "Paul, what *is* the matter? Have

319

I taken off on the wrong foot? *Do* you want to bust things up?"

He protested. "No, no, no! I'd better tell you the whole tale. I don't want to go back to the University, I couldn't bear it – it's such a circumscribed, safe little life, all rules and conventions, and I simply couldn't live it. I've been writing a lot – I told you – and I've been in touch with a great many theatre people and film people and men who know about publishing. And they seem to think I could make a living at it. Only . . . it wouldn't be a safe, certain sort of living, at least for some years. . . ."

Marion turned to him, her eyes alight. "Oh Paul, how marvellous! You doing something you really want to do! And me making the safe and certain living while you're feeling your way! Is that what you were trying to say?"

He nodded. "I feel rather a clot . . ."

Marion cried out, "I think – as Joan would say – it's a simply enormous idea! Give up the old house, and live somewhere reasonably rural and not too far from London, and I'll get a Public Health job of some sort with regular hours."

Paul, between laughter and embarrassment, said, "You're a good size, yourself, when it comes to ideas."

They swaggered home together in the gathering dusk.

Also published by
Greyladies

LADY OF LETTERS
by Josephine Elder

Lady of Letters explores many of the themes familiar from Josephine Elder's popular girls' school stories; friendship, love of learning, being true to oneself. It tells the story of Hilary Moore, as scholar, history mistress in a girls' high school, university lecturer and writer.

Thoroughly at home in her academic life, it is in Hilary's friendship with an older science teacher and her romance with a young doctor that tensions arise and her ideals are tested.

The intriguing disclaimer, 'The characters in this book are might-have-beens not portraits' invites speculation on how much of this story is based on Miss Elder's own life.